SPECIAL MESSAGE TO READERS

Ruth Dugdall is an award-winning British crime writer, whose debut novel *The Woman Before Me* won the CWA Debut Dagger Award and the 2009 Luke Bitmead Bursary. She worked as a probation officer for almost a decade; two of those years were in maximum security prisons in Suffolk, and she also worked with children who had been convicted of murder. Her writing is heavily influenced by her professional background. Ruth currently lives in Luxembourg, and volunteers at a local prison.

You can discover more about the author at www.ruthdugdall.com

NOWHERE GIRL

When Ellie goes missing on the first day of Schueberfouer, the police are dismissive, keen not to attract negative attention on one of Luxembourg's most important events. Probation officer Cate Austin wants a fresh start; along with her daughter Amelia, she moves in with her police detective boyfriend. But when she realises just how casually he is taking the disappearance of Ellie, Cate decides to investigate matters for herself. Soon she discovers that Luxembourg has a dark heart: due to its geographical position, it is at the centre of a child trafficking ring. As Cate comes closer to finding Ellie's whereabouts, she uncovers a hidden world, placing herself in danger not just from traffickers, but from a source much closer to home . . .

Books by Ruth Dugdall
Published by Ulverscroft:

THE WOMAN BEFORE ME
THE SACRIFICIAL MAN
HUMBER BOY B

RUTH DUGDALL

NOWHERE GIRL

Complete and Unabridged

CHARNWOOD
Leicester

First published in Great Britain in 2015 by
Legend Press Ltd
London

First Charnwood Edition
published 2016
by arrangement with
Legend Press Ltd
London

A catalogue record for this book is available
from the British Library.

ISBN 978–1–4448–2995–2

Published by
F. A. Thorpe (Publishing)
Anstey, Leicestershire

Set by Words & Graphics Ltd.
Anstey, Leicestershire
Printed and bound in Great Britain by
T. J. International Ltd., Padstow, Cornwall

This book is printed on acid-free paper

For my friends in Luxembourg,
who made the city feel like home.
And for the Scheen family.

Day 0
SCHUEBERFOUER, AUGUST 2015

Ellie

The ferris wheel dominates the Luxembourg skyline. A show-stopper, luring the tourists away from the city's cathedral and the Duke's palace, dazzling them with its brilliant rainbow of lights. It turns slowly, gaudy and bright, higher even than the supermoon that glowers above the city.

Sugar and smoke fills the air, the ground is littered with greasy wrappings and scrunched-up napkins as the whole landscape of Glacis car park is taken over by waffle stalls and beer stands, roller coasters and rides. Terror Train is especially intriguing, the crowds push but only a few actually step forward to pay. Terrified children look up to where men in black masks patrol the balconies, wielding axes that they know must be fake, but look real enough, beckoning down, daring them to try the ride. A sign across the ticket booth, where a ghostly figure takes the money, informs that *Terror Train is a 4D show*, and wiser parents steer their children away, to the regal carousel with its golden camel and ivory swan, where the youngsters can be observed at all times.

Unlike Ellie.

Unseen by the customers, around the back of these attractions, are twenty or so tightly parked caravans. Homes to the builders of the ferris wheel and roller coaster, men who are working endless shifts now the fair is finally open, swaggering through the crowds, scrutinising tourists for the heaviness of their wallets, balancing boxed Wii machines on their broad shoulders to persuade the gullible punters that winning big is actually possible.

Above it all, the iconic wheel is the pride of Schueberfouer. More London Eye than ferris wheel, each gondola has four seats to transport the delighted and nervous up, far above a comfortable height, to peer across the night sky to the forests and rivers where Germany, France and Belgium begin.

Around the Glacis, all the roads are gridlocked. Drivers have left their seats and can be seen tapping fists against the car roof, looking ahead for any signs of movement in the traffic. Some lean in to speak to their children within the car, trying to allay their frustration by pointing up at the wheel, glittering with lights and moving majestically above them, tantalising them with the possibility of fun.

'When we get there,' they say, 'we'll go on that.'

Impatient children squabble in the back seat, complain about feeling sick and being hungry.

'Are we there yet?'

'Soon.' Parents try to keep their patience. 'Then we'll be up there in the sky. Would you like that?'

Despite the drizzle that has just started. Despite the six euro cost. Because a promise is a promise.

When, finally, the traffic shifts, overlarge cars nudge into spaces, jut out into the road with front wheels on kerbs. The locals arrive by night bus, put on especially for the three-week event that is as extravagant and bright as tradition demands. They walk past and watch smugly as the Land Rover brigade, the ex-pats, argue over spaces and who forgot the umbrella.

At the top of the wheel, the passengers in the highest gondola find their hearts quickening, as the metal box sways. The ground below is terrifyingly far away. They see now that the gondolas are not sealed around all edges, that there is a gap between the floor and the door, and they are rocking more than they expected to, spittles of rain pricking flushed cheeks. But their fear is not the greatest on the Glacis, they aren't screaming like those on much faster rides, or the brave souls fastened into the giant perspex ball being bungeed into the sky, only to be yanked back on thick ropes. Last year, a rope broke, a tourist ended up in Kirchberg hospital trying to negotiate for an X-ray with only a European Health Card, it even made some of the papers. Not that business has suffered, the search for an adrenalin high is powerful and after a few beers or sugary snacks, the dangers seem diminished. Screams can be heard too from the more traditional rides, the sickening waltzer and roller coaster, this year named for a mouse though nobody timid would dare.

Between these attractions the crowd pushes and twists, seeming from above to move as one being, an octopus of human activity that spins out for candy floss and chips with mayonnaise, or the more traditional deep-fried potato cakes, *Gromperekichelcher*, served on disposable plates with a puddle of apple sauce. Trays are fought for then struggled with, Belgian beer and local wine flows quickly and profitably from the many pop-up bars dotted between rides. Cold and strong, and very welcome for adults taking respite from children, for nervy teenagers on the pull, and for those who are taking a break as they peruse the rich pickings of the fair: over stuffed purses and dangling car keys, bottoms and breasts in tight clothes. Opportunities of all kinds exist at Schueberfouer.

But where is Ellie?

Near to the caravans, and in the furthest corner of the fair is a smaller attraction, but a crowd is already gathering, several people deep despite the drizzling rain. There she is, in the midst of people. Her blonde head bobbing as she strains to full height. But Ellie is short for her age and gets lost in the fray. The balletic poise she's crafted since she was three, and her desire to seem older than her seventeen years is soon abandoned as she stands on her toes in a frustrated attempt to see over the shoulder of a man with skin like tanned leather, a rubbery neck like a bulldog's, who has just stepped in front of her. Eventually she moves around his bulk, ignoring and not understanding what he says to her as she slips in front. Because she has to see.

4

At first glance the size of the crowd is a mystery. There are no rainbow lights, no banks of Christmas Day presents, no prizes to lure the gullible. There is a simple metal stand with a bar, like the monkey bars that line the walls at her school gymnasium, and men, young and fit looking, some her own age, are lining up to hang from it by their hands.

Two minutes and you win 100 euro fair token! the sign crows, in Luxembourgish, so it takes Ellie a few seconds to work out that the prize isn't actually cash but a gift card to use at the fair. Still, there is a bigger reward at stake and the men around her want it, she can sense them watching intently with a mixture of jealousy and then relief as each punter starts well but soon drops to the ground, landing in a muddy puddle that is gradually forming. Each of them imagining the delicious pride of being strong enough to win. The kudos.

The bulldog-necked man moves closer, breathing heavily beneath his dark bushy beard, she can hear him rasping asthmatically, his sour stench is directly behind her. She can't imagine that he would last long dangling from that bar.

Ellie's attention is drawn to her left, where a couple of teenagers, arms draped across the scaffold of the attraction as if they own it, are watching the event from the raised position of a double-sized wheelie bin. They lean and mumble to each other, cracking jokes from behind their hands so there are odd eruptions of hysteria. The girl is beautiful, she has a perfect oval face and skin like mocha, and she wears a tight red dress.

She nervously twists her silky black hair in her fingers, and Ellie can't stop staring. The boy is as handsome as the girl is beautiful, and she wonders if they are siblings. But then the girl says something and the boy looks down, shy and vulnerable, and she sees that he isn't comfortable with her, he's not oblivious to her face; not siblings, then. She wonders if they are lovers, but sees the girl is scanning the crowd, looking for better pickings. The girl knows her own worth and pulls away from the boy, as if to indicate that she is not with him.

Ellie judges the boy to be older than her, maybe as old as twenty. He seems vulnerable without his companion, who is now talking to a man in a designer raincoat with pasty skin and a bald patch. The girl threads her arm through his and they begin to wander away, to a passageway nearby. She sees the man touch his hand to the hem of the red dress just before they disappear from view.

The boy steps up to the man in charge of the attraction, who nods and places him so his turn is next. A few watchers in the crowd jeer at him, and he waves, friendly banter as if they know him. She hears one call out, 'Go, Malik!'

The crowd give Malik encouragement but also taunts that he won't be able to succeed, but their jeering turns to cheers when he pulls off his t-shirt, flexes his biceps and grins at them. Naked from the waist up, he hooks his fingers into the waistband of his massively oversized trousers and waits for the boy currently taking his turn to drop.

Malik does not seem to pay, and he has not queued as long as others, but no-one stops him as he walks steadily towards the bar.

Ellie watches as he spits on his palms then reaches up, revealing the full definition of his torso. He isn't overly muscly, he is lean, but he also looks fit. His face is narrow, feline, his eyes dark and intense. The crowd presses forward in anticipation, she can feel the bulldog behind her, he's too close and she can feel his stomach against her back. Holding her breath against his stench she ducks down, separating a cuddling couple, and squeezes between two boys in American football tops as she makes her way to the front.

Now Ellie can see properly.

The boy is hanging from the bar and the fluorescent numbers above his head are counting the seconds: eleven, twelve, thirteen. He winks to his beautiful friend, who has returned from the alleyway and is now watching from back near the bin. She calls, 'Bonne chance, Malik.'

His arms are already shaking. Ellie knows he won't win the money, but he still looks strong to her. She wonders how long she would manage, she's done gymnastics in the past and the ballet has made her arms muscular. But she hasn't seen any other girl try, and she'd be too self-conscious to be the first.

The boy looks up, his black hair is wet from sweat and he flicks it from his eyes, staring directly at her as he does so. A long moment passes between them, and Ellie thinks how sexy he looks, how his brown skin shows that he's enjoyed the sun this summer, she imagines it as warm to the touch, like melting caramel. The thought makes her self-conscious; she's pale, too blonde to tan. Not as beautiful as the girl he's with, nor as cool as others she's seen wandering around Schueberfouer, teenagers with baggy, ripped clothes and elaborate silver piercings, cool kids whose parents aren't crazy, who are allowed to do as they please. Ellie is dressed more simply in black jeans and a yellow t-shirt. She hadn't been sure about wearing the t-shirt, a recent birthday gift from her mum, but her sister, Gaynor, had said it made her hair look pretty. But now Ellie feels too clean, too prissy, when this handsome boy is naked from the waist up and sweating and his hair is ragged and dark and he is still staring straight at her. Ellie believes that the only thing interesting about her appearance is her nose, which she pierced herself on her seventeenth birthday last week. It's still sore and her mum hates it but she refuses to take the stud out, it's a small act of defiance. She hopes the boy can see it, that he doesn't write her off as a total loser.

Fifty-two seconds and the boy drops, landing neatly in a crouch, then stretches up. He re-adjusts his loose jeans back to their position on his hips and pulls his t-shirt on when it is thrown back to him by the man running the attraction. His beautiful friend smiles but he doesn't return to her, he walks towards Ellie. She looks around, flustered. Where are her mum and Gaynor? She can't see them in the crowd.

There is no avoiding the boy now, he is almost

in front of her, and his gaze stops her from turning away.

'*Salut*, Uncle,' he says, and then she realises that he is not greeting her after all, but someone else, someone close by. She turns and sees the bulldog man, whose scraggly eyebrows are furrowed as he looks down at her. She hadn't realised he had moved, that he is once again right behind her.

'*Salut*, Malik. You did well.'

As she shifts out of his way the boy does notice her, and looks her yellow t-shirt over. Ellie curses Gaynor for suggesting she wear it. It's damp from the spitting rain, and her bra is visible, she should have brought a coat like her mum said.

'*Bonjour*,' he says, and she gives the same greeting back though her accent betrays her.

'English?' he asks, baffling her that he has established so much from just one word.

'*Oui*,' she confesses. Though she doesn't know much about the country, she has never actually lived there and they only return at Christmas, a duty trip to her mother's relatives. She'd like to finish her A-levels in Durham, live with her grandparents, but her mother won't agree. It's been the source of arguments.

She's actually half German, after her father, and has lived most of her life in Heidelberg. But now she lives in a country where she can't speak more than twenty words of the dialect, the locals treat her like a tourist and she has never studied the history. A wanderer, a mongrel, she feels she belongs nowhere in particular. Home is somewhere else, but she hasn't found it yet.

9

'Vous êtes français?' she asks.

Malik shakes his head, though his face seems to say he's pleased by her mistake. 'Algerian.' His eyes flick her up and down, taking in the rain-damp clothes sticking to her body. She can't begrudge him this, she has spent fifty seconds scrutinising his torso.

Just then she hears her name being screamed, loud and shrill. 'Ellie! El-lie!' Her mother has found her.

Ellie sees Gaynor's red jacket, then her mother's equally red face, beyond the crowd. They still haven't seen her, she's hidden by the bulldog man's bulk.

'You come with me,' Malik asks, or commands, she's not sure. Then he moves closer so his breath is warming her lips. 'We can have some fun.'

Ellie's mother sounds hysterical, calling her name again and again, but moving away in her desperate search. Ellie knows she should go to her, put her out of her misery, but she's punishing her too. Ellie wanted to come with her friends from school, with Joe, not her kid sister. Her mother was so mad that Ellie was planning to see him again, after all the recent trouble, that she confiscated her phone. She's seventeen, sick of being treated like a child; it's another reason she wants to live with her grandparents in England. And this boy, he's lovely, his smile makes her smile back and she recalls how flat his stomach was, the colour of his skin.

Suddenly, she feels a small tug on the bottom of her t-shirt, she turns around and her sister's face is looking anxiously up at her. 'Ellie! We've been looking everywhere, Mum is going to kill you.'

Ellie bites her lip, fearful for a second but then defiant. 'I'm seventeen, Gaynor. Mum should chill out.'

But when she looks back the crowd has once again closed in on itself and she can no longer see the cute boy, or his beautiful friend, or even the bulldog man. Her chance for some fun is gone.

Gaynor tugs hard at Ellie's t-shirt, her face scrunched. 'We've got to find Mum, Ellie! She's going nuts.'

Gaynor's red mac flaps in a gust of air like a flag.

'Okay, Gaynor. Calm down. I wasn't lost, I was just here.'

'I wanted to go on the ferris wheel,' Gaynor says petulantly, her eyes narrowing now she realises her sister wasn't even lost, that all of the worry and shouting was for nothing. 'But we were too busy looking for you. Mum's dragged me everywhere, screaming your name. I've had a rubbish night and it's all your fault.'

Gaynor's lower lip wobbles and Ellie sees that she might cry. This trip was a treat Gaynor had been looking forward to, she'd spoken of nothing else the whole three weeks they'd watched Schueberfouer being constructed.

Ellie looks up at the wheel, huge and majestic, glass boxes taken around at a slow pace that even she might be able to cope with. Gaynor especially wanted to ride it but Ellie has no head

11

for heights, like her mother.

'I never got to go on,' Gaynor pouts. 'I wanted to, but Mum said we had to find you and I shouldn't be so selfish. But it wasn't me who was selfish, it was you.' Gaynor is teetering on a tantrum now, the panic and then relief at finding her sister has turned to anger. 'It was all a lie. You weren't even lost!'

Ellie juts out her chin, but her defiance is now only for show. Gaynor has made her feel guilty.

'I'm sorry, okay. Look, why don't I take you on the wheel now, to make up for it? But first we'd better find Mum.'

* * *

When they find her, their mother's face is strained, her eyes almost popping with tension and her voice is hoarse from screaming. She tried grabbing a bored-looking fair official, begged for help, but he wasn't interested in a seventeen-year-old who's wandered off for a few minutes. She's rung Achim, but he took that calm, measured tone that made her want to scream and told her she was overreacting as always. Bridget feels that she is the only one who cares that Ellie is lost, and her relief at seeing her daughter is both powerful and explosive, a force she cannot contain.

She hugs Ellie to her chest, once and hard, then pulls away and nips her chin in her fingers, shouting at her daughter with the last of her breath.

12

'Don't walk away like that! What are you playing at?'

She braces Ellie by the shoulders, shakes her with pent-up anger, then hugs her with immense relief again, longer this time, kissing her cheek with lips as strong as a punch so Ellie jerks away.

'Mum! Stop fussing.'

'You scared me! Why do you do that to me? Don't you know how it hurts, how it terrifies me?'

'Lighten up, Mum. This is Luxembourg, not some war zone. Remember?' Ellie is turning away when her mother grabs her, harder than before. Pulls her so mother and daughter are face-to-face, eye-to-eye.

'Don't speak to me like that!'

Ellie's response is as loud and angry. 'Then don't overreact. I don't need your help! I'm fine!'

Her mother slaps her across her face. 'Stop being such a little bitch or I'll teach you a lesson you won't forget!'

Ellie flinches, reels back. She senses that other people close by have heard the exchange and are watching too, and thinks she sees a mother from the school. She is used to shouting, even slaps are not rare, but her mother only swears when she's drunk. Looking at her mother's dilated pupils it occurs to Ellie that this might be the case.

'There are things you don't know about the world. And I am trying to protect you.'

Ellie pulls away, she wants to free herself, shaken as she is by her mother's intensity.

13

Gaynor is unruffled by the angry display, she's used to seeing her mum worked up with Ellie, and the swearing hasn't registered. She cares only about the promised ride.

'Can we go on the wheel now?' she natters her sister, demanding and feeling justified. 'To make up for your selfishness?'

She sounds just like their mother, Ellie thinks.

Bridget.

Bridget tries to get a grip on herself, shakily opens her purse in a valiant show of normality, sighs at how little remains and pulls out her last two twenty euro notes, thrusting one at Ellie with a shaking hand.

'Go then.' She tries to smile at her daughter, but Ellie is refusing to look at her. She is ashamed now, of calling her daughter a bitch, of the slap. But still she feels aggrieved. 'I'll wait for you over there.'

She points to the wine stand, set on a rotating platform, some hundred yards away. After the search for Ellie and fighting through crowds like a crazy woman, she could do with a drink. She had a small beer twenty minutes ago, when Gaynor said she was desperate for a juice, and drank it quickly. It's gone to her head.

'Have fun,' she calls to both her daughters. It sounds forced, a limp afterthought, even to herself.

Bridget carefully watches Ellie and Gaynor make their way to the queue and turns towards the wine bar, deciding she deserves to sit down. For the past hour she's dragged Gaynor around the whole of the Glacis, and now she feels guilty. Ellie was fine all along, Bridget had overreacted. 'Like usual' Achim had said on phone, when she'd called in the midst of her panic. This has proved him right, and he will gloat when she tells him.

But Ellie's disappearance has wrecked Bridget, ruined the night for Gaynor too, who had wanted to go on everything, to taste all, and knew nothing of the money it cost or the fact that no amount of ping-pong balls in jars or arrows in boards were ever going to win that jelly board or huge teddy or quad bike. It was all a con, all part of the fun of the fair.

Bridget orders a glass of Crémant, pays with her final twenty euro note, and takes a seat on the wooden turntable, half under the plastic roof so random spots of summer rain prick her face but her body remains dry. The wine, disappointingly, is over-sweet for her palate and the fix makes her feel slightly sick, especially as she hasn't eaten yet and it's almost ten o'clock. Still, the hit of the alcohol is welcome, it numbs the edge of the tension. She should relax, she hasn't seen anyone else screaming at their kids. She feels the threatening pulse of a migraine around her eyes, maybe because of the wet weather, maybe the flashing lights and smells of hot machines. She shouldn't finish the drink, but she does and buys a second even though she knows she is skirting the drink-drive limit.

She sips the dregs, wincing but swallowing just

the same, watching the wheel turn slowly. Bridget is unsure which gondola her daughters are in, thinks the wheel is the only thing in the whole damned fair with proper beauty. On a stall nearest the wine bar plastic flowers are for sale, and wooden ones tinted purple and pink, but she finds them tasteless and hates the way the sellers push them under her nose so she is forced to swallow the stench of pot pourri. At least the Crémant drowns out the flower smell with citrus and grape. Bridget checks her purse, though she knows just coins remain now.

When they are off the wheel she will take the girls home and get Gaynor straight to bed, so that everything is quiet and peaceful when she tries again to talk to Ellie. That girl needs to learn about the dangers she refuses to see, about how vulnerable a teenage girl is in this world. Ellie used to listen, there was a time she respected what Bridget said, but recently she has been so difficult. Sleeping with boys, experimenting with drugs, acting like life is one big joke. Bridget has felt keenly what it means to have a husband who always works late, who comes home only to disappear into his study where he reopens his beloved laptop. It would be wonderful to share the parenting burden, just once, but this was the life she chose when she agreed to give up her nursing career and move to Luxembourg. She has to be resourceful, as she learned to be out in the field, nursing in a war zone. Ironic, she thinks, that it was easier than being a mother.

Bridget suddenly feels as though she's being

watched, her neck muscles tense and there are goose bumps down her arms. Then she turns and knows for sure, a man is staring at her. His dark face, his thick body, is familiar to her. She feels she has seen him before, and he is looking at her with such familiarity that this must be true. She plays her fingers on the stem of the empty glass, thinking she should go and fetch her girls, but before she can leave he moves towards her.

'Please forgive me for watching you,' he says, and then she sees that he has a fresh glass of wine in his hand. He removes the empty glass from between her fingers and replaces it with the full one. 'I had to be sure it was really you. I was not even sure you were still alive.'

It is then that she remembers who he is. 'Jak?'

He smiles, and his eyes crinkle at the edges. It is an older face, and back then she never saw him smile. He's larger too, but he was a soldier when she knew him. The first time she met him he had a gun, and was wearing a uniform. And he was holding a baby.

The conversation ends as the third glass of wine is finished. No longer feeling so wretched, Bridget gathers herself and begins to walk slowly towards the wheel. The queue is longer now and she has to step aside, communicating with her hunched body and upturned eyes that she is not waiting for a turn, but rather for someone on the ride. There is a gated area in front of the wheel, accessed only by purchasing a ticket, and despite the fake grass and illuminated plastic benches the atmosphere is one of cattle being herded into a van. Three men, all security-bouncer beefy, are opening the door of the empty gondolas, letting new riders in. The customers who have finished their ride have already exited on the other side, which is not nearly so attractive, no grass or bench, just a muddy track leading behind a fence.

Realising her mistake, Bridget tries to backtrack, much to the annoyance of the people behind her who are impatiently brandishing their tickets. She ignores dirty looks as she moves around to the back where groups and couples and families are pouring out of the gondolas, shaky-legged, in a continuous stream.

Through the fence she watches expectantly for Ellie and Gaynor. One gondola opens and a group of teenagers run out, all wearing hats and oversized shirts, some carrying skateboards. Even the girls are dressed in the shirts workmen favour the world over, worn cotton in tartan check. One boy, handsome but angry, knocks into her. Meekly, Bridget steps aside, making herself small, and wills her daughters to be in the next box.

She sees Gaynor's red mac before the glass box comes to a halt and is already turning to leave the awkward place where she is forever in the way.

Then she sees that Gaynor isn't with her sister, but with a mother and daughter, whom she recognises from the school playground. As soon as Gaynor is close, Bridget asks, 'Where's Ellie?'

Irritated that her elder daughter has once

again ignored her instructions, so soon after getting lost, she tries to steady herself but the wine sloshing around her stomach is making her feel sick and her throat is still sore from shouting. If Ellie has wandered off again she has no more reserves left.

Gaynor, unconcerned, says, 'I wanted to ride with Amelia. You remember, Mum, she started at the end of last term? She's in my class.'

Bridget struggles to take in Gaynor's answer. She is struggling to process that Ellie has once again gone off on her own. Ellie was supposed to be with Gaynor, and she couldn't even do this. She's worn her fury out and sadness seeps into its place. Where did she go wrong, that Ellie is so wilful and selfish?

'So Ellie let you ride without her. Which box is she in, then?'

Gaynor is distracted by her friend from school, chatting happily with Amelia in the afterglow of the ride, but Bridget crouches so she can see Gaynor's face and impart the seriousness of the situation.

'Where is your sister, Gaynor?'

Gaynor looks around to where a couple of teenagers are standing, a handsome brown-eyed boy and a beautiful girl with hair as sleek as oil, messing around in a way that could quickly become violent. The girl is watching them, a strand of black hair in her mouth, her impassive face unreadable.

'She went on with them, on the gondola behind mine,' Gaynor says. 'I think she fancies that boy over there. She was watching him

19

earlier, he didn't have a t-shirt on.'

She smiles naughtily as she says this and her friend joins in. They are being cheeky, but Bridget feels cold, the tips of her fingers tingle.

'We'll wait here for Ellie to come back,' Bridget says, disappointing Gaynor yet again, who wants to go on another ride with Amelia.

Instead they stand side by side as the next glass box came to a halt, but Ellie isn't in that one either. Or the next one.

Bridget is distracted, but is vaguely aware that Gaynor's friend, Amelia, the little blonde girl who arrived from England halfway through the summer term, is waiting too. Amelia's mother, a petite redhead in terrible clothes, has been busy untying a black Labrador from where it was tethered to a post, but now she comes up to Bridget, the dog wagging its tail eagerly at the girls. 'Hello. Shame about the rain, isn't it? The seat was soaking! Is your other daughter still on the ride?'

'I hope so,' said Bridget, as she fights to keep the tone in her voice calm. Looking back to the crowds of surging people she has the hysterical thought that she'll never find her and curses herself for confiscating Ellie's iPhone, punishment for Ellie spending the night with Joe last week, and then making plans to meet him here even though Bridget had expressly forbidden any further contact. The phone was practically attached to Ellie's head, and taking it away was the only way Bridget could really make her see that there were consequences to her thoughtless actions.

'I'm sorry,' she says to the British woman, who appears to be waiting until Bridget finds Ellie. 'But I can't remember your name.'

'I'm Cate,' replies the other woman, offering a hand to shake. 'Cate Austin.'

The gondolas keep emptying and filling, and Bridget's hysteria increases with every one that doesn't contain her girl. Amelia and Cate stand dutifully, the black Labrador pulling impatiently at his lead while Cate makes soothing suggestions about teenagers and fairs and her turning up soon. But Ellie doesn't turn up and by the time the wheel has completed yet another cycle, Bridget can recognise people getting off as those she saw getting on. She is trying to control it, but tears are mingling with the raindrops that fall from the sky.

She rings Achim's mobile a second time, tapping her foot and looking left to right as she waits for him to pick up. He doesn't. So she rings again, counting the rings to almost fifty until he gets the message and finally answers.

'Bridget, I'm in a meeting.'

'I'm still at the fair.' She tries to stop the tears being heard in her voice. 'Ellie's run off again.'

A pause. Could she hear a sigh? Or was he speaking quietly to whomever he was in a meeting with. 'But you found her last time?'

Bridget tells herself that she's not being hysterical, really she's not. 'Yes, eventually. But she's gone off again, she's not here Achim. I can't find her anywhere.'

'So call her mobile.'

21

'We confiscated it, so she wouldn't contact Joe. Remember?'

Now the sigh was audible. 'Bridget, I really don't know what you expect me to do. I'm in the middle of a Skype meeting to America here, and it's important. We've just heard the budget is going to be cut.'

'But I don't know where Ellie is. Please, Achim.' She wants to say 'help me' but stops herself. 'She went with Gaynor to get on the ferris wheel, and then she just disappeared.'

'Well, when you find her you tell her she's grounded for another week. I'll speak to her when I get home, or tomorrow, as I may not be home before midnight the way this is going. Now let me get back into this meeting before they decide that one way to save money is to sack me. Okay?'

It wasn't okay, but what else did she expect him to say? Bridget ended the call, surprised when Cate touches her arm, she hadn't even registered the other mother was still there.

'Maybe we should find someone from security?' she suggests. 'Put out an alert for her.'

Bridget hesitates, she's reluctant to do anything that will look like she's creating a fuss, but Cate seems to know what to do and Bridget allows herself to be guided through the crowd. Behind them, Gaynor and Amelia chat happily about school and which stand has the best prizes, calling to their mothers to look at certain things, asking about going on more rides. Bridget hardly hears; she hardly feels the push and swell of the crowds. She just wants to find Ellie.

Cate has collared the same official whom Bridget spoke with earlier.

He looks at Bridget with an assessing expression, and she sees what he thinks of her: *overanxious.*

'This is the second time you have spoken to me, yes? And last time, your daughter, she was okay?'

Bridget has to concede that she was.

The man waves a hand dismissively. 'So she will turn up again.'

For him this must seem normal, a teenager lost in the crowd, probably wilful, but Cate insists that he sends a message out on his radio, an alert for Ellie. She says Ellie has been missing for almost half an hour now, it's dark and the rain is getting heavier. They need to find her, to go home.

Seeing that the redhead will not leave until he agrees, reluctantly the man presses the talk button on his radio and speaks into it in quick Luxembourgish, breaking off to ask Bridget, 'What is she wearing?'

The question jolts Bridget because for a second she doesn't know. And then she remembers the yellow t-shirt. The security official gives this information over the radio, still unmoved, and around them the crowds begin to shelter in the awnings of stands selling waffles and candy floss, they continue to scream on the ghost train and roller coaster.

The wheel continues to turn.

23

'In here,' calls Olivier, hearing them arrive home in a fumble of bags and coats and heavy yawning.

Cate leaves her keys in the pot for items that get lost and walks through into the open-plan lounge where he is curled on the sofa, typing on his laptop, the TV is switched onto a local news channel, but the volume is off. General beats her to Olivier's side, sniffing at his master's legs until Olivier gives him a brisk rub on his flat head.

'You're late. How was the fair?' he asks, looking up so that General whines at the sudden lack of attention.

'Busy.' Cate sits on the sofa, and begins unlacing her trainers.

'But good,' adds Amelia, plopping herself cross-legged on the rug and reaching for the TV remote. Within seconds she has found a channel she likes and American chatter fills the room. 'I saw my friend, Gaynor. She's in Mr Z's class with me. Can I go to hip-hop class with her on Wednesday?'

'Mmmm.' Olivier isn't really listening, his attention is back on his computer screen.

'That's why we're so late,' adds Cate, her feet now in socks as she pushes them across his thighs. He puts his laptop aside and cups her toes with his hands, finally engaging eye contact. She can see Olivier is tired, the skin under his eyes is slightly dark. 'You okay?'

'I'm fine. Tell me about the fair.'

'We met Amelia's friend, Gaynor, and went on

24

the ferris wheel with her. Her sister got on the gondola after us, rode with a couple of local kids. But when her ride ended she just walked off, we couldn't find her anywhere. You should have seen her mother, she was pretty upset, I almost had to carry her to the security guard to report it. I felt bad leaving her, but someone from the fair came over to help. And Amelia needs to be in bed.' This last sentence she pointedly directed to her daughter.

'How old is this sister?'

'Seventeen.'

'Ah,' said Olivier, giving a knowing look as if that explains everything. 'At that age I used to get lost at Schueberfouer whenever I could. So, do you want something to drink?'

★　★　★

The evening unwound, Amelia yawned one too many times and was sent to bed, despite her protests that it was Sunday tomorrow, no school. Olivier and Cate chatted sleepily about how to spend the day.

'If the weather has cleared let's drive north, to the lake.'

'I'd like that.' Cate kissed him. 'But I want to go to bed now.'

'You're tired?'

'I didn't say that,' she replied, nibbling his earlobe.

It was still a novelty, being able to look forward to not sleeping alone. After three months everything still felt new for Cate, just landed in Luxembourg, newly liberated from her career. Newly in love.

★ ★ ★

As Cate fell, exhausted and happy, into a deep sleep, beyond the flat the rain had stopped and a fog had started to descend over Luxembourg. By the time the super moon was eclipsed by the grey smog, the lights of the fair were being turned off for the night. In the Glacis car park a trickle of travelling folk made their way to their caravans, stepping over puddles as they greeted each other, sharing stories about the punters. On the hoopla stall, one Japanese customer had spent 100 euro on hoops and still walked away without a prize. On the ghost train a kid had got so terrified he threw up on his seat and they had to close the ride while they cleaned it up. Other fair folk didn't stop to chat, but as they walked to their caravans they totted up in their heads how much money they had made, others thought nothing, were simply looking forward to getting their head down for the night.

One man remained awake, sipping a coffee as he thought about the next trip, the next fair. Planning the step beyond Luxembourg, beyond Europe and back to Algeria, the place where his story and many others began. He thought of the majestic Djurdjura Mountain, its tall white crowns and hidden places, and wished himself back there though he knew he had left that life behind. He was not a soldier anymore, and the baby he had saved was now a man. Both of them were a long way from home.

Amina

When she reached the far side of the commune she stopped running, resting a moment as she checked that no-one had seen her leave. Beyond was the olive plantation where she and her brother and sister had played when they were little, sheltering from the too-hot sun under the lush protection of its whispering canopy. The brown earth was warm and soothing between her toes and the air had a sharp lemony tang as she breathed it in. She heard a rustle behind her and turned in case a jackal was about to pounce, but could see nothing but the yellow flowers with their stringy petals, the thin and twisted branches of the *ouzou* plant, the white-blue sky above. Then a small hand slipped inside her own and her sister, Pizzie, pressed against her.

'Oh, Piz, you shouldn't have followed me. You know we are not allowed to be here alone.'

'We're not alone now,' she said, though both girls knew that without a male escort this was the same thing. Pizzie looked quizzically at her big sister. 'Why are you crying?'

Amina squatted down so her nose touched that of the six-year-old, gazing into her half-moon-shaped brown eyes, wondering if she would see her again.

'Because I'm leaving you.'

Piz frowned, which made her face so serious

that Amina had to look away to avoid laughing. 'But you are going to a better place with food and money and school. A place for freedom, Omi says. Where police will not call in the night.'

Amina kissed her sister's grubby forehead and forced a smile.

'I hope so, little one. It is what has been promised.'

She avoided looking up, towards the mountain. Hidden in Djurdjura's rocky folds was danger, and maybe even their brother, Samir, though they couldn't be sure as rumours are not to be trusted. The elders said he was still in Paris.

Pizzie followed her sister's gaze. 'Is he watching us, Amina?'

Amina's eyes travelled the mountain as she never would, rising to the peak, Tamgut Aalayen, where men hid and waited, fighting a war for Allah.

'I hope not,' she answered quietly. She willed her brother elsewhere, because she was scared of what it would mean for Samir if he was back with the Brotherhood. What it would mean for her mother and sister, when she was no longer at home to care for them. Since January the Algerian police had knocked almost every week, and if not them then there were visits from the mosque elders, asking about Samir, making Omi cry with their accusations and their threats.

Omi said she had no idea why her son had gone to Paris, she knew nothing of the friends he had made there who were now dead. It was a shock to her, as much as to anyone else, that eleven people had died in that city, eleven more had been injured, and that his friends had wielded the guns. But Samir was not connected to this, she was certain, it was impossible. He was a good boy.

Even when she searched in his bedroom after the police had left, and found a pile of comics, the drawings on the covers of Muhammad. The drawings were shocking. She looked closer and saw names, realised that they were drawn by men who were now dead. No, Samir was not involved. It could not be so. Omi was sure of it. And yet she began to plan for her daughters to leave Algeria, to go to a safe place where they could not be touched by the things their brother may have done.

Uncle Jak had agreed with Omi. Yes, this was the best way. But Pizzie was too young to travel without a parent. It was not her time yet. Amina would have to go alone.

★　★　★

Back in Amina's modest home a party, subdued but hospitable, was under way. On the rough ground behind their domed stone house, three wooden tables had been erected in a line, and bowls of food were displayed like flowers; every colour of rice, green leafy delicacies, yellow fruit and, of course, meat. Amina's mouth watered at the sight, until she saw Uncle Jak helping himself to huge amounts with thick fingers, piling his bowl high.

Uncle Jak had arranged everything, as he had for others who had already left the city of Tizi Ouzou, so Omi said they could trust him. He was known to be a good man. Rumour was that he had saved a baby once who would have perished without his help, and now that baby was living with Jak in Europe, as his son. Jak was a man of honour. Plus, he had shown them letters, written by some of the girls, that described big houses on golf courses, wealth beyond their wildest dreams and — most important of all to Amina — reading books and learning. Things that Samir had started to say were unseemly in a wife, whose role was set down by Allah and not to be questioned. On his last visit he had said other things too, about Allah's wishes and what should happen to those who did not follow the righteous path. He had said that as the head of the household, Amina's husband would be a man of his choosing, one of his brothers-in-arms, and that even if Amina was left a widow it was an honourable state. Soon after, when Samir had once again disappeared suddenly with no warning, Omi spoke to Amina of Uncle Jak. This was the beginning of the plan for her to leave.

Uncle Jak was not a relative, but he was Kabyle and that amounted to the same thing. He had been a soldier once, like Samir, and now he lived in Europe. He returned twice a year with his truck, and took the eldest child of some families away, for a better life.

★ ★ ★

30

Amina watched how he eased himself into his seat, chatting in rusty Kablye to the relatives Omi had trusted to invite, his stomach wobbling, and jowls like rubber tyres around his hairy neck and chin, though his mouth was strangely small and delicate. He jumped when the chickens scratched near him, and became irritated when their goat, Lila, tried to nibble his shirt. He lived in a foreign city now, their ways must seem strange to him. But Amina only knew to trust the soil and the animals and the mountain. She knew nothing of shirts with starch or hair with gel or stomachs with too much food. And it made her scared.

★ ★ ★

Omi sat on a stool at the head of the women's table, a position of honour as she was saying goodbye to her daughter. The white material of her *haik*, which covered her body, shaded her completely, but underneath its folds Amina knew she was fragile as a bird. Amina knelt by her side, breathing in the aloe scent of the oil she used on her skin.

'You look very pretty, Omi. But you should eat.'

Omi was wearing her best *haik*, which had delicate embroidery and bright beading along each edge, carefully washed after each wear so only slightly grey. It was the same *haik* she had worn for her wedding when she was just a girl, and for every party since. But five children, three still living, had taken their toll and the dress hung on her loosely, some of the beads had been lost along the hem. Inspired, Amina kissed her mother's sallow cheek.

'The first thing I buy in the city is a roll of silk for you, Omi. I'll send it here.'

Omi smiled sadly, coughing with a hand to her chest. 'And what would I do with silk? I want you to go to school, Amina. I want you to know yourself before you know a husband, and I do not want you to be a widow.' She addressed her guest, her frail voice rising with emotion. 'She will go to school, Jak? You have promised me.'

'Do not fret, Omi.' Uncle Jak laughed deeply, as he swallowed a large mouthful of food. 'Only the best school for our Amina! I shall see to it, Madame. *Viva harraga!*' Then he wagged a finger as if Amina were a spoiled creature. 'But you must work too, little lady. In Europe it is expected.'

Omi sat higher on her wooden stool. 'My daughter is not afraid of work, she has helped me for many years with the animals, and with the vineyard when her father was alive.'

There was silence, and Amina wondered if anyone else at the party was thinking of the day her father was killed, all because his vineyard produced wine, dark enough to stain the tongue purple, and alcohol was forbidden by Allah. Samir, his own son, had said the death was just, even though since then the grapes had rotted on the vines, and there was no money for food. Samir did not think about this, or the hardship that followed. He was on a higher path.

Uncle Jak bowed his head. 'You have my word,

Madame. Amina will go to school. And I will protect her as if she were my own daughter. I was a soldier once, and it would not be the first time I have saved a child. Amina is safe with me.'

Day 1

Ellie

Ellie's head hurt, even opening her eyes made her wince. She must have drunk a lot, because her limbs felt heavy and she didn't know where she was. This had happened before, waking with black holes in her memory. Last time she had been with Joe, she'd passed out in his bedroom after too much vodka and missed her curfew. Mum would kill her for doing it again.

'Joe?' she murmured, sending her weak voice into the dark room. There was no reply.

Gingerly, Ellie lifted her head and looked around. She was lying on her back, fully clothed but for her shoes, with one leg hanging off the side, but the mattress was too narrow for her to shift position without toppling to the ground. She felt sick, she could barely move without her stomach threatening to empty itself. She inched her hand along to feel the other side of the bed, expecting to find Joe's sleeping body but instead there was a wall, though it made a hollow sound when she knocked her hand against it. It was metal. Was she in a caravan? Where was Joe?

Sitting up as much as she could manage, Ellie saw that above the narrow bed was a tiny window, half-covered with a ragged curtain. It was still dark outside. *Okay, good,* she reassured herself. She was finding it hard to string one thought to the next. What she felt more than anything was exhaustion, and it was anaesthetising any fear. *You've had too much to drink but you won't be home late.* She tried to sit up properly, but simply didn't have the energy. Her stomach heaved and she was forced back down, lying as still as she could until the wave of nausea passed.

Slowly, the memories of the night began to drip through. She remembered she hadn't been with Joe, but another boy. Malik. He had called to Ellie as she waited in line for the ferris wheel, he and the beautiful girl had gestured her over, and because Gaynor had found a friend from school and they were chatting happily, she had gone. Ellie couldn't remember much after that, though she knows she had a drink from the way her head hurts. Just a bottle of Diekirch. Or was it two? She had been nervous, she remembered that, both about the possibility of being spotted by her mother wandering off again and being revealed to be a goody two shoes in front of this exotic couple, who didn't have a parent watching over them like an hysterical hawk.

Ellie swallowed, her throat hurt and her tongue felt like sandpaper. *God, I need some water.* Her mum would be worried, she should call her. But then she remembered that she couldn't, because her iPhone had been confiscated as punishment after her mum found her texting Joe. She'd been forbidden any contact ever since she spent the night at his

35

house. Her mum had slapped her when she returned home, hungover the following morning, and called her a slut. She'd taken her to the doctor for a morning-after pill even though Ellie told her again and again that she'd been too drunk to have sex. At least the doctor was sympathetic, requesting that her mother leave the room so she could have some time alone with Ellie and then, when it was just the two of them, asking with genuine concern if everything was okay at home.

The thought of her mother's rage last night triggered a dull fury at the injustice of it, a recollection of that barbed insult, *little bitch*, and the slap. She felt some satisfaction that her mother would be suffering now. Bet she wished she'd not taken the phone away. And just because Ellie wanted to be with a friend rather than her snotty sister.

Gaynor.

Ellie felt a pinch in her gut that did nothing to ease her sickness as she thought about her sister. She should have ridden the big wheel with her, she'd promised. But the cool kids, Malik and the girl, were calling her over. She was about to climb in the gondola with Gaynor, Amelia and her mum, looking like some dorky family.

Instead she'd walked across to Malik. She'd made a choice. It was only now, waking up in the caravan, that she wondered whether she'd made a bad one. *Where is Malik now? Where the fuck am I?*

Head throbbing with each tentative movement, Ellie lifted the ratty piece of fabric from the window that may once have been a curtain, wiping the condensation with her palm. All that was visible was wire fencing, the same fence that wrapped around the Glacis to keep the fair secure when it was shut, and a white van that was decorated with some advertising. In the distance the ferris wheel was still and unlit. Without the glamour of lights or music, it looked abandoned, like a half-finished building project.

Ellie's limbs felt stiff. Her yellow t-shirt looked grubby as did her bare feet. She saw now that her elbows were caked with dry soil and under her fingernails was something dark, which looked like dried blood. She inspected herself for scratches or cuts, but couldn't find any.

She got off the bed, and needed to support herself on the table. There was nothing on the shelf but a small bottle of Viva. She grabbed for it. *Oh, thank God.* She drank the whole bottle in one greedy gulp, coming up for air with a crunch of the plastic and a gasp.

Hydrated, though still unsteady, Ellie reached for the door handle, twisted it. Nothing happened. She twisted in the other direction, but still the door remained stubbornly closed. She turned again to the window, but when she searched for a clasp she saw it was solid and didn't open.

She was locked in.

Panicked, Ellie explored all the hidden places of the caravan but found nothing, just empty cupboards and a bone-dry sink. Her head began to pound and her thinking slowed, sluggish, so she grasped onto this one thing: *I must find my trainers*, as though that was the most pressing problem. Apart from the water and a bottle of bleach under the sink, there was nothing else. She sat back on the pull-out bed, woozy and thinking she was going to be sick, bile was already stinging her throat. She breathed slowly to master the feeling, but it wouldn't go away. She was soon spitting into her hand, phlegm-like strands of moisture, then running to the sink and heaving.

Her meal from last night, the potato cakes her mum had bought her, came up in a liquid burst. Both hands on the side of the sink, Ellie panted and gasped, unused to vomiting. When was the last time? That holiday in Morocco, after she'd had Coke with ice from the beach vendor. Later the staff at the hotel told her mum that the ice cubes would have been the problem. Ellie had lain in the hotel room, the curtains half-drawn and watched the ceiling fan whirl, gasping in the cool air like it was liquid because she was so parched and couldn't even hold down water. And all the time her mum had sat by her side, stroking her forehead, reading to her. Holding her when the retching took over. Ellie had never questioned that her mum would always be there when she was ill.

But not now.

'Mum,' she called weakly, to the empty caravan.

Then she lifted her head and looked herself square in the mirror. Barely recognising the pale face that stared back at her.

Bridget

Across the city, Bridget was sitting on the sofa in her front lounge, holding a wristwatch in her hands and watching the second hand turn. For seven hours and forty minutes she had done this, ever since Achim had made the call to the police.

Whoever he'd spoken to had told him that a missing person would not become a police matter until twelve hours had passed. There were still four hours until he could officially report their daughter missing. Achim had argued with the police operator, and put Bridget on the phone, demanding that she explain exactly what had happened.

Bridget had made it worse then. She'd only told the truth, that Ellie had wanted to be with her boyfriend, that she had stayed out overnight with him before without permission. Even to her ears it sounded like a teenage strop, a bit of normal rebellion, and the woman on the other end of the line said as much. Trying to reassure her but coming across as patronising.

Achim had been furious, with the police, but with her too. After he'd put the phone down, giving up on any police help just yet, he'd proceeded to call every one of Ellie's friends. Most didn't pick up, so he'd resorted to texting:

Is Ellie with you? This is her father. I just need to know she's okay.

The answers had been swift, sympathetic, but none of them knew where she was. He'd called Joe first, waiting until he picked up, but Joe said he had no idea where she might be, that he had finished with Ellie anyway. The night Ellie and Joe had spent together had not meant so very much, it seemed. He didn't even sound surprised that she had failed to come home.

After making the futile calls, Achim had gone upstairs. Bridget had wandered up just after midnight and again at two and both times he had been in their bedroom, laying on their bed, fully clothed with his hands behind his head, staring at the ceiling. He didn't say anything, but she could feel the waves of anger rolling off him with increasing intensity. He'd always babied Ellie, which was part of the problem. She'd been so spoiled, overly protected.

'I think Ellie will be okay,' she'd ventured, stepping closer to the bed. 'She'll be home tomorrow, sorry she's caused us all this worry.'

He didn't respond, but she saw his jaw clench. He didn't agree with her.

'She's seventeen, Achim. When you were that age you didn't even live at home.'

'That was different,' he protested, 'I was a boy. And it wasn't the same.'

★   ★   ★

Achim had been at university, so he was right, it wasn't the same. A bright boy, he had got a place at Heidelberg University, a three hours' drive away from his family home. After graduating he'd moved to England to study for his Masters in business studies. It was where they had met, in Durham. Bridget had just arrived back in England after a nursing placement in Africa, and was itching to get away from her parents' home, sleeping in her childhood bed, until a new assignment was offered to her. She longed to be back overseas, the excitement of the unknown. Being home was a trial, as neither parent understood her need to get away. 'Aren't there sick people here in Durham?' her mum would ask, and Bridget knew that there was no proper answer for that.

She was only in the bar because it was cheap, a student hang-out, and Achim had appealed to her because of his German accent. Even in Durham she wanted something different and foreign, and that was what he seemed to offer. But still, her work came first, and when Médecins Sans Frontières offered her the posting in Tizi Ouzou she took it without even thinking of him. The relationship should have ended there. It would have ended there, if not for his persistence. Meeting up on rare breaks, showing her a different world from the war-torn camp where she tried her best to mend what was broken.

That last placement, the one in Tizi Ouzou, she had nearly taken a very different path. She had been devoted to the country, and its people.

Achim had graduated by then, got a job in Heidelberg. It seemed that they would never even meet again.

Of course, when she discovered she was pregnant, she knew a baby would mean she had to give up her job. An abortion was the only option, and this meant arranging a trip back to Europe. It was all in place, and she had no doubt it was the right decision.

And then the solider arrived with the baby and thrust it in her arms.

It changed everything.

Once Bridget had decided to keep the baby she resolved to give birth in Algeria in order to continue working as late into the pregnancy as possible. Achim would not hear of it, a child of his being born in an area where tourists were warned not to travel and healthcare was basic. There was no counter-argument, either, from MSF. A pregnant nurse was a liability; her work with them was over. So Bridget turned her back on her vocation and moved to Heidelberg, to start a life with Achim, even though she knew they were from different worlds. It wasn't what she had planned, but she came to see that Achim had given her a gift.

He had given her Ellie.

In Heidelberg, Bridget was restless, and also bored. Having a toddler was no substitute for the adrenalin-filled frenzy of working on a MSF camp, so when Achim had suggested she get a job at the university hospital, she leapt at the idea. The vacancy was in a new department, the Ion Treatment Programme for cancer sufferers, the first of its kind in Europe. Once she started to work she felt needed again.

They should never have left Heidelberg.

Achim's company had offered him a promotion to Luxembourg and it seemed he simply couldn't say no. She had hoped her nursing skills would be useful there too, but Luxembourg was the one country where she couldn't practise, because she lacked the necessary language skills. French, she had, but after years without use it was rusty, and she had no knowledge of Luxembourgish. For MSF the fact that her French was poor had never been an issue, it was the language of nursing that was so desperately needed, and she had developed both skills at a rapid rate in Tizi. But in Luxembourg she was grounded, relegated to a housewife and recent evidence was that she wasn't cut out for the job.

How could she be? When her daughter had now been missing for eight hours. Just four more until the police would become involved. *Let it be over by then. Bring her home now.*

$\star$　$\star$　$\star$

By four-thirty Bridget's body was exhausted but her brain was still running the same thought: *Just wait until it's morning. Everything will be okay, it's always better when it's light.*

The second hand on her wristwatch kept moving, and slowly the time was spent.

At ten to seven she heard movement upstairs, the shower being run, and Achim eventually appeared, his hair wet from a quick shower. He looked exhausted.

'Did you manage to get any sleep, Achim?'

He shook his head. 'You?'

'I've been sat here by the window all night. Waiting for her to come home.'

He frowned, his mouth twitched and she willed him to say something comforting, something that would make all of this feel

43

different, better somehow.

'Coffee?'

She nodded, thinking how strange it was, that if someone peered in the window right now it could almost look like a normal day. Then she saw that he was wearing his work jacket.

'You're not going in to the office?'

Achim shook his head, looking angry again. 'Of course not. I'm going to the police station, to make sure they do something. I thought it would be better to go in person, and I don't think it hurts if I look professional.'

Achim was a senior partner with his bank, he was used to being listened to.

'Don't leave me with this,' she begged, panicking. 'Ellie will be home soon, I know she will. Please just wait here with me. Please, Achim.'

He looked at his watch. 'I'll be back as soon as I can, okay? Look, Bridget, if Ellie arrives home you call me, straight away. You're right, she'll probably be back before I am.'

'That's what she did last time, remember?' said Bridget, desperate to make him wait, to give Ellie more time. The idea of the police being involved terrified her. It escalated things to another level.

'But that was different,' he reasoned. 'We knew she was with Joe.'

Ellie had stormed out after a row, about her wish to study her A-levels in England and to live with her grandparents. As if Bridget was going to let her move to another country, at her age. After she'd gone, Bridget received an angry text saying she wasn't coming home. But the text had been sent from Joe's phone, so Bridget had known she was with him. The following day, Bridget had taken Ellie to the doctor for a morning-after pill, something Achim didn't know.

'Are we totally sure she's not with Joe now?' Achim said.

'He told you she wasn't,' Bridget replied. 'Besides, he finished with her. Remember?'

'He could be lying. I think I'll drive past his house on the way to the police station.'

Achim was collecting his keys, his phone. He paused and for a moment she though he was going to kiss her, hold her. But no comfort came.

'Call me if Ellie comes home,' he said.

Cate

Cate Austin's first waking thought was to wonder where she was.

Living in Luxembourg was still so new to her that her brain had not fully registered that she had a new life. She sometimes woke feeling confused, expecting to be in her Ipswich semi with a pressing need to get a move on because she was once again late for work. She no longer had to worry about that. Not for the immediate future anyway.

Cate stretched an arm across the bed, but Olivier was gone. She had learned that he was an early riser, and would likely have been up a few hours already, tapping away on his laptop and taking calls. For a city with the lowest crime rate in Europe, her detective boyfriend seemed plenty busy.

Unlike Cate. Leaving the probation service was a relief, like finally putting down a heavy load she had been carrying for so long that she had become too used to its weight. Cases, reports, prison visits. And her last case, Humber Boy B, that had made the decision to move abroad so easy. She didn't have to think about any of that now.

Her leaving party had been just six weeks before, at her manager Paul's house. The party had been in full swing, the house crowded with people she had worked with over the years, when she found her old police pal Stephen Flynn in the kitchen. He looked comical, clutching a colourful cocktail, and gave her a hug to congratulate her on escaping. He'd been flirting with the diligent office manager, Dot. They seemed to be getting on famously so Cate made her excuses and went to find Amelia and her half-sister, Chloe.

Paul had shepherded the girls into the front room in front of a massive screen, and played the box set of *Miranda* on a loop, so they were happily watching and squealing at the TV.

'You okay, Amelia? Having a good time?'

'Yeah, this is so funny. Stay and watch, Mum.'

Cate was glad to see Amelia that way, had been worried that this leaving party would upset her. After all, Amelia was saying goodbye to Chloe as well as her father, and that was a huge thing for a twelve-year-old. Tim had been opposed to the idea from the start, and tension

46

was running high between them, but Luxembourg was only a fifty-minute flight from
London and Cate had promised to bring Amelia
back to Suffolk every school holiday. Cate would
have to stay with her mother while Amelia was
with Tim, which wouldn't be a bed of roses, but
that was the deal she had struck and what she
had gained was a chance of a new life. And for
now, at least, Amelia was enthusiastic about the
plan.

Elsewhere in the house, adults chatted,
disinhibited by drink and the assurance of being
surrounded by friends. Paul waved Cate over to
his chair, pointed to where Olivier was fighting
the throng to get to the bar that was actually a
wallpaper table with a white cloth over it. 'He's
getting himself a beer and something with soda
for you. So we have a moment.'

'Thanks for organising this, Paul.'

She smiled at him but Paul's face remained
serious.

'I think you could be making a mistake,
sweetheart.' He touched her earlobe, where a
diamond earring sparkled under the lights, a gift
from Olivier. 'This is very pretty, but it may not
have much depth.'

Cate had known Paul for years and she trusted
him, but that didn't mean he had a right to rain
on her parade. 'Don't, Paul. Please, not when
everyone is having such a great time.'

'You not want to hear it?' He cocked his head
to one side, but his eyes were steely and she
recognised his stiff posture from when he was
broaching difficult news at the team meeting, or

47

taking on a mouthy member of staff.

And she didn't. She knew what he'd say; that she hadn't known Olivier long enough to move in with him, that she was giving up her career. Add to that Tim's fury that she was taking Amelia to live in another country and pretty much no-one thought it was a good idea.

'I feel responsible,' he continued. 'I encouraged you to give that sexist Frog a chance, and now he's stealing you away to Luxem-bloody-bourg. The only time I've heard about the place is in the Eurovision, *douze* bloody points. Where even is it anyway?'

'It's in the middle of Europe. A great chance to travel.'

'The middle of nowhere,' retorted Paul. 'And you can travel anywhere you like from Stansted, you don't need to go abroad to do it.'

Cate felt Paul scrutinising her and knew he was peering beneath the recent auburn highlights, the glossy make-up, to the real woman she was. She dreaded what he would say and looked over his shoulder, longing for Olivier's return.

'I think you'll be bored, sweetheart. You hate the Eurovision.'

This broke her resolve to keep a dignified silence. 'You know what, Paul, I'd love to be bored. I'd love to have nothing to think about except what cleaning product or pasta to buy. I'm sick to death with the probation service. Sick of violence and crime and poverty and abuse.'

Paul looked uncomfortable. 'Oh come on, Cate, you love it.'

He was trying to lighten things now, but she

48

was angry. When Paul saw this he said, 'Oh, sweetheart. You always did take life too seriously.'

'Exactly. I do. And I'd like just a year — my career break is only for twelve months! — when I don't have to ask someone why they killed their baby or ate their lover or chucked their best friend off the Humber Bridge.'

'Come on, Cate. Not all your cases were that interesting.'

Cate was irritated now, and just a bit exhausted. 'I don't want interesting, Paul. I want normal.'

Paul gave her a chaste kiss on the cheek and pulled away to look solemnly into her eyes that felt dangerously moist.

'Yeah? Well I'll give it a month before you get your sticky paws into something. I know you, Cate. You think you want to be a housewife or whatever but in your soul you're a probation officer. You'll find someone to fix, even in Luxembourg.'

★ ★ ★

So, here she was.

There had been a touch of frost on the ground when they set off from the city, yet just an hour later the sun made an appearance, proud as it should be for August in central Europe.

'The ice saints are late this year,' said Olivier, as they drove along winding roads flanked by pines, the sun warming by degrees with every minute.

'What's an ice saint?' Amelia said, leaning

49

forward between the seats in front of her so that General had to scrabble his paws to keep a purchase on the back seat, where he was laid out.

'A saint from spring, when you can have frost and sunshine in the same day. Just like today.'

Amelia grinned at that. 'I like it. Ice saints sounds like a pop group or something. Gaynor and me are going to sing together, we could call ourselves that, and audition for *Britain's Got Talent*.'

Cate, who had heard her daughter sing, smiled as she looked out of the car window. The road was higher now, the forest was behind them and instead, the landscape was flat. She could see for miles, down ravines, up to churches propped on crevices. Then the road headed downwards again, towards the lake.

★　★　★

Picnic blanket, hamper, Amelia's *Maze Runner* book that she had already read twice, and Cate's sketch pad that she had recently brought out of retirement. As General excitedly ran around, barking at a triage of geese flying past, they laid out their patch on the grassy banks of the reservoir Esch-Sur-Sûre. Cate set about slathering Amelia's pasty white skin with suncream, despite her protests.

'Mum! I'm not going to get a tan with factor 50.'

'No, and you're not going to get sunburned either.'

50

Amelia rolled her eyes, impatiently waiting until the job was done and she could swim. Cate then covered her own body with the thick white sunblock, much to Olivier's amusement. She held up the bottle, offering him some, but Olivier laughed and rejected the offer. 'I think I'll take my Vitamin D neat, thanks.'

He stretched back on the grass and sighed in contentment, a moment that was swiftly interrupted by his phone beeping. In one elegant movement he was walking, phone to his ear, away from them and towards the shade of the trees, standing under their dappled shadow as he spoke in quick French to whomever had disturbed their Sunday outing.

'I'm going to swim. Come too, Mum. You never get in the water.'

'Because it'll be freezing.'

'But it's boiling!' Amelia protested, grabbing Cate's hand and leading her over the flinty beach to the water's edge, much to General's delight. He didn't need any persuasion, and bounded into the water, his black fur turning sleek, seal-like, as it became drenched with the waves of water each bounding jump produced. Cate stepped in, crocs and all, and winced.

'See?' she called. 'Lake water takes a while to heat, even in August.'

Determined, Amelia waded deeper, so the water was at her knees then her thighs. General barked, and she splashed some water at him, making him even more excited. Cate stayed at the edge, watching her daughter play with the dog. Blinking at the water, it's silvery blue-green sheen, transparent and beautiful. The lake was edged by fir trees that graded in colour from lime to deep moss green, flanking the hills around them. Cate felt lucky to have escaped the past and Suffolk and all that had meant for her, but she found that even in this place she was still herself. Unable to shake the pensiveness, her habitual tendency to see the glass as half-empty. That trait had always been something she had associated with her work, or her marital struggles with Tim, more latterly with her sister, Liz, reappearing in her life. She shivered, no longer from the cold, but now thinking about the court case against her father, which she was avoiding by being here. The first day of his trial was tomorrow.

She was miles away from all that, she had escaped all the darkness of her past and her career. Yet now, she realised her need to seek the darker side of a situation was habitual to her. Because rather than enjoying the beauty laid out in front of her she was straining her ears, and her terrible French, to try and decipher what Olivier was saying so urgently into his phone.

'Mum, look!' Amelia turned slowly, her face full of delight, and Cate saw the butterfly that had landed on her forearm, the copper wings and black body, no doubt attracted by the bright white of Amelia's skin or the salty sheen of the factor 50.

The butterfly stayed put for so long that Amelia gave it a name, 'Valeria, like the girl in my class,' and asked if she could take him home. Olivier was still in conversation under the tree, and the weather had not yet changed but the ice saints were there, in Cate's mind and heart, the sudden drop from hot to cold that was so swift it could not be accounted for or predicted. *Something has happened.*

Olivier stopped talking, the phone was returned to his pocket, and then he was on the foreshore with Amelia, marvelling as the butterfly flew away in a flash of gold, and showing her how to choose the flattest flint to skim across the silvery surface.

Luxembourg was so different from the Suffolk landscape of yellow rape fields, its huge skies and brown marshlands. Cate was now in a setting that seemed straight from a fairy tale, unending forests of Hansel and Gretel, pretty stone turrets of chateaux and ancient castles. It was all unreal. Beautiful but strange. And the man she was with, she did not yet completely understand why he had asked her to come. Even now, six weeks after arriving in Luxembourg, she was unclear as to why he had invited her. It didn't seem that they were in the midst of a great romance, though each night they made love, because each day his activity was a mystery to her. Paul had been right, she did not leave Suffolk because she wanted to be with Olivier; she was with Olivier because she needed to leave Suffolk.

She should really call home. Liz and her mother would, even now, be preparing for court. Her father, whom she had not seen in almost two decades, would be going over his statement, thinking through his defence, probably meeting his barrister for a final time before the trial. This was what she was running from.

And here she was, by a lake watching a white dingy sail past with baby blue sails, red buoys, yellow flags marking a path through the flat water. Isolated from all that was familiar, from her mother and Liz, from the career she had spent so many years working at. This was a chance to start again but also a blank page and whatever came to be written there, she was the only author. She was no longer a child, no longer subject to managers or budget cuts. There was no ex-husband breathing down her neck. This realisation was fascinating yet frightening.

Olivier rejoined her, sitting heavily on the grassy bank, looping an arm around her waist.

'Everything okay?' she asked him, picking up her sketch book and drawing the lines of the lake, trying to capture the way General's hefty bulk became lithe and graceful once he began to swim.

Olivier paused for so long that she thought he wasn't going to answer. Then he called to Amelia, 'Amelia? What did you say her name was, your friend's sister? The girl who got lost at Schueberfouer?'

Amelia called back. 'You mean Gaynor's older sister? Her name's Ellie.'

'What's their surname?'

Amelia thought for a moment. She had only known Gaynor a few weeks. 'Scheen,' she said. 'Like the cleaner, Mr Sheen. I think their dad is German.'

Cate leaned to look at Olivier's phone, but he moved it from sight.

'Why are you asking? What's happened?'

'Achim Scheen just called the police station in Hamm to make a missing person report. He tried to make a statement last night, but was told to wait twelve hours in case Ellie returned on her own.'

Amelia, still listening, shouted across, 'Gaynor told me Ellie wanted to go to the fair with her boyfriend, but their mum wouldn't let her. She said she might be with him.'

Olivier leaned forward. 'Did Gaynor say anything else?'

Amelia splashed her hands on the surface of the water, ready to jump in again and bored with the conversation. 'Only that her mum was really mad at Ellie, because she'd already wandered off once but they had found her. And Ellie has run away before. Last time she was with the boy all night.' Amelia says this last part with a shocked whisper. *Children*, thought Cate, *are always such prudes*.

Olivier was poised, listening intently. Cate had the unnerving feeling that Amelia was being interrogated.

'When she ran off before,' Olivier asked, 'what happened?'

'Ellie was with a boy from upper school, and they were drunk.' Amelia raised her arms to the sky, ready to dive. 'Her mum was really angry. Gaynor said she hit her.'

'Are you sure about that, Amelia? It's a serious accusation,' Cate said quickly, aware that Olivier was taking all of this in. She had seen that look on his face before, when they were discussing a case at a risk-management meeting. He was acting like a police officer now, everything Amelia said was under scrutiny.

'I'm sure. Gaynor said that Ellie was hit so hard she had a swollen face for weeks. They thought her cheekbone was broken, but the doctor said it was just bruised.'

And then Amelia ended the conversation, disappearing into the water with such grace she left only ripples.

Amina

Amina did not mind travelling with the cattle, it was the three other humans in the truck that made her nervous, and so she found a place in the corner near where the heifer was tethered. The press of warm fur, the sweet smell of her udders, the sharp acrid smell of manure that soiled the floor of the truck, all reminded her of home. She sat on her wooden box of possessions, trying to keep steady and not slide to the floor, her cheek just inches from a solemn bovine face that watched her as the truck made its rocky way through villages.

Uncle Jak had stopped at two other houses before they left the commune. Picking up a boy and a girl at the first stop that looked so alike, they could only be brother and sister. Amina recognised them from the festival of Eid Al-Fitr, they both had the distinctive ivory skin and fine flaxen hair of the Berber people, but she did not know their names. The boy, with one protective arm around his sister, greeted Amina in Kabyle, and may have tried to say more, but the noise of the truck and the tiredness weighed down her bones and kept her silent.

The last girl to be picked up was the most lovely and also, at nineteen, the oldest. She was talkative, and moved her lithe body quickly, waving her long arms as she spoke, her eyes darting from the brother and sister, then back to Amina. She told them that her sister was supposed to make the trip but had fallen in love with a local boy.

'Fool her!' she scorned, looking around at the other four passengers. 'So I said I'd come instead, make money for my family. If she wants to marry that farmer boy than she's made her choice, but me, I want Paris, London, those places. I want to speak like lady and know things.' Her dark eyes glittered and she swished her silky black mane over one shoulder as she said this scandalous thing, making Amina hope that maybe this was indeed a gift they had all been given and that she, like this pretty vivacious girl, should be grateful. But she missed Piz, already ached to hold her sister's small body within her own and snuggle the back of her neck.

'Hey, you with face as long as this here cow creature, who you?'

Amina jolted, aware that the girl was addressing her. 'I'm Amina.'

'And I'm Jodie. Not my real name, this my European name, for this new life we are all here going to. Amina . . . hmm. Maybe you should be Tina, like Tina Sugandh. Smile big, Tina, like you're a star or you will be thrown off truck before we reach Paris, London.'

'I don't know who Tina Sugandh is,' Amina said, but she still forced herself to do as Jodie asked and smile big. It felt uncomfortable, like she was trying on a garment that was the wrong size.

'Good girl,' said Jodie. 'We'll have time to catch up with *The Newlyweds* when we arrive, then you'll see why it's better to be Tina Sugandh than Amina from Tizi Ouzou.' After pulling a sour face at the filthy floor, she moved her possessions onto her lap, kept safe by a wooden box that Amina recognised from the market as usually containing soft fruit. The box had no lid so Amina could see a folded *tapis d'prayer*, and a wooden comb with an intricately engraved handle. There was dried fruit, too, and a bottle that must contain oil. Oil was good for anything, cooking, cleansing the face, removing stubborn marks. Jodie's items were useful, but there weren't as many as Amina's, sealed away in her box, which was now her seat. Omi had packed it, and from the whispers she guessed that Piz had put a surprise inside too. Amina would open the box when she arrived in her new home, it would make her feel better. The things she needed for the journey she held on her lap: her own tapis d'prayer and a gallet stone, smooth and pale grey, for cleansing herself five times each day before she knelt on the mat and prayed to Allah. She also had a pocketful of almonds, and another pocket of figs, which Omi had told her to eat slowly, spacing each mouthful so she

58

never got so hungry she felt the need to eat all she had. It was uncertain how long the journey would last.

Jodie sighed, looked around the truck to where the brother and sister were sitting close together, talking quietly to each other, yellow heads pressed close. Jodie began speaking again as if Amina and she were in the middle of a conversation.

'You ignorant, don't know who Tina Sugandh is or that this a big chance for us? Uncle Jak, he tell me one girl he took last year she now live in house with swimming pool and she has her own bathroom. You can imagine such things, long-face?'

Amina couldn't. She often washed at the stream and sometimes she had paddled when she was hot from scrubbing the clothes in the river, but she had never been in a swimming pool. She didn't even know how to swim, as the river only came to her thigh so what was the point learning? It was enough, back when the vineyard thrived each season, and they were one whole family. It was her father who first spoke to her of getting an education, using the money from the wine to send her abroad to study. He wanted his children to benefit from his success, to have chances that he had missed. But now he was dead, and that dream had died with him.

Jodie began to hum, a French song Amina knew from the schoolyard, and after a moment she joined in. Before long all four teenagers were singing the songs of home as the truck arrived at the water. *Harraga* would continue on a boat.

59

Amina was glad of the cave made by the rocks, it gave protection from the sand that was being whipped up by the wind. She pressed anxiously against Jodie, who told her that the plastic square machine Uncle Jak kept peering at was a GPS, a type of radio, and he was awaiting news of the boat. The young travellers had become a sort of group, not through conversation but from the shared experience of getting this far, the hope of arriving safely. Amina shared her figs with the others, marvelling at the yellow hair of the brother and sister, which was not unheard of among the Kabyle, but rare enough that she envied it. The girl's name was Safiyya, and her brother was Reza. They were not just siblings, they were twins. His hair was not quite so light as hers, though they shared the same grey eyes and pale skin.

They too were leaving because of the activity in the mountains. Reza, as he was now eighteen, had started attending mosque with the men and there had been talk of him being recruited into the Brotherhood. He had told his father, who had begun immediately to think of ways to get Reza away from the possibility. Not all families wish to have a martyr for a son.

There was silence after Reza told his story. All four of them thinking of the life they were leaving, the unknown possibilities to come.

★ ★ ★

Though she was glad to be out of the truck, the water crossing was the part of the journey Amina most feared. She couldn't swim, and they would be three hours crossing the Strait of Gibraltar, more if the weather was bad. She had heard whispers back in Tizi Ouzou, of other people who tried *harraga* and ended up lost in the waves. Samir had spoken of this too, he had said it was Allah's punishment to them for leaving their homes. What would the punishment be, she wondered, when he found out that Omi had organised for his sister to leave? She shivered and Jodie put an arm around her shoulders.

'We 'burn' together,' Jodie said. 'You know why they call it this, Amina? Is because if we see we are getting caught then we burn our papers. Is better that way.'

But Amina knew nothing of papers, and she had no way to start a fire.

'What would happen to us?' Amina asked.

'We would be locked up, in a prison they call an immigration centre,' Reza said. 'And then they would decide what to do with us.'

'So they could let us stay?' Safiyya asked him, and Reza gave an encouraging nod.

'They would send us home, fool!' corrected Jodie. 'Think about it, Safiyya. Why you think the good people of Europe would want your Muslim self in their country? Stealing they jobs. Your exotic-fruit sister stealing their men.'

Safiyya blushed bright pink and looked down, but Reza glared at Jodie. 'I don't want anyone else's job, I only want to work to better myself.

61

And Safiyya is a good girl, she will marry only when it is right.'

There was a silence. Amina thought of her own dream of learning things, of being free. If she stayed in Algeria her future would become part of a secret world, she would be married to a man of Samir's choosing and there would be no escape.

Amina prayed, softly saying the words of the Qur'an, and finding comfort in them: *You alone we worship, You alone we ask for help.*

Just then they heard a sound, a put-putting noise that heralded the sight of a boat. It was much smaller than Amina had imagined, an open vessel with a small motor at the back. The man steering it was wearing a baseball hat and had a full black beard like her brother when she saw him last. She felt comfort that, baseball hat aside, he looked like the men back home, unlike Uncle Jak, whose beard was less full and who was much fatter too. Uncle Jak shook hands then kissed the man on each cheek. They spoke in Arabic, then rapid French, and yet made no move to go.

'What happens now?' asked Safiyya, this time directing her question not to her brother, but to Jodie.

'We have to wait until the coastguard is not watching,' answered Jodie.

'How you know all this?' Reza asked, still irritated.

'My brothers, they have all made this trip. Twice they came back but on the third time they did not return.'

'So which country are they in?'

'God's country,' said Jodie. '*Inshallah*, they are safe now.'

Amina shivered, and found that she could not stop.

When the bearded man came close, Uncle Jak told them that they must call him Captain, and that he was an experienced seaman and they were lucky to have him guiding their ship. Captain looked to where Jodie and Amina were sitting holding their boxes. 'You must only bring what you can carry, those boxes will weigh the ship down. Here . . . '

He pulled plastic bags from his pocket and gave them one each. Amina clutched at the box, thinking she could never part with it, but Jodie immediately began to empty hers, tipping her belongings into the dirty black bag. 'Hurry, Amina,' urged Jodie. 'They will not wait for us. Our families have already paid for us to burn, and the captain would think nothing of two less in his boat. A lighter vessel is quicker, and we should do as he says.'

Amina had already left her sister, her home. Omi. Now she left the box, in the protection of the rocky cave. She felt that with each part of this journey she was losing one more piece of her self.

The small boat rocked, banging against each wave as if looking for a fight, but every time the wave won, splashing over the side and adding to the puddle that was forming at the bottom of the boat. Reza held his sister's head as she vomited over the side, her blonde hair darkened by sea and sick. The sight made Amina feel ill too, but Jodie told her to watch the horizon and to breathe only through her nose, which seemed to help for a little while. The captain did not flinch, he kept accelerating until the boat was more like an unbroken horse jumping fences.

Amina wanted to kneel, to face Mecca and pray, but there was no way of knowing which way was east and the floor of the boat was now sloshing with water. As the journey progressed the twins weren't faring too well, before long both brother and sister had been sick so many times that now all they did was retch, dry-stomached, a sound that was thankfully drowned out by the waves. Because Reza was now unable to help his sister, Amina held Safiyya's hand, stroked her bony back. It was what Omi would do when Pizzie or Amina were unwell, she knew that comfort was a free thing to give. As the pink sun rose, the siblings were exhausted but at least no longer sick. Reza was hunched like a dog, barely able to lift his head, while Safiyya let Amina cradle her. They were still tightly huddled when the boat finally hit Spanish sand.

They had survived the terrible journey. Amina felt herself close to tears until she remembered she was not a child any more, and that she must act in a proper way, as Omi would will it.

★   ★   ★

After the boat they travelled in a grain truck, and all four were too exhausted to worry that they

64

must sit on a floor crawling with beetles. The twins had been so ill that they fell asleep as soon as the truck began to move. Amina too was soon dreaming, rocked to sleep by the truck's movement down pock-marked roads. Hours passed, with no food or water.

She dreamt she was back at home, in the village, and Omi was combing her long black hair with oil so that it gleamed, hair as slick as a bird's wing. And then she became a bird, huge and black, her wings open and she took to the sky. She was free.

* * *

The truck comes to an abrupt halt and she wakes to discover that freedom was only a fantasy. Here is reality, a truck full of stowaways, the stench of their sweat and recent sickness, their fear, is stifling.

When the door opens Uncle is there, and a familiar face is good to see, so good that Amina finds she is smiling.

Jodie has regained her composure. Though she's pale, she manages to encourage Amina, 'Keep grinning, Tina. That's my trick too.' Then Jodie says to Uncle, 'So, this our new home, Uncle Jak? What language they speak here, then?'

Uncle stands aside as the group find their legs, Reza helps Safiyya climb down from the truck, to the grassy ground. Amina wants to kneel and kiss the ground, thank Allah for her safe arrival, but no-one else is doing this so she doesn't.

When she stumbled, Uncle touches Jodie's

waist to help her from the truck. 'Only one language you'll need here,' he tells her with a wink. 'We are in Luxembourg now.'

Amina doesn't know what language he means, but she knows she doesn't want to learn it. She wants to learn other things. She wants this to be the start of good things.

Around her is green, though a different type from her home. And muddy, which is the same. The building, though, is tall and concrete. It is not pretty, not like European homes in her imagination, but there is a white van parked outside the house and there is a swimming pool painted on the side, just like Jodie spoke about.

The back door opens and a woman stands there, well-fed and wearing a colourful apron over black clothing. She is also smiling, and half-hidden behind her back is a boy, younger than Pizzie, but still Amina's heart softens to see him. She can only see one cheek, one eye, and a mop of dark hair, but she has the impression of a smile across his almost hidden face.

'Say *Salam alaikum* to your new auntie,' Uncle Jak tells them, and they all lower their heads in respect.

'*Salam*, Auntie,' they say, as they enter the house that smells of spices, turmeric and cayenne pepper. Amina takes this as a good sign. The boy watches them carefully, his face still half-hidden by the fabric of Auntie's flowery apron, but as she turns back toward the stove the boy's whole face is revealed. One eye is dark brown and seems to be smiling. The other is completely covered by a white bandage, sealed at

66

all four edges with white tape.

'*Salam alaikum,*' whispers Amina. 'Hello, little one.' Hoping that the boy understands. He lifts a hand to wave, but his hand is skinny and the wave is a limp-wristed attempt. Though he is smiling, Amina senses that he is unwell. He moves back, as if wanting once again to hide his bandaged eye from view.

Auntie becomes irritated with his clinging, trying to ready the meal, and she pulls her apron free. 'Are you hungry, Fahran? We'll eat soon, but you could go and wait in your room. Go and play.'

Amina can see he is reluctant to leave, with the excitement of new guests, but there is much pushing and commotion as Uncle brings in only two bags, Jodie's and Amina's.

'What about Safiyya and Reza?' Jodie says suspiciously, and Amina is glad to hear her ask the question she herself was wondering. 'We only have one spare room,' snaps Auntie, over her shoulder. 'Just space for two of you. The boy will work with my cousin in Germany. The girl will be more useful in Belgium.'

'You can't separate us!' Reza places a hand firmly around his sister's shoulder. She looks close to tears, but her brother is angry. 'We won't go to different countries!'

Uncle sighs. He considers the boy closely.

'The Belgian border is just fifteen minutes away, and Germany isn't much farther. You wouldn't be so far apart. You need to work, Reza. The work is building a café at a swimming pool in Germany.'

'But we stay together,' insisted Reza, and Amina wished that she too had a brother who would fight for her in this way.

'Impossible!' says Uncle. 'I cannot have a boy in a nail salon in Bastogne! This is Europe now. With motorways and fast cars so you can forget your village idea of what is a long way to travel. We are in the heart of Europe, everything is possible.'

Auntie intervenes, she can see that the boy will not be persuaded. 'Jak, let them stay together. He can work, and she can be helpful in other ways around the swimming pool. When they are settled, then is the time for the girl to move to Bastogne. But not now.'

Reza's face relaxes, just slightly. Safiyya has her head on his shoulder, her eyes are closed, but tears run down her pale cheeks.

'Okay,' says Uncle, grudgingly. 'You will both go to Germany. For now.'

Auntie reaches for Safiyya and lifts her head. 'Do not cry, girl. You are now in Europe and like Uncle says, everything is possible.'

Safiyya manages a small smile and Uncle leads the twins out, back to the van.

Auntie is turned towards Fahran now and her face shows all her love, also her hope that what she has just said is true, that everything will be possible for the boy with the bad eye.

Day 2

Ellie

She won't be sick again. And she won't cry.

Ellie took the bottle of bleach, the heaviest thing she could find, and held it like the P.E. teacher said to throw a javelin, hurling it straight at the window. The bang was loud, ricocheting around the caravan, and that spurred her on. Again and again she picked up the bleach bottle and threw it with all her might but the window didn't break. Her arms ached, her breath caught, and she felt anxiety threatening to overtake her, but she pushed it down and ran at the door, the weight of her seventeen years bashing against it. She began to yell with each push, and to shout again and again, hysteria taking hold now. 'Help, help, help.'

She returned to the tiny window, banging her palms and screaming in frustration that there was no opening. She pulled the mattress from the bed, threw it, slammed the empty bottle of water at the door, then the bleach again. She did everything she could to attract attention, to break free.

And then, just when she was giving up hope, the caravan door opened.

Bridget

Meanwhile, Bridget stands at the window, staring out onto the street. Waiting. Her eyes, unblinking and wide with exhaustion, scanning the empty road, her ears straining for a van or car, but finds nothing. Her thoughts are running, fast, faster, until she cannot contain them. She sees then that her hands are shaking. *I have to do something with my hands*, she thinks. Remembers how the doctors would give the patients paper and pencils, and ask them to draw. It seemed so simple, so pathetic, but to Bridget's surprise, it worked. A drawing, a story. Solace for the boy who had lost his mother to AIDS, whose sister was raped because she was a virgin. An old woman, mad with grief, and seven children to care for. A piece of paper, that was all she had been able to offer them. It had helped.

She remembered there was a notepad in the coffee table drawer, last used at Christmas to keep Scrabble scores, and she found it, still with the biro slid into the spiral binding. Bridget put the pen in her shaking hand, telling it to move, because she didn't want to go mad. This was how she started: *I could go mad, Ellie, with this grief.* But then she strikes through this line. It was not good enough. If she was going to write to Ellie she was not going to be self-absorbed, every word must count.

Dear Ellie, she begins again. Then: *Oh, my girl, I would give so much to be able to talk to you, to* say these words rather than write them. But Ellie, would you listen? Can you hear me now, thinking these thoughts for you?

Bridget paused. The pen hovered above the paper.

There are things about me you should know. And then the words flowed, because this was what Bridget really wanted to say to her daughter, all these months of conflict, but had been unable to. These were the things she most wanted to say:

I know how you see me. And you're right, I am tense, I do worry. I shout and swear too. I want you to forgive me, but I think that will only happen if you understand.

It's just that I don't fit. This person, the one you see, the parts of myself I can't escape, worked well in other places. Are you bored of hearing my stories of sick people in sick places? But there, I wasn't angry or stressed, I was the one who fixed things. I had answers, medical and moral ones. I had skills.

I wonder if my skills have gone, since I haven't used them in so many months. In all the seventeen years that you have been alive I haven't been the person I was best at being. Instead, I have been your mother and it seems I'm not very good at that. I've failed you.

I'm sorry, Ellie. You should be home. You should already be here and I don't know what has happened, what has gone wrong, or what to do to stop it.

★   ★   ★

As Bridget waits for the police to arrive and take her statement, she does not cry. She simply stares at the words she has written to her daughter and hopes that Ellie can understand.

Ellie

The caravan door swung open and Ellie's moment of elation was stolen as soon as she saw the man, his size, his thick neck, and realised that it was the bulldog man from the fair. He had been directly behind her. Speaking with Malik, after he had dropped from the bar. And later, when she had followed Malik and his beautiful friend away from the ferris wheel, this man had been there, at a distance, but watching.

'Where's Malik?' was the question that came first, though there were others crowding in, like why was she locked in a caravan, and why she couldn't remember anything of the night before. When the man stepped forward she had to steel herself to keep her stance, to keep her eyes fixed on his almost black pupils, squashed as they were in his doughy tanned face. His arms were thick and strong. She wouldn't let him know she was frightened.

'Malik is working,' the man said, and his voice sounded cautious, as if she were a wild animal he had caught in a trap that may bite. 'He asked me to come and check you were okay.'

'Of course I'm not fucking okay!' yelled Ellie, her resolve to keep control becoming lost to her fear and rage. 'I've been sick. I've been locked in.'

'I'm sorry,' he said. 'But the door was not locked, simply stuck.' Here he turned, twiddled the caravan door as if to prove the point, and held it open for her. 'Come on, girlie. I'll take you to Malik.'

'I'd rather just go home,' Ellie said, inwardly pleading that she had simply misunderstood and that it really was possible.

'*Oui*, home, of course. Come on then.'

She went to the open door, expecting fresh air and the gravel ground of the Glacis, but instead the door opened slap-bang into the open side of a van. Inside the van was a wooden bench and blankets on the floor.

Ellie froze, adrenalin pumped her with fight or flight energy. There was nowhere to run, so she turned, prepared to fight, but the man was solid in front of her.

'Get in the van,' he ordered.

'Fuck off!' she yelled, loud, then she screamed and kept screaming, her legs kicked, her arms thrust from her body and she fought as hard as she could.

Bridget

Bridget placed the notepad in the drawer and leaned back into the sofa, her body sinking into it gratefully though she still gazed towards the window, clutching the soft pink rabbit that Ellie had loved as a toddler and still kept on her pillow. It smelled of her daughter. Not the scent she now favoured or the acetone of her nail-polish remover that permeated her bedroom, it had her girlhood scent, talcum powder and vanilla, and Bridget couldn't let it go. She couldn't get showered either, or change her clothes. She was still wearing what she had worn to Schueberfouer and deep in the weave of her jeans and jumper was the smoke, the oily stench, of the Glacis car park. It was as if to shower and change was to move time away from when she last had Ellie close, and she couldn't do that, not until Ellie was home.

Achim had visited all of Ellie's friends, he had been to Joe's home three times, and had finally accepted that she was not with him. Now he was back home, upstairs in his study, and she could hear him speaking on the phone, an insisting command that she was familiar with. He must be calling the police again, urging them to do more. He had spoken with the school and insisted that they send an email to all parents. Hoping that by doing so someone would remember something, maybe a friend they weren't aware of would share a secret.

Bridget knew it was a waste of time. She knew that Ellie should already be back and things had gone wrong. While Achim was driven to act, she could do nothing but sit and wait for her daughter to arrive home.

The police had eventually called at the house. A detective named Olivier Massard had told them that cases like this were often resolved by the teenager arriving home of their own volition.

Achim had become furious, and Detective Massard has assured him that they were indeed taking the matter seriously, that everything was being done according to procedure. Achim didn't accept that, so now he was busy doing his own detective work upstairs when she wanted him to sit beside her, to comfort her. This could be a moment that united them; God knows they needed it.

Bridget feared that if she went upstairs and saw him in his study she was in danger of grabbing the laptop and smashing it into his face, just to make him bleed. Make him wounded like she was, because she could do nothing. Life could not carry on for her until Ellie was home, and all she wanted from Achim was love, tenderness. Not his activity, his futile phone calls and trips out, scouring the areas that Ellie loved.

She took the notepad from the drawer again, finding the permanence of ink on paper, of the words, comforting. The only comfort she could find.

Dear Ellie,

There are other things you should know about me, and forgive me for not telling you before. You don't always hear my voice, so I stay silent, but once my voice was important. Or not even my voice, but my hands. Back when I was an MSF nurse my skills were valued, I was respected.

What we had to work with in the field was so basic, you wouldn't believe it, even if I showed you photos. How could you, with your privileged life, even begin to understand how people live in houses built of tin sheets, how they clamber on rubbish heaps for food, how they lack shoes. It was amazing to behold, and I saw it often, how tough the soles of their feet became, as if the foot took on the thickness of leather. Maybe their hearts had the same protection, because I honestly don't know how so many people continued to shuffle forward with such huge burdens of loss. I remember a woman shouting at gunmen, and seeing behind her the shape of a boy, blood seeping beneath him. Yet she had the energy to shout. Maybe she was asking them to shoot her too, I know I would have.

Even then, and this was years before I had you or had even met your father, I knew that I could never bear such loss. So many nights I would torture myself with the images of the day, and I would add up my failings with this patient or that. If I had made a different decision, had more energy, palpitated the heart for longer . . . Each evening, late, I drank and I smoked, like we all did, because it was something to keep the demons at bay.

If you were here now you'd call me a hypocrite. I was so mad at you when you came home after that night at Joe's house with a hangover. And furious when I smelt the cannabis in your bedroom. But you never asked how I knew the smell, and I should have told you. So I'm telling you now that I used drugs often, because it helped.

But what excuse do you have? What suffering

have you seen, what life-changing decisions have you made? I know it's not your fault, but I got angry with you, and I'm sorry for that.

I've always tried to protect you, Ellie. I never want to be that woman, standing over her child and crying out for mercy. I've seen, first hand, the very worst of human behaviour and it scares me. I've always done what I can to protect you from that, but you won't listen. You won't have me tell you that world is a dangerous place, you had to discover that for yourself.

Well, now you have, so you can come back to me.

Can you hear me shouting out? Can you hear me calling you?

Please come home.

Cate

The first sign that anything was different happened when Cate pulled up at the 'kiss and drop' section of the school car park. She was approached by the regular security guard, who acted as bouncer of the school campus. This time, rather than simply waving her on, the guard came and opened the car door to let Amelia out.

'Moien. May I check that you will be collecting her tonight?'

'Of course.'

The second sign was the pained look on the other mothers' faces, who were standing in tight groups talking, rather than dashing off to the gym or café or shops.

Rather than driving back home, where General would be waiting with his legs crossed, desperate for his morning walk, Cate pulled into a parking space and got out of the car. She wandered deliberately close to a gaggle of women in designer jackets with sunglasses propped on their glossy manes, to see what they were discussing with such stricken faces. The group wasn't speaking English, but even though Cate couldn't make out most of the words, which sounded Russian, the same name kept repeating on their glossy lips: *Ellie. Ellie Scheen.*

Now that Cate looked around she noticed that the security guards were doubled in number, and even grumpier looking than usual. All wore orange day-glow jackets over their dark suits, despite the nineteen degree heat, and this at eight thirty in the morning.

Amidst the gaggle of women, Cate saw a face she recognised, a nervy Canadian woman who had been designated by the Parents Association to meet her for coffee in the school canteen when she first arrived, one of the group's welcome services. That she had the task suggested to Cate that the woman wasn't high on the pecking order, had not yet risen to the heights of organising the wine-tasting event or the autumn charity ball. Cate racked her brain for the woman's name and once it clicked she called out, 'Mary-Ann!' No response from the Canadian who was walking swiftly towards the school entrance, so Cate yelled again, 'Mary-Ann!'

She turned, saw Cate and gave a feeble wave.

She seemed to be distracted by the security officers. Cate saw that Mary-Ann's face was drained of colour and she looked anxious.

'Hi, Mary-Ann. Do you know what's going on?'

There was a moment when Cate saw that, along with anxiety, Mary-Ann was also experiencing the sense of importance that comes with holding privileged information. Her eyes sparkled and she paused before she spoke.

'This morning the Parents' Association received an email from the principal. A girl from school went missing from Schueberfouer. One of the older pupils, a bit of a rebel apparently.'

Mary-Ann spoke quietly, but the gaggle of Russian women stopped talking and moved closer.

One said, in an awed voice, 'It is not the first time! A boy was taken before, just outside of Luxembourg. In Ikea. A Swedish boy, just seven years old, with very blond hair.'

'What happened to him, Katrina?' asked one of her friends.

The woman adjusted the Gucci sunglasses on her head. 'A store detective found the man, before he got away. He was in the toilets, dying the boy's blond hair brown.'

All the Russians began a shocked protest at the thought, and Cate tried to think about how many times she had heard this particular story. Why did no-one ever question the sense of taking time to dye hair instead of just scarpering? The mess alone made it unbelievable, but none of the women had cottoned on to the fact and it wasn't Cate's job to enlighten them.

Another woman leaned into the group and said confidentially, 'My daughter said that this missing girl is playing Game of 72. It's all over the Facebook, teenagers are signing up for it, agreeing to go missing for three days.'

'You need to tell the police about that,' Katrina said, and the whole group nodded collectively, enjoying the vicarious thrill of their conspiracy theories, their urban myths. If only Ellie's disappearance was a myth. Over twenty-four hours, and still missing.

'Could she be with friends? Or family?' Cate asked Mary-Ann, knowing this was the most likely scenario. But Mary-Ann could only shrug helplessly.

'The Parents' Association has called an emergency meeting, I should really go now or I'll be late and Carol hates latecomers. We don't know what to tell the other parents, we know so little ourselves, but we're going to come up with a strategy. We'll probably schedule a seminar on dealing with teenagers. Shall I put your name down?' she added, hopefully.

'Thanks, Mary-Ann. That would be great.'

$$\star \quad \star \quad \star$$

Arriving back at the flat, Cate busied herself with loading the dishwasher, going room-to-room to straighten beds, folding towels. The activities, domestic and simple as they were, soothed her and she may have spent the whole day reorganising drawers if not for General's

80

insistent whining, reminding her that there was a routine that must be followed, unless she wanted to mop the floor too.

She took him to Merl park, a place where he was certain to meet many other dogs, usually smaller and wearing delicate rhinestone collars, as seemed to be the fashion in Luxembourg. 'Don't have your head turned, General,' Cate advised him, as he began to inspect the bottom of a handbag-sized dog with huge bulging eyes and thin shaking legs.

She knew that, back in England, her father's trial would have started. She could imagine him officially entering his 'not guilty' plea, and the prosecution calling the first witness, her sister. Poor Liz. Brave Liz, braver than Cate, who was a refugee in Luxembourg rather than witnessing the family tragedy being exposed before the eyes of twelve good men and women. She should have called, that morning. But what could she have said? 'Good luck' seemed too flippant. There was no luck, no winning to be had. Whatever the outcome, the damage had been done. She resolved not to torture herself with thoughts of England, and instead wondered what it would be like to own a dog no heavier than a bag of sugar.

As someone who had always worked in an office, Cate was surprised at how quickly the time passed at home, how a load of washing, a trip to the shops, used up the time so she had to rush to collect Amelia from school.

* * *

81

She could have totally forgotten that anything was wrong, if not for a disturbing conversation with Amelia, just after they arrived back at the flat before the rain started coming down.

Amelia was seated at the long walnut table which was the pride of Olivier's flat, strategically placed to give a view over the balcony and across to Merl park. General was standing at the patio window, maybe looking out for his tiny doggie friend, or watching the ducks fight for cover in their pond home, or the turtles hide under their shells as the rain dripped on their backs, but Amelia saw none of this. She was preoccupied with the school books open in front of her, the homework she had brought home.

'I can't do it, Mum. There's too much homework here. It wasn't like this in England.'

Cate leaned over her daughter to see. The worksheet was in German, and required Amelia to name the animals.

'Sorry, sweetheart. I'm not going to be able to help with that. But Olivier will, he's fluent.'

'But he'll be back too late! This needs to be in tomorrow.'

Amelia folded her arms on the table and hid her head inside, then started to cry.

'Hey, stop.' Cate sat beside her, and coaxed Amelia's head up. 'You're just feeling a bit overwhelmed, what with starting a new school in a new country. We've both had a lot of things to adapt to. But this is only homework, Amelia.'

'And I can't do it.' She looked genuinely devastated that she couldn't complete the work, though Cate suspected it was more to do with fitting in, to adjusting without her father and half-sister around. She hugged her daughter tight and looked down at the worksheet.

'Okay, let's give it our best shot. Your teacher must have covered this in class today? She wouldn't expect you to simply know the word for pig in German.'

'She started to,' sniffed Amelia, wiping her nose with her hand, 'but then she asked us how we'd stop a stranger getting us in his car.'

'Hey?' Cate said, stroking her daughter's hair. 'What's that got to do with German?'

Amelia sat up straight, her forehead wrinkled as she thought back to the lesson. 'I know, it did get a bit odd. She started by checking that we all got collected after school, y'know by an adult. But some of the class walk home on their own so then she said what would we do, if a stranger said our mum was in hospital and we had to go with him. Then she started writing on the board, ideas like kicking and poking him in the eyes. I said I'd kick him between the legs. I saw that happen to Dad once when he was playing football and he was in agony.'

Cate touched her daughter's chin, turning her face so she could see her worried expression. She felt a wave of anger at the German teacher, for causing this. 'Listen, Amelia, this is important. It is very, very unlikely that anyone would ever approach you. But if it ever happened your best weapon is this mouth, okay? You scream and shout and you don't stop. And then you run. Do you understand?'

Amelia nodded seriously. 'I'm a fast runner,' she said.

'You are,' Cate agreed. 'And you are also very excellent at shouting. But you shouldn't be thinking about things like that. I'm going to call the school . . . '

Amelia looked up in panic. 'No, Mum!'

'But Amelia . . . '

'Please!' Amelia looked close to tears.

'Look, it's okay. You can listen. You'll see that I don't make a scene. I'll be as nice as pie.'

Under Amelia's tense gaze Cate bit her lip before she pressed the contacts icon on her phone and scrolled down to find the school's number. When her call was answered she recognised the voice of her favourite security guard, the only one who felt permitted to smile.

'Good afternoon.'

'Hi, it's Cate Austin, Amelia's mum. I wonder if I could have a quick word with Madame Schroeder, please?'

Madame Schroeder may not have taught Amelia the German names of farm animals, but she had certainly been trying to teach her something.

After being asked to wait she was put on hold and had to endure the screech of a violin being played very badly. Hold music courtesy of the school orchestra. Nice touch, she thought. Amelia had abandoned the language homework and was now working on her art project. She had been asked to capture a moment from her summer holiday, and her drawing was of Felixstowe, smiling children playing on the beach. Her carefree picture hardly matched with the idea of children as vulnerable, needing to know about self-defence. She was still admiring Amelia's drawing when a voice came on the line.

'Hello. You wanted me, Madame Austin?'

Though the teacher was abrupt, Cate decided to be gentle. 'Good afternoon, Madame. We're new at the school, so my daughter is probably a little sensitive, but she didn't seem to understand her homework. She's a bit upset.'

'No need to be.' Madame Schroeder sounded relieved that this was the reason for Cate's call. 'I can speak with Amelia at lunchtime tomorrow, and go through it again.'

Cate continued, more cautiously, 'I wonder if I could ask you about something else? She said that during class you gave some instructions on self-defence. Is this something to do with the missing teenager?'

There was a silence, and Cate could hear the teacher's rapid breathing.

'I am sorry, but your daughter misunderstood. I was speaking in German, so maybe it was not clear to her, but I was simply giving the word for hands, legs, kicking, pushing. That is all.'

Cate looked at her daughter, thought back to how much detail Amelia had just given her, and knew the teacher was lying. 'Please, Madame Schroeder, I'm not criticising you. In fact I think it's a useful topic for all the kids to learn. I used to work in a prison, and we all had to take a course on personal safety.'

Now Madame Schroeder sounded surprised,

but also very interested. 'You are a prison officer?'

'Probation. But I resigned to move here. If it would be useful in any way I'd be happy to share what I learned about self-defence.'

'Thank you, Madame Austin. I'll bear that in mind.' Madame Schroeder had softened, there was an expectant pause as if she was about to ask Cate something else.

Cate seized the moment to say what she really wanted the teacher to understand. 'If there is something to be aware of, something that's happening in Luxembourg, I'd rather know.'

Now there was only silence. Cate felt herself defeated.

'I am sorry, Madame Austin, but I do not know how to answer you. And now I have some work that must be done, for classes tomorrow.'

With that, and saying a brief goodbye, she ended the call.

Cate had gone as far as she could.

★ ★ ★

That evening, Olivier, rather unusually, arrived home at five o'clock. Amelia was still working on her drawing and Cate had not even begun to think of what to cook for tea.

'No more homework for you tonight! I thought we'd go to Schueberfouer,' he said to Amelia, making the trip a *fait accompli*. 'Tonight is the family event, so everything's half price, which means we can go on double the rides! We can eat there too.'

Amelia dropped her pencil like it was a stone, her concerns about German homework long forgotten.

* * *

They managed to get close to the Glacis, parking the car and walking for just a few minutes until they were next to the ferris wheel, the focal point of the fair and their first destination. Olivier wanted to ride, but Amelia pulled a face and said, 'But I went on that already, with Gaynor and Mum. I'd like to try something else.'

The trio walked around, Amelia leading the way, deciding what to ride next. She stopped at the water ride, so abruptly that Cate walked into her back. They both looked up at the long stretch of water climbing upwards then becoming a downward waterfall, all to be travelled in a circular boat.

'Can we go on that?'

Cate looked to where large round dinghies were being pulled up a waterslide, then sent spinning down in a tumble of splash and rapids, and saw that everyone who left the ride was drenched. She was wearing a new summer dress in pastel blue, her first Luxembourg purchase after she'd noticed that women here never wore jeans. Or, God forbid, trainers.

'Okay, but let's make sure we put on the rain macs.'

The rain macs didn't help, being thin as a plastic bag and already soaked by many customers, but Amelia tugged one over her head without complaint, laughing as Olivier put a red one on.

'Like Superman, *n'est-ce pas?*'

'*Oui,*' agreed Cate.

Amelia waited in line, hopping from foot to foot with growing excitement as they drew nearer to the front.

'See?' Olivier said smugly, taking Cate's hand. 'In Luxembourg we know how to do fairgrounds. Better than your mini-golf or fake ski slope.' He winked at her, referring to the destinations of their first dates, though she thought all of these type of things were much of a muchness, apart from the grandeur of the big wheel which couldn't be eclipsed by any fairground ride she'd seen before.

★　★　★

The fair was filled with younger children and parents indulging them at a reduced rate. Cate saw the familiar slow walk of mothers carefully pushing prams over rough terrain, boys weighing up the potential prizes of hook a duck over the rifle range. It was comfortingly familiar, the universal appeal of plastic toys that weren't worth the price of the game, the stalls of fudge and hot roasted nuts, the irresistible appetite for sticky and sweet and fast. Olivier was right, it was a cut above Felixstowe seafront or any of the other local attractions from her home, yet it made Cate ache in the pit of her stomach, just once, hard and fast. And then she thought about everything else that England meant for her and pushed the thought away.

'Shall we get something to drink?' asked Olivier. 'What about you, Amelia?'

In the drinks department too Luxembourg was a cut above, with a white marquee giving views of the fair, seats around tables with potted flowers on them. Amelia ordered 'kids' champagne' then looked disappointed that it was only fizzy orange. Olivier ordered Cate a glass of Crémant, and himself a beer then turned to Amelia.

'What about a *barbapapa*, after we've finished our drinks? To make up for the orange champagne.'

Cate leaned onto her daughter's shoulder and whispered, 'He means candy floss,' and Amelia's eyes immediately lit up. 'Though it's not exactly what I'd call a nutritious meal.'

'Yes, please!' Then, to Olivier, '*Merci*.'

'She's getting the hang of it,' Olivier said to Cate. 'Soon no-one will know you're not native.'

Cate smiled and sipped the Crémant, as once again, Olivier studied the screen of his phone.

'Your phone hasn't stopped beeping since we got here. Anything wrong?'

He put it carefully back in his pocket, took her hand, kissed it and said, 'Remember when we first met, Cate? I said that when we are together it must not be about work. It is only me and you.'

Not quite true, though, Cate thought to herself. *Not when the calls keep coming and you absent yourself from us to take them, then refuse to talk about it.*

Amelia was twisted in her seat, admiring the little wooden huts that served food, having already worked out which one served the most generous portion of spun sugar.

★ ★ ★

Olivier took another call, this time leaving the table and walking a short distance apart. Cate wouldn't say anything; Olivier had given them this, a space that felt like a holiday, a chance to travel. If he took work calls throughout the evenings and weekends that was something Cate would have to learn to accept.

So far, it was the weekdays that had been the biggest adjustment. After she had dropped Amelia at school the day yawned ahead of her, and that accounted for her pathetic offer earlier to Madame Schroeder, to help teach self-defence. As if she could teach. *In fact*, she thought, the alcohol making her maudlin, *what am I good for?* She'd never learned to cook properly, and had no interest in traipsing around supermarkets or local markets squeezing fruit. She certainly wasn't up to being a trophy wife, running from the gym to the beauty salon to be botoxed or waxed, and anyway, her savings didn't stretch that far, much less her tolerance for pain.

When Olivier returned to the table she had given up on her resolve to bite her tongue.

'Whatever's going on at work, Olivier, you can tell me. It's not as if I'm going to breach any confidentiality, I hardly know anyone here. And I might actually be able to help.'

Olivier gave her a warning look, assisted Amelia down from where she was perched on a bar stool and manoeuvred her to the sweet stalls. As Amelia ordered her candy floss Cate asked him, 'Are the calls about Ellie Scheen? She's still missing, isn't she?'

'Between us, Cate, this is just a simple case of a teenage runaway. She'll turn up, like she did before. Teenagers are rebellious, we know this. And for Ellie it is not the first time, plus she was last seen talking to a boy. I think we know this story, very well. But her father has given a statement, and he is a very persistent man, so until she decides to come home, Ellie is a missing person. We have to go through the motions.'

A thought occurred to Cate. 'Is that why we're here at the fair? Is this you 'going through the motions' of investigating it?'

'Partly. I wanted to see Amelia experience something I've enjoyed since I was a boy. But also I wanted to get a little sense of this place.'

'In case Ellie is still here?'

'In case she needs a little persuasion to go back home.' No more was said and Cate tried to enjoy their time at fair, a family picture that she had never really experienced before. Tim had left when Amelia was just a toddler, and though Amelia had been on many outings with Tim and Sally, when she was with Cate it had only ever been just the two of them. The new family trio walked tentatively through the mirror maze, knocking into glass and each other as they felt their way to the exit. They got giddy on the waltzers, though Cate couldn't relax when she saw how the lecherous ride worker ogled all the females as they bent to climb into the circular cab, even looking at Amelia's bottom in her tight leggings, though she was only twelve. Cate gave him a hard stare, which he returned, knowing but not caring that he had been caught.

If Olivier saw the leery man he said nothing, but focused on turning the cab as fast as possible until Amelia was laughing hysterically at the manic spin of the ride.

It was only later, back at home, that Cate began to think of Bridget. As she readied herself for bed she reflected that Ellie had now been missing for forty-eight hours, which seemed rather long for a show of teenage rebellion.

Amina

Uncle Jak took Auntie to one side, into the dimly lit hallway and away from the four teenagers. After speaking with her in a low voice he handed her a roll of money, kissed her on the cheek, and left, taking Reza and Safiyya with him. Amina was pleased to see him go, glad to be in the company of only females, though sorry to be saying goodbye to her friends so suddenly. Then Auntie looked them over, Amina and Jodie stood close together, each clutching their bag of belongings. Auntie swiped a hand down Jodie's body and said, 'Very fine. A pretty girl.' In the same way Omi might have appraised a goat or her father would announce a good crop of grapes from the vineyard.

Outside they could hear Uncle Jak starting the van, the engine hesitating as if too tired to begin travelling so late, and then it slowly pulled away. Amina tried not to think about Reza and Safiyya being driven over the border to another country, to Germany, or to ask herself if she would ever see them again. Instead she kept her head bowed respectfully, though really she was studying her surroundings and wondering if this could be a place to call home.

The kitchen was small, with the back door leading directly to the yard where the van had been parked. It was pleasantly cluttered with steel pans and herbs hanging from string on door handles, and there was a lamb tagine slowly charring on the burner that smelt of cumin and garlic. Amina's mouth watered for the tastes of home, though she wasn't sure that Auntie was from Kabyle, and the few words they had shared had been French, not Arabic, so she couldn't place her accent. Auntie dressed in a Western way, so her clothes gave nothing away either. Now she had taken off her flowered apron, Amina saw she was wearing a black top advertising Beauty Asiatique.

Jodie had noticed too. 'What this place, Auntie?'

'This here the beauty salon we run from the front of the house,' Auntie said. 'I'll show Amina tomorrow. She'll be working there so I can spend more time with Fahran.' She did not say where Jodie would be working.

Auntie busied herself setting out bowls for the two girls, and one for the boy too, who had still not spoken though he had not left to play in his room, either. Amina smiled at him, and he looked at her with his one good eye, as they set about eating their food. His bandage was very clean, even though the day was almost done, so it gave no clue as to what was behind it. It did not seem to bother him though, and he ate hungrily, licking his lips and smiling so cheerfully that the bandaged eye was soon forgotten. Amina reached a hand to give him a gentle tickle and he gave a surprised laugh, so she tickled him faster until he doubled in a fit of giggles. Auntie whipped around from where she was busy washing pots at the sink and gave Amina a glare. 'Eat your food, girl. Then I'll show you your room.'

When Jodie raised her eyebrows and gave Amina a warning look, she understood; Auntie did not want Fahran to get close to the girls. Or maybe she did not want him to play too physically because he was sick. Either way, Jodie's eyes warned her that she should not encourage him.

She finished her stew, peering around at the hallway beyond the kitchen, which was brick-floored, narrow and long. Along the walls were red and gold hanging charms, and on the kitchen door was a hand-drawn picture that said, *Mama et Papa*. The picture was of a round woman with a red scarf scribbled around her head, and Amina saw from the swirly crayon hair, the purple dress, that it was Auntie, alongside a stick-figure that she guessed was Uncle Jak but bore no resemblance. Fahran must have drawn it, and Amina wondered if he went to school. He seemed to be the right age for it, but that would surely only be possible if Uncle and Auntie had papers, at least for the boy. During their journey, Jodie had told her that they could apply to be naturalised, but first Uncle Jak needed a job contract, and he hadn't established enough links for that yet. How long they had been in Luxembourg, she wasn't sure, but Jodie said it wasn't very long. Amina wondered if Fahran made the same journey she had just travelled. How could a child so young survive that?

Fahran finished his food and left the table, burying himself in Auntie's softness, his face pressed against her t-shirt, but his dark hair was sticking up and the bit of his face he did reveal showed his good eye, wide and alert. He was watching Amina.

'Bedtime now, *habibi*. Be a good boy and go up to your room. I'll be up when I've seen to the girls, to tell you a story.'

Jodie and Amina's empty bowls were taken from them, and they were each given a glass of water and a white tablet. 'This medicine will help you feel relaxed. You can take your water upstairs, if you like.' Amina swallowed the tablet with a mouthful of water and wanted to finish the drink straight away, she was thirsty from the spices, but it was best to do as Auntie suggested. 'Come on. I'll show you your room.'

She led the way along the hallway, past a narrow table with a light, draped over the light was a red scarf with gold thread woven through it, another scarf was pinned along the staircase railing. Up they went, to the next landing, passed a closed door where Amina guessed Auntie's own bedroom was. The hallway's red walls, the colourful scarves and trinkets, the smell of spices. It felt safe and Amina allowed herself to relax a little.

At the end of the hallway was an open door, and inside Fahran was lying on a mattress on the floor. Though the room was small it had been painted a pretty shade of blue and there were a stack of soft toys and plastic cars on the carpet. Fahran was lying on his stomach, and seemed to already have fallen asleep.

After checking on her boy, stroking his hair and giving him a gentle kiss, Auntie took a key from the pocket of her apron and said to them, 'Come, follow me. You are at the top.'

Amina looked at Jodie and together they went up the final flight of stairs. The key wasn't for the first closed door though, that opened freely and then they were on a landing that was so narrow that Auntie had to turn sideways, and it was dark too. Amina felt the floorboards were wonky, open wooden slats that moved as she placed her foot. This was not a proper level, but some kind of attic or roof space.

She pressed her body softly against Jodie's back, for comfort, as Auntie found the key deep in her apron pocket, opening up the door that was smaller in height than even Amina. It was a surprise that Auntie could even make it through, and she looked uncomfortable, stooped in the attic room, blinking as if she had forgotten what it looked like in there. Jodie too could not stand fully upright, but Amina was small enough to walk easily. The blessing, the thing she noticed first, was the small window, at floor level, but offering light and a view of outside. It didn't look like it opened, but Amina was still counting her blessings, she so desperately wanted this new life of hers to be a good one and for Omi's sacrifice to be worthwhile. The cost of *harraga* had been great. Omi had sold the vineyard, and though the burned grape vines were worthless, the land itself was shaded by the mountain and had good soil. It was their only asset, sold secretly and quickly. When Samir came back down from the mountain or returned from Paris, he would discover her gone, and the land sold. Omi would be in trouble, there would be consequences. But she had told Amina to leave, to be safe.

The attic room had two mattresses on the wooden floor, each with a blanket thrown on it. There was also a bucket, and Amina knew immediately that this was their toilet. A wooden crate served as a small table, and on it was a carved hand-held mirror that was so much like her mother's she wanted to hold it to her chest. That was all the room offered, yet with Jodie alongside her, Amina felt it might be enough.

'Thank you, Auntie,' said Amina, offering the woman a smile.

Auntie accepted the thanks with a nod and a quick slick of the eyes over her body and face. Then she said, 'I think you'll do very well, Amina. You seem a nice well-raised girl.'

This made her happy. She could write and tell her mother this, when she found a way to send a letter. Her mother would be pleased.

'Settle now, and sleep. You have had a long journey.'

Auntie left and Amina tried not to hear the key being turned into the lock. Jodie threw herself down on the mattress nearest the window and said, 'I take the bed with the view, okay, long-face?' She then picked up the mirror and studied her reflection. Neither girl had washed for three days and Amina hadn't been to the toilet since they left Spain. She looked at the black bucket in the corner, but couldn't bring herself to go. She thought things were supposed to be more civilised in Europe, not less. She contented herself by going to the window.

★ ★ ★

Lying on Jodie's mattress, side by side, both girls looked out of the low window. They saw the road, with cars, the tall houses opposite and, to the right, a church spire. Not like the rounded mosque with its smooth white walls in Tizi Ouzou, this was like a stone dagger inserted into the sky, sharp and serious. Amina could not imagine praying in a temple as spikey and unwelcoming as that.

'What country you think this is, Jodie? Is it Paris?'

Jodie made a dismissive sound, and Amina though she might spit if they were outside. 'No, not Paris. Not anywhere in France. This here

Luxembourg, Uncle Jak said.'

Amina tried the word, found it difficult.

She had never even heard of this country that was now her new home. She placed her bag of belongings at the foot of her mattress, wishing again she had been able to keep her wooden box and wondering who had it now. Someone, surely, would have rescued it from the cave on the beach. She thought about emptying her belongings onto her bed though she would have preferred to do this alone. Jodie was already lifting the few items from her bag and placing them in a line on the floor.

Amina opened the bag, hoping that nothing had been damaged by the journey. Inside, folded so neatly, was a beautiful corn-yellow Kabyle dress that she hadn't seen in her haste when she opened the box on the beach. But now she could see that this was a gift, and a very precious one. Omi must have been embroidering the neck and hem secretly when she was asleep, and it would have taken many hours. The threads were intricately beaded and made from bright silks, it was the most beautiful thing she had ever seen. The gift made her want to weep.

Jodie was watching. 'Where you think you going to wear that dress, Amina? To the local nightclub?' She laughed, but on seeing Amina's stricken face she stopped and frowned. 'I'm sorry. It is very beautiful.'

Amina put her face down so Jodie couldn't see her tears, and unpacked the rest of her possessions. There was also her cotton night-dress, a comb that had once been her grandmother's and had a piece of coral in the centre, a precious stone bought with the first harvest from the vineyard. Then she saw a pink soft blanket that was folded small at the bottom of the bag. She lifted it and raised it to her face, breathing deep.

'Your baby blanket?' asked Jodie.

'My sister's.' Amina felt a pain around her ribs, her heart swelling with longing for her family. She breathed steadily until the pain eased. *You'll see them again*, she promised herself. *When you are educated and rich. You will go home and show them what you have achieved and Omi will be proud.*

Something hit her head, made her flinch. Jodie had tossed her own comb at Amina. 'No daydreaming,' she said, and it sounded like a warning. 'We have to do what we can with what we have, not disappear into dreaming. Okay?'

Amina agreed, though she didn't know why dreaming was bad. She just knew that Jodie was wise, she knew things, and she resolved to do exactly as she said, then she wouldn't go far wrong.

'What do you think of Auntie?' Amina asked.

Jodie touched her teeth with her tongue, something, Amina had come to realise, she did when she was thinking. 'She made us a good meal, and this room has been recently swept. So, it seems that she will treat us well. I think she wants us to like her, and that's good for us. We should try and please her because women often have the power in situations like this.'

'Like what?' Amina asked, sure she was

missing something. 'In what situation could a woman have power, Jodie?'

'This situation, us, being here in the house. Auntie will have to say that we are her children, to everyone else we must look like a family. It is the woman who must spin the tale, if it is to be believed. But this is dangerous for both her and Jak, it could attract talk. We won't be allowed to leave, not to walk freely about. People may be watching.'

This was not a surprise for Amina, who was not supposed to go anywhere without a male chaperon, but Jodie sounded annoyed. It must be different in her village. Jodie lifted Pizzie's baby blanket and put it around her own shoulders, which Amina didn't like but she didn't stop her.

'Let's hush now, Amina. I'm half-dead from travelling and I need to sleep.'

Amina wanted to ask more, she had so many questions, but she knew that Omi would tell her that if your friend is honey, don't eat it all at once. And so she lay down and closed her eyes, hoping that tomorrow would bring some answers.

* * *

Despite her exhaustion from the journey, Amina found it hard to sleep. Instead she thought of home, and wished she was there. Jodie snored like the friendly boar kept as a pet at the tavern in Tizi Ouzou. All the children would pet the boar, laughing as it enjoyed its daily drink of beer, straight from a bottle like a baby. That must be different now. 'Algeria is not an Islamic state,' Samir had told her once. 'Muslim, yes, but not Islamic. Not yet. But one day soon it will be so. Allah wills it.'

It was just before the vineyard was set on fire, and though no-one was ever blamed, Samir said it was an act of god. Would the same thing happen to the tavern, and would they still keep the boar as a pet if the bar was shut? Amina shook her head, trying to free these bad thoughts that could not be answered just by wondering. It was best that she didn't think about home, it made her sad, and Jodie was so relaxed in her sleep that Amina felt sure that everything was going to be just fine, and the mattress beneath her bones may be thin but it was bliss after sleeping in the van, pressed up against the sides as it rocked across Europe.

★ ★ ★

The following morning, Auntie unlocked their room early, when the sun had not yet risen, but Amina comforted herself that at least this meant they didn't have to put up with the stinking bucket as the day warmed and the air in the small room became thick with dust. Amina couldn't help but think of her home, of stepping out with bare feet into the canopy of olive trees, calmed by the call of the dunnocks, occasionally spotting a small brown head as they jumped from branches.

Auntie led them to the floor below and

showed them the bathroom. 'A shower each, yes? But quickly, everything costs money here and you too-skinny things won't take more than two minutes to clean your arses.'

Omi would be shocked at Auntie for using such a rude word, she would never say such things. But this was Europe and so things were different here, and the water was like rain, soft and cleansing. In the lukewarm shower, Amina let her hair go slick and straight, the water run through it until it squeaked. The blessings did not end, as her dress that was filthy and torn from when she jumped into the van was gone and Auntie had placed on the chair a pair of leggings and a t-shirt, both black. They seemed to Amina to be the softest, most modern clothes she had ever worn, but the leggings clung to her skinny legs and made her feel silly, like a scrawny kid. The t-shirt was too big and fell shapelessly to her waist. She didn't mind this so much, but when she saw Jodie in her red dress, also from Auntie, she realised what was possible. Jodie's fat stomach and wobbly thighs, her rounded chest, all looked beautiful in the tight cotton, but also made Amina blush. She assumed that Jodie had a different uniform because she was prettier than Amina, she would have looked skinny and silly in the red dress.

Jodie tugged at Amina's t-shirt. 'This is no good for you, Amina. We'll have to ask Auntie for a thread to bring it in at the waist or you'll never find a boyfriend.'

'I don't want a boyfriend,' Amina quietly answered. 'I want to go to school.' But the logo on her t-shirt did not mention any school. Just like Auntie's own t-shirt it said: *Beauty Asiatique*.

★ ★ ★

Clean and dressed, the girls made their way to the ground floor, where Auntie was waiting. She looked both girls over and nodded her approval. Then she asked them to fetch their prayer mats. They formed a line in the hallway, faced East, and prayed together. Amina was glad when Fahran put his prayer mat next to her. He sneaked a smile at her, but he still didn't speak.

For breakfast, the girls were allowed to sit in the kitchen, where Auntie had put out tea and bread, a baguette that seemed half full of air and hardly dented Amina's appetite, a packet of cheese slices that tasted like plastic. Amina wanted to ask what was wrong with Fahran's eye, but Auntie seemed preoccupied, checking her phone regularly as if waiting for an important message, so she thought she'd better stay silent.

Once they had each eaten a small piece of bread and one slice of cheese the plate was whipped away and Auntie ate the rest while telling them what their jobs would be for that day. 'Work is important, for both of you girls. It is how you pay for this here food, for the roof over your heads. Once you have paid for that, then the money will come to you, as your wages.'

Wages! It was a magical word, and Amina

wondered how much this would be, and how often they would receive it. But neither of these questions were answered.

'You,' she said to Jodie, 'will be picked up soon by Jak and Malik. But Amina, she has nicer manners and will stay with me.'

Despite what Auntie said about her manners Amina felt that it was because she was too gormless and girlish to leave the house. Of course Jodie would get a better job, she was prettier and sophisticated.

'And so,' Auntie thumbed Amina, her mouth still full of bread as she spoke, 'we'll train you up to work in the shop. You be nice and happy for the customers, and make sure everything is so clean, Allah himself would be amazed. Okay?'

Amina hadn't seen the shop yet, and was nervous about dealing with customers, but she nodded eagerly. She wanted Auntie to know that she was willing to work, but there was a question that could not go unanswered. She thought of Pizzie and Omi and took a deep breath.

'Please, Auntie, what about school?' she asked, tentatively.

'The shop will teach you everything you need,' said Auntie. 'You learn maths, from working till. You learn science, from the beauty products we use. And you learn languages from the customers. What more you think you need?'

Jodie laughed like this was a big joke, but Amina told herself that if she could learn all of this it may indeed be all she needed.

★ ★ ★

Auntie takes Fahran upstairs, leaving Amina to wash the pots. Jodie stands by the window, waiting to be collected, tugging at the hem of the red dress to try and pull it down. Though she doesn't speak, Amina can hear her breathing, fast and heavy, like it was when they were on the boat. She knows Jodie is scared.

The white van finally arrives and Amina wonders where Uncle Jak had spent the night, or if it is simply that he woke before them. He is sitting in the driving seat and another man, who looks younger, is beside him. Whilst the younger man jumps out, Jak remains in the van, dabbing at his cheek with a tissue. Amina sees him use the rear-view mirror as a guide, he licks the tissue then dabs again. When he pulls it away Amina sees that Uncle Jak is bleeding.

Now that the other man has left the van, Amina can see that he is not much older than she. He has curly dark hair, but most of it is hidden inside a green woollen hat. His eyes are like the gorse in the winter, a very fine copper, and his skin is as dark as Amina's. He could be Samir, if not for his smile, which Samir stopped doing long ago. Jodie has noticed the boy too, and as he walks into the kitchen she stands taller and sucks in her stomach. She thrusts out her hand to him. '*Salam alaikum.* I'm Jodie.'

He takes her hand, holds it for what seems to Amina to be too long, appraising Jodie in her tight red dress. '*Wa alaikum.* I'm Malik. I think you are coming with us today.' He barely notices Amina, shrunk as she is against the sink.

Jodie looks over her shoulder at Amina and

winks, following Malik back to the white van with the swimming pool picture on the side. It is then that Amina remembers to call, 'Ask them about Reza and Safiyya. Please find out where they are.'

But the van door shuts and Amina is not sure if Jodie heard her. She returns to tidying the kitchen.

* * *

Satisfied that everything is clean and neat, Amina heads to the stairs, wanting to return her prayer mat to her bedroom and to comb her hair through now it is dry. On the first landing she sees that Fahran's bedroom door is open. She slows, eager to see him, resolving to speak with him this time.

But when she looks inside the room Fahran is lying on his bed and Auntie is cradling him. Beside her, on the floor, is a white tub of water and a roll of bandage, some scissors. She is trying to soothe him but the boy won't be soothed, his mouth is open in a silent scream. Auntie looks up to where Amina is standing, revealing the desperation she is feeling. It is something Amina recognises, she had seen it on Omi's face when Pizzie had the fever. And also more recently, when the Algerian police came and asked questions about Samir. Both times Omi had looked desperate, fearful that she was losing a child, and Auntie now reveals that same madness in her eyes; she would do anything to help her boy.

107

'What's wrong with him, Auntie?' Amina asks gently.

Auntie shakes her head, as if even saying the words would be bad luck. Seeing her like this, and thinking of her own mother, Amina takes a brave step forward, longing to comfort her or help the boy if she is allowed. Fahran is barely moving, his face his pressed into the bedding as he emits a long, low sound of suffering. If she was at home, she would run to the elders for help, as Omi used to say, 'Ask the experienced one, not the doctor.' The elder would boil herbs and make a poultice to take away whatever curse has taken hold. But here, in the west, it is the doctor that knows best.

'Why you not take him to the hospital, Auntie?'

Inside her gnarled hands she holds her son's smaller pale hands. She rubs them gently, as if to bring the blood back there.

'I am afraid.'

Amina understands then, that they are in Luxembourg without papers. They are illegal. And if Auntie takes her boy to the doctor she would have to tell them so. They would send them all home, and the local Brotherhood would punish her for trying to leave, for breaking sharia law. And then there would be no schools and no jobs and no better life. Not ever.

'You are afraid of being sent back to Algeria,' Amina whispers, but Auntie looks at her like she is a fool.

'Not that,' she says, in her usual voice, the one she reserves for reminding the girls how stupid they are. 'I am afraid to hear what is wrong.'

And this is something Amina finds harder to understand, but she is not a mother, and she reasons to herself that maybe she will one day.

'But the doctor would give medicine, Auntie.'

She looks at Amina again. This time there is nothing but unbearable sadness in her eyes. 'I don't know if there is enough medicine, Amina. I fear this is an illness that even the clever doctors here cannot cure.'

It scares Amina, what Auntie says. Surely the clever doctors here can cure every illness? And how can the boy be so very sick, when he is so young? There must be something that can be done. She moves forward, hoping to comfort the boy, and hearing her approach he lifts his head. Auntie is quick to place a bandage, skilled with snipping and taping it in place, but it is too late. Amina has already seen. Where an eye should be is a black space, a hollow hole rimmed with yellow pus.

Day 3

Ellie

'Fuck you!' she screamed, again and again, as loud as she could. She used her nails, and when one cut the bulldog's cheek, making him yell in Arabic and then French, she stabbed him again, this time into his eye, and was glad that he screamed. As he doubled over, she kicked him in the groin.

'You fat fuck,' she yelled, pushing past him to where the back of the van was open, but squeezing in the tight passageway between the van and caravan, jumping down and landing in a heap on the gravel.

Other caravans were packed together, closed doors and drawn blinds, and Ellie could see it was very early. No-one was looking out, though someone must have heard her scream. She knew the fat fuck couldn't wedge himself easily to follow her, but she could hear him breathing, speaking in swift French into his mobile.

She ran, down and through the maze of caravans, turning at each corner, to find a way out of the Glacis. She was so close to home, just a few miles away, if only her pounding heart and pumping feet would take her there.

She could see the ferris wheel, high above. If

she could make it there she would be close to the road, she could make a car stop for her. The fairground was a ghost town, all of the rides boarded up and she pushed herself on, though the sickness was back, her head pounded and her muscles ached. She ran, passing the roller coaster, the waltzers, energised by her freedom which was so close, so close she could hear the cars on the road, and also the blood in her ears, the beat of her heart in her throat.

The fairground was surrounded by a metal barrier, but she could climb it. She had to climb it. She reached the grill, her trembling fingers finding the holes in the metal and her feet stumbling, straining to climb, but there was nothing to grip. The cars went past too fast, she screamed at them for help, sore-throated and open-mouthed, but if they could see her they couldn't hear, and didn't stop.

She slammed her palm onto the wire, pressed her face to it as if she could push her body through the metal, turned at the sound of running feet, bracing herself for a fight.

It wasn't him. It was Malik. Relief flooded her, made her weak, she slid as he put his arms around her.

'You're shaking!' he said. 'Ellie? It's okay.'

And, needing to believe him, she let him hold her, support her as she stumbled away from the fence as the bulldog rounded the corner, stopped, put his hands on his knees to draw raggedy breathe.

'It's okay, no need to be scared,' Malik said again, and she thought he was speaking to her.

But then he added, 'I found her for you, Uncle. But I think it's time we left the Glacis.'

Bridget

Her mother stood at the lounge window, still waiting. Watching the street, though the only movement was people leaving for work, a couple of keen joggers.

Bridget felt like screaming, she was so close to it that she had to put Ellie's rabbit into her mouth to stop herself. And she had to stop herself because if she started screaming she feared she'd never be silent again. The feeling started when Achim announced that he was once again abandoning her.

'The Parents' Association are having a meeting at the school, so I'm going to go. The more attention we can get, the quicker we'll find her.'

'Don't leave me, Achim.'

'There's nothing I can do here,' he'd said reasonably. But nothing about this was reasonable, and the fact that he could have sat with her, for him to simply share her pain, would have been doing enough.

But he had disappeared, out into the world that hid Ellie, leaving her to wait by the window with only the police officer for company, returning with no news, but looking a decade older, and disappearing upstairs to his study.

She bit the rabbit again, driving away the frustration she felt towards Achim. He was so busy pushing the police to do something, hounding Ellie's friends and the school, pacing the city, that he had forgotten her. He hadn't given her any of the attention she so desperately needed, not a moment of love. In fact, he acted with the same disregard and absence that had defined their relationship since they had moved from Heidelberg to Luxembourg. She knew their marriage was in trouble, but she had believed it was fixable. Until now.

And still, life had to go on. Gaynor had to be taken to and then collected from school, and thank God that Cate had offered to do that for her. Bridget simply couldn't face seeing the other mothers, their sympathy and pity. Achim may be able to handle it, but she couldn't.

Bridget could only continue to watch at the window, screaming silently into the body of the plush rabbit, until Ellie came home. All she could do was try and explain, and hope that it wouldn't be long before Ellie would read her words. She took the notebook from the drawer.

Dear Ellie,

Maybe tomorrow you will come home.

You are lucky, to have that sense of home. It was one of the things I lost, with all my travelling. When I was out in the field, the locals were usually polite and glad to see me, but they also kept a respectful distance, which reinforced that I was a visitor to their country. I asked my driver once why this was, why none of the locals came for a drink after work, why they never invited us to their homes, and he said it was because they knew we'd leave. They were protecting themselves from any more pain, having already felt more than enough for one lifetime.

My first placement was in Botswana for nine months. I had a break, and then was sent first to Tunisia, and then to Algeria. It doesn't sound much, three placements in my short career with MSF, but it was enough. Each time, before and after, I'd go to Brussels for briefing and support and then board a plane back to England. That flight was the worst time for me. I still thought Durham was home, but when I was back, everything felt wrong. How was it that the buildings stood derelict, yet still more were being built? How could people be buying things with such ease, as if money was meaningless? All the wasted food. I was a stranger in my own land. Friends drifted away, and I didn't care. They were frivolous, shallow. My parents, your grandparents, weren't interested in hearing my stories, my mum would say it was too sad to hear of families torn apart by disease, but really I think she just didn't care. More concerned that her neighbour Sheila had just bought a caravan in Hartlepool, or with my father's dangerously high cholesterol level. They hadn't seen what I had seen, and after a short time I learned not to speak about it. I went on the temporary nursing register at the local hospital and waited for my next mission to come through.

Waiting is hard.

What I feel now, Ellie, as I wait for you to come home, is that same desperate aloneness that I felt between missions. MSF had a policy

114

of enforced breaks, they gave us this space to avoid burnout, but I couldn't cope with normal life. I drank and I smoked then too. This is full disclosure, Ellie, I'm not going to hide anything from you, not anymore. I feel I've been pretending for too long.

I want to drink now, I'm desperate for something to numb my brain, but I'm scared that if I start I won't stop. The last time I had wine was at Schueberfouer and I bitterly regret that now. It affects the judgement.

Instead I go to your room, telling myself I'm searching for your cannabis stash, but really you are the drug I need. Your smell is everywhere. The hair bands, still with strands of blonde silk caught in the nylon. I lie down on your bed and hope that, wherever you are, you are comfortable. That you are being looked after with the same care I used when I was caring for the children in Tizi Ouzou. I ask a god I don't believe in to give me this, it is all I ask in return for those months I spent nursing strangers. Please, God, let my daughter be safe and well.

Let her come home now.

Cate

'Hello, Cate. It's Eva Schroeder speaking. You may recall that I teach Amelia German . . . we spoke yesterday afternoon?'

Madame Schroeder. The teacher who had been giving tips on self-defence. Calling her at ten thirty in the morning and sounding tense.

'How did you get my number?' But even as she asked, Cate realised that as a teacher, Eva would be able to access all parents' details. Then, quick on its heels, another thought. 'Is Amelia okay?'

'She's fine. I'm not calling about her, it's about Ellie Scheen.'

Cate was surprised, but also keen to hear news of the girl. 'Has she returned home?'

Eva made a sound that made Cate think she might be close to crying. 'No. I'm afraid not.'

'I'm so sorry. Bridget must be beside herself.' Cate had thought about getting in touch properly, after seeing how distressed she was, but knowing that Olivier was now working on the case and that it was one of a teenage runaway, plus Amelia's comments that Gaynor had seen Bridget hitting Ellie, she thought it was wiser not to get involved. Who knew what family dynamics were ticking away under that particular time bomb?

'So, what is it you want, Madame Schroeder?'

There was a surprised pause. 'But you said you'd help.'

'I said I'd help with self-defence class, but I may have been . . . '

Irritated, the teacher cut her off. 'You're the only person I know with any direct knowledge of criminals. You told me, you're a probation officer. And you want to help.'

'Hang on, Madame . . . ' Cate had meant that she could give a talk to the children on avoiding danger, something like that. Her offer was limply constructed, and now it was coming back to bite her.

'Ah, there is the bell. I must go to my next class, but let's arrange a time to meet. The Fischer café near the school, under the Bouillon car park? I have a free period after lunch for lesson preparation, so we can meet for an hour and a half. That should give us enough time.'

'Enough time for what? Honestly, Madame, there's nothing I can do to help find Ellie. Teenagers run off all the time. I did it, for a few days. My sister did it. Ellie is sure to come home soon.' But even as she said it Cate remembered that her own sister had been gone for sixteen years before she returned.

There was a pause on the other end of the phone.

'Okay, Madame Austin, I really must go. But you should understand that Ellie's mother does not believe she has run away. I will tell you more when we meet. Twelve o'clock, yes?'

Cate slid her phone back into her bag, immediately regretting agreeing to meet.

*   *   *

The Fischer café was ugly. Even though the sun was blistering, the interior was gloomy, the tables by the window closed off by strategically placed chairs so the only free table was near the toilets. Madame Schroeder was already seated in the corner, sunglasses on her face despite the dull light within the place. She was not what Cate had expected from her voice. For a start, she

117

didn't look German, with her small features, her dark eyes and chocolate-brown hair pulled into a girlish ponytail. She looked young, too young to be so serious. And she seemed nervous when she offered Cate her hand to shake.

'Please, call me Eva.'

'Cate.'

Cate ordered a bottle of Rosport water, a small one as she wasn't planning on staying for long, and joined her.

'It's so hot,' Cate said, sliding into the seat. 'I'm not used to it.'

'A mini-heatwave,' Eva agreed. 'Dogs die on days like this. But you wait, later there will be a storm.'

Eva nursed her glass of freshly pressed orange juice, waited until Cate was seated and launched into a speech. Cate liked her directness, though it puzzled her too.

'Thank you for meeting me, Cate. I knew you were not lying when you said you would help Ellie. She was in my class for eighteen months, ever since she first arrived at the school. German should have been her mother tongue, given that she was raised in Heidelberg and it is her father's nationality, but she was too used to speaking English at home, so I gave her some extra help. She was a pleasure to teach, very vivacious, she had a real spark to her personality. I think people always say things like that when someone is missing, but it is true.'

'Nice girls still run off, Eva.'

But even as she said it she regretted her flippancy; she'd seen the impact around the

118

school that very morning, immense and immediate. Word had spread among the ex-pat community and Cate guessed from the lack of cars in the kiss-and-drop area that some parents were keeping children at home until more was known about Ellie's disappearance.

Eva and Cate sat across from one another, occasionally the waitress glanced up from her newspaper, but no-one else was there. Most locals went to the bistros for lunch, and the café's main trade was in takeaway coffees for those about to jump on a bus. Cate noticed Eva's hand was tight on her glass and when she removed it she left a paw of sweat; whatever her motivation was for getting involved, it was powerful. She had the zeal that Cate had seen in social workers before they burned out.

'I'm guessing,' said Cate, 'that you haven't always been a teacher.'

Eva looked down at her glass. 'I am from a small village in Belgium, but I was ambitious. First in Arlon, then in Ghent, I worked in local government, public relations mainly. I enjoyed it, in the main. Until Brussels. There I worked for the mayor, as his PA, and I saw many things.' Here she glanced up and Cate saw a steely determination in Eva's face. 'Public relations was more of a challenge in the capital. It was no longer school fêtes and charity galas.'

'Missing children?' ventured Cate.

Eva sighed. 'Information would arrive, and my job was to put it somewhere, anywhere but in the public eye. Kidnapped children, spirited across Europe. The victims were usually

119

travellers from Africa, not 'us', you understand? Children from government homes, refugees, people with no fixed address. People with no papers who did not officially exist. They simply disappeared, and to us, to the people in charge, they did not matter.'

'But they mattered to you,' Cate said softly, watching Eva closely, warming to this strange and intense woman.

'Very much. I blew the whistle, doing an interview with *Prospect*, a current affairs magazine, which attracted some interest and was shared online. Not that it did me any good. Or the missing children, more importantly. So, I was no longer a PA, and I trained as a language teacher. At least I did not have to hide things like this. I have always been good at languages, and this is how I met my husband. He's German, and was working in Brussels, trying to learn Flemish. He enrolled on my night class, he was not a good student but I could tell he was a good man. We hadn't been married long when my husband got transferred to Luxembourg and it seemed a wonderful opportunity, a chance for me to get away from all that sickness.'

Cate thought of the children she had known about, back in the UK. The 'missing', the ones that ended up on a poster, or at the Centrepoint hostel in London, but never made it as far as *Crimewatch*. She had known of children being collected from the local authority home by their drug dealers, their pimps, and the social workers on duty did nothing, said they were powerless. It was children like that who went missing, and everyone just gave a figurative shrug as if nothing could be done.

'Not all kidnappings are equal,' Cate stated evenly, sad though the fact was. But on this basis, if that was indeed what had happened, Ellie's case should be high profile. An ex-pat, from a successful, high-achieving family. Why had it not ground the city to a halt, why had the international press not descended on Luxembourg? 'So, why is Ellie's case not in the news?'

'To be fair, the media here is not what you will be used to in England. We have stricter guidelines, and the police would not share so much with journalists. But even so, there has been nothing yet, not even in the local free paper. This is curious, especially as Achim is very high up in the banking district. My husband knows him from work and says he is much respected, a man with great ambition.'

Eva finished off her orange juice and collected a massive stainless steel pot from the chair next to her that Cate had not noticed before. Eva struggled to pick it up, and balanced it over her slender rib cage.

'So, you see that something is wrong with the way Ellie's case is being handled. And we must go now, because I have just an hour left before the school will notice I am missing and twenty-two children have to learn the German names for farm animals without a teacher.'

Cate pointed at the steel pot. 'What's inside?'

Eva tapped the lid. 'Our ticket inside Ellie's home.'

Ellie's house was on the edge of the old city, in the area directly leading up from Grund at the point where tall medieval buildings and cobbles made way for perfect square houses in delicate candy colours, that would have been better placed in California or Spain than the Petrusse Valley. Eva checked the number of the house she had scribbled in biro on her wrist. She adjusted the pot so it was across her chest, and led the way to the front door of the pastel-pink house.

'Here we go, number eight. As my husband says, Achim Scheen is doing very well for himself. Ellie lived in the best house on the street.'

Cate didn't comment on the past tense, though she silently acknowledged that either Eva's English grammar was not perfect or she didn't believe Ellie was coming home.

* * *

The door was opened by a tall, well-built man in a police uniform. His white shirt immaculate, and his navy trousers perfectly creased; a poster boy for the police, though not a man who had got his hands dirty, at least not today. He greeted them in deep Luxembourgish, and Cate was glad to have Eva with her, who spoke with him in the Germanic language, endearing herself to the officer. Cate's own thoughts were scrambled by the sight of his uniform. What if Olivier was here, how the hell would she explain herself? Eva was smiling sadly, then pointing to herself and Cate, to the large goulash pot, and the police officer was nodding pleasantly, gesturing for them to wait. Clever Eva. Who would turn away a couple of women bearing the gift of food?

★ ★ ★

The police officer didn't return to the doorway, but Bridget did. Cate saw how altered she was, how the anguish that had started just two nights ago had multiplied into sheer despair etched on her face. Her hair hung lank and unwashed, and her clothes were crumpled and too warm for the day's heat. Cate suspected they had not been changed since the night of Ellie's disappearance. In her hands she held a limp pink rabbit with long ears. Its eyes were closed, as if in sleep.

Bridget hovered in the hall, not moving to let them pass, her posture was broken but a flash of hope had shone in her eyes in the instant she first came to the door, only to be extinguished when she saw Eva's cooking pot. That same hope that must surely have sparked every time the phone rang or someone arrived at the door, only to be cruelly dashed. A torturous emotional journey, from hope to hell, that would define her existence until Ellie was back home, safe and sound.

She looked at them with such naked desperation that Cate felt crushed by it.

'I'm so sorry, Bridget,' she said. What else was there to say?

She was a mother whose child was lost, whose

spine was now made of string, whose brain obsessively processed only one thought. It was the nightmare every mother knows too well, but one they usually wake from. This woman had now lived that nightmare for sixty hours.

Eva thrust the goulash pot into the woman's empty arms, and she clutched it automatically.

'Please, Bridget, accept this. It's all I could think of to do.'

'Oh, Eva, thank you . . . '

And Bridget, too polite to tell them to go away even though they had nothing for her, nothing she wanted anyway, invited them inside.

★   ★   ★

The police officer was seated in the dining room, at the round mahogany table. Arranged in front of him was his radio and police notebook, all at perfect angles, which he was scrutinising with a short black pencil. Olivier had a similar notebook that was never far from his grasp. All police officers kept notes in case they were later required to give evidence in court.

Bridget ignored him, he had already become part of the furniture. She walked past the dining room to the kitchen where she opened the fridge, standing uselessly in front of it as if she had suddenly forgotten why she was there. Her thoughts were elsewhere.

Eva went to her, took the casserole pot from her hands and moved some items around to find a place for the pot, lingering a moment to rob some of the cold air before closing the fridge door. Then, with a hand cupping each shoulder, she guided Bridget to one of the bar stools at the kitchen counter. Cate perched alongside as Eva returned to the fridge for juice, then found glasses. All the while Bridget watched this other woman move around her kitchen as if she had no idea where she was.

Finally, Eva took a stool opposite Cate and gazed at her expectantly, Cate understood: Eva had done her best, she'd found Bridget's address and cooked the goulash, now she was passing the ball to Cate.

Cate glanced to the hallway, thinking that just yards away in the dining room the police officer would be making notes in his book, about their arrival. He should have taken their names, surely? Or was he assuming that woman bearing food could never be significant to any investigation?

'We want to help, if we can.' Cate leaned forward, both to establish eye contact with Bridget and so she could speak softly, though the police officer was surely too far away to hear their conversation. 'If there's anything we can do . . . '

The sentiment was as limp as the mother's body, as empty as she must feel inside.

'I just want her home,' Bridget said, plaintively.

'Do you have any idea where she could be?' asked Cate, gently.

Bridget's head jerked as if Cate had said something shocking and then she quickly shook her head. Her lip wobbled and her eyes welled with tears.

'What about any friends or boyfriends?'

'Ellie has not run away,' Bridget answered firmly. 'We are a close family, we love each other. She would not do that to me.'

Cate thought that though this was undoubtedly how she felt, it could not be entirely true. Teenagers were selfish beings with secret lives, even Amelia had picked up that there was tension in the home. And hadn't she said that Ellie had indeed spent a night away before, with a boyfriend? She felt uneasy, remembering also that Bridget had apparently slapped Ellie.

'Whoever Ellie is with, there will be some connection.' She meant that it was unlikely to be a stranger, but didn't feel able to state this so bluntly. 'Maybe someone you disapprove of?'

'Are you a police officer?' Bridget asked sharply, as if seeing Cate for the first time. Once again, hope darted through her expression, held there, waiting to be dashed.

'Sorry, no. I was a probation officer, back in the UK. So I know about criminals, I suppose I have some knowledge about what makes bad people tick.' Cate felt a fraud even saying it, but she also knew it was her only ticket to ride. 'And I would like to help, if I am able.'

Eva put her hand on Bridget's wrist. Her own role more clearly defined than Cate's, as a supportive and nurturing friend. For a second, Cate envied her.

'Talk to us, Bridget,' she urged. 'Maybe we can help, and maybe not. Either way, what do you have to lose?'

There was a long pause, until finally Bridget

said, 'We should never have left Heidelberg. We've been in Luxembourg for almost two years and I still feel like I really don't belong. Before this it was other things that made me feel this way in Luxembourg, like dealing with people in shops or in the banks. The way they saw me, as a privileged ex-pat housewife, not as anyone who had anything valuable to contribute. But Ellie's disappearance is something else, everyone I speak to, it's as if they don't even accept that it has happened. The whole situation feels beyond my control. The police aren't listening. Their presence will stop Ellie coming home.'

Cate raised a meaningful glance towards the dining room, where the police constable was seated. He must be able to hear. But Bridget didn't care about offending him, she was too angry.

'What is the good of him just sitting there? It's just a gesture, probably to appease Achim. He's been very insistent,' snapped Bridget. 'But it will stop anyone from returning her, it will scare them away. And they won't tell me anything.'

'This is usual with the police, isn't it?' Eva tried to sound positive and looked at Cate expectantly. 'They play things very close until they have something concrete to share. It is us, us mothers, who must think the worst has happened, but it can often be fine in the end.'

Bridget looked towards the landing that led to the circular staircase, as if checking it was still empty. 'Achim, my husband, has called everyone on Ellie's phone at least twice. He is wandering

127

the streets, demanding that the school increase their security. He's driving himself crazy, yet he hasn't spoken with me once. He hasn't even held my hand.' She was holding her own hand, clasping it in a grip that was so tight her knuckles were white. 'I thought situations like this were supposed to bring a couple together, not drive them apart.'

Bridget looked so lost at that moment, so confused by her husband's behaviour that Cate winced for her. She had seen how relationships suffered when a child was hurt, had experienced it after her sister, Liz, went missing. After the accusations and the blame her parents had divorced, both convinced that the other was responsible for their runaway daughter. Even now, back in England, they were establishing who was to blame in court as Cate's father tried to defend himself against claims that he had abused Liz. *I'll call this evening*, Cate thought. *I'll find out how Liz and Mum are, how the court case is going. I'll offer more support than I have.*

Liz had run away for a reason, and maybe Ellie had too. Thinking that Bridget herself may be to blame, if it was true that she hit Ellie, Cate had no comfort for her and looked away. She saw a police business card pinned with a magnet to the fridge. She recognised it as Olivier's. Would Bridget throw her out if she knew she lived with him?

'It's the police's job to find Ellie,' she said, as much to the card as to Bridget. 'You must trust them.'

Bridget turned in a fury of energy, following Cate's eyeline, and snatched the card so the magnet went spinning on the ground, tossing it onto the granite worktop.

'This man,' she spat, 'Detective Massard. He tried to imply I abused my daughter at the fair! Some crazy idea he got from someone that I swore at her, that I hit her. That's why he thinks she's run away. Why he's not taking this seriously.'

It stung, to hear Bridget verbalise the very thought that Cate had just had, and of course she was right, Olivier did believe that. And Olivier's source was Amelia.

For the sake of disclosure she should tell Bridget, right now, that Olivier was her boyfriend. She should make her apologies and leave. But she stayed silent.

*   *   *

Eva had to be back at work and Cate said she had things to do too, not admitting that her list consisted of walking General and shopping for milk. She had told Bridget that she'd collect Gaynor along with Amelia when school finished, save the poor woman the ordeal of the school run. It was the least she could do.

Waiting outside the school entrance, with General straining at his lead, Cate saw the first trickle of school children run out onto the playground. In the corner, shaded by a single tree, Mary-Ann stood with a group of women and only when Cate drew nearer did she sense the panic being whipped up. By then it was too late to turn away.

Katrina was regaling the group with a story about a boy who was taken from the school bus stop one morning, only to be found later that day, naked in a field. 'But he had a scar,' she said, in hushed awe, indicating the place where a kidney would be.

'Well, I've bought my daughter a tracker,' a diminutive but beautiful Japanese woman said proudly. 'She wears it on her wrist and I can see where she's at.' She flashed her gold iPhone, which showed a map with a red dot bleeping in the centre. Presumably the dot indicated the very place where they were now standing.

Jesus, was this what it had come to?

'Where did you get it?' Mary-Ann asked timidly.

'Tokyo. But they sell them on Rakuten.com,' her friend added helpfully.

Ellie's disappearance had united the mothers, blurring the boundaries of nationality and language and given them a subject in common. She gathered from the chatter that Ellie's father had attended the meeting, and implored them all to be extra vigilant.

As Cate was backing away, tugging General so she could simply wait for Amelia and Gaynor on her own, the woman who'd bought the tracker thrust a flyer into her hand.

'The Parents' Association are issuing these to every child,' she said bossily. 'The Ministry of Education has issued the same message to all schools in the city.'

No doubt the result of the emergency meeting that morning. In Cate's hands was an official-looking missive in bold print:

Try to be accompanied by an adult to and from school.
Do not accept a lift from anyone, if it has not been agreed beforehand.
Avoid talking with anyone you do not know.
If anyone approaches you, tell your parents and/or a member of staff.

Cate didn't realise she was holding up a line of women, eager for their copies of the flyer, until they tutted her out of the way. She folded it into quarters and slid it in her pocket, thinking she'd show it to Olivier later, *See, people don't believe this is just a teenage rebellion. You can't contain this.*

Since Saturday she'd tried to talk to Olivier about Ellie's disappearance several times but he'd been unwilling to share anything with her. It was not yet an equal partnership, she was reliant on him for a home and it still felt as though she was his guest. She knew that by moving to Luxembourg, she was escaping the trial. Even if she didn't want to admit it. Since her sister Liz was taking their father to court, the abuse finally in the open, Cate felt unable to see any of her family. It was just too painful, the guilt about not being the victim, the endless wondering if she had failed Liz. The complicated feelings she felt for her mother, who had colluded with the abuse, but who was also a sad alcoholic. Cate vacillated between pity and contempt, but being in a different country, just as the court case commenced, brought her a distance that she grasped with sheer relief. She was yet to even contact home and find out how things had gone on the first two days of the trial.

Frankly, she had wanted an escape and Olivier had offered one. But that respite was now in danger of becoming something else.

★   ★   ★

Olivier was late home. He wasn't interested in the pasta and jar of sauce she'd heated, and she could hardly blame him for that, but he opened some local wine and they took it outside, to the table and chairs on the balcony, savouring the warm evening. From where Cate sat it seemed the moon was directly above them, camouflaged by a smoke screen of mist. The street lights were orange love for the mosquitoes and gnats that buzzed around the glowing bulbs, the lamps set down the street so it was like a runway into the city.

'Napoleon, he planted trees in lines like this,' said Olivier, pointing to the equidistant oaks, 'so his soldiers would have shade as they marched.'

Cate mulled this over, watching as the only soldiers left were the gnats.

As they sat in the warm night there was a grumble of thunder, some distance away but lengthy, a signal of what was to come. General knew it too; less brave than his namesake, he cowered at Cate's feet, his nose pushed deep between his forelegs.

★ ★ ★

She waited. Waited until they had finished the wine, until the evening was almost done and the rain had started, making them move to the living room where Olivier was nursing a stubby bottle of beer as he resumed tapping on his laptop. General was laid out like a rug at Cate's feet, one black furry paw rested across her toes.

'Any developments today with the Scheen girl?' Cate asked, as innocently as she could though her face was burning. 'Has she been found?'

Olivier looked up, sipped his drink. 'No, she hasn't come home yet.'

'You still think she will? On her own, I mean.'

Olivier put his bottle down, the glass clinked on the table, and leaned back in his seat, arms behind his head and eyes closed. He looked tired, and also less certain now.

Cate moved next to him, dislodging General's purchase on her feet, bringing her knees up and resting them in Olivier's lap, his arm came down, around her shoulder. She placed her head against his chest, listening to the rapid throb of Olivier's pulse.

'What if this isn't just a case of teenage runaway?' she asked, feeling how much she longed for it to be. It was with dread that she said, 'What if it's a kidnapping?'

133

She felt Olivier's chin rest gently in the crown of her head. 'Mmm. It may not be as straightforward as we first thought. But we're checking things out.'

'What things?' she probed, thinking the physical closeness was an invite, that this time, maybe Olivier would open up about what was actually going on.

But she felt him shift his position, move her away so he could focus back on his computer screen. 'I told you, Cate. Work is not something we can discuss. Why don't you go and read Amelia a book while I finish off here?'

Ellie had now been missing for seventy-two hours. Cate wanted to talk to Olivier, to know what was going on, and how much the police had found out about Ellie's disappearance, but what struck her most was that not once in their conversation had Olivier said the girl's name. As though he didn't want to invest too much emotion in this case.

Now, before she could stop herself and even though Amelia was close enough to hear she said, 'Do you think she's dead?'

'No! God, Cate, please don't say such things. What if Amelia hears you?'

'There's nothing we could say that she won't have heard at school. Everyone's in panic, spreading rumours about other kidnappings. Some of her friends aren't even coming to school until the case is solved. Are you solving it?'

Olivier rubbed the bridge of his nose with both thumbs. 'Of course. But I cannot talk about an active police investigation with my girlfriend.'

Girlfriend. He made their relationship sound so trivial.

'But she isn't dead?' pressed Cate. 'You know that for a fact?'

'Cate, what I know is that we are in Luxembourg, not America. She will be alive, wherever she is.'

'So where is she then? With an old boyfriend? Some estranged family member, maybe?'

'Yes, for sure it is something like this. She is somewhere, and we will find her.'

Somewhere. It may as well be nowhere.

There was comfort, though, that Olivier was certain Ellie was alive. He must know something, of course he couldn't give her details. Whoever Ellie was with, it didn't have to be the most sinister scenario, not the kidnapping she and every other mother she'd met that day feared and had nightmares about.

She kissed Olivier's cheek. 'I'll go upstairs and read to Amelia, then I'm going to have a bath. Don't be late to bed.'

He smiled up at her. 'I'll be as quick as I can.'

★   ★   ★

Cate stopped at Amelia's bedroom door, and saw her daughter was already in bed, the duvet pulled high to her face so only her nose was visible under the tousled blonde mop of hair. 'Goodnight, love.'

Instead of a reply there was a sniff, and Cate went to the side of the bed, stroked her daughter's hair. Amelia snuffled further into her

135

duvet and Cate saw she was crying. 'Amelia, I'm sorry. Were you listening to Olivier and me just now?'

She moved her head so her mouth was exposed, reminding Cate of a baby bird in a nest, and nodded. 'Is Gaynor's sister dead?'

'No, babe. Olivier just said she isn't.'

'So why can't they find her then?'

'I don't know.' Cate moved in next to Amelia, cradling her and giving her all the comfort she could offer, and tried not to imagine how Bridget was feeling right now, seeing one daughter into bed while another one was gone.

When Amelia's breathing became heavy and steady, Cate gently untangled herself, and went to her own bedroom.

★   ★   ★

In their en-suite bathroom Olivier and her each had their own sink, with a three-shelved cabinet below. Cate had no right or reason to sift through Olivier's shaving creams, razors and cologne, only she had heard him, opening the cupboard each morning and night and heard the following sound of a blister pack of pills being opened.

Inside was packed with a pharmacy supply of drugs, various types, some still in their boxes and others in silver strips with several pills already popped. She lifted the nearest box and took out the leaflet, searching for English words. By the time she'd read four different leaflets she understood that the different drugs all treated the same thing: Olivier had a stomach ulcer.

She got into her nightdress and climbed into bed, knowing that any conversation with Olivier would end badly the way she was feeling. She wanted to talk to him, about Ellie, about his stomach ulcer, about why he hadn't mentioned it to her and about the way he was freezing her out of every possible conversation.

And across the channel, her father's trial would be progressing.

She tried to lose herself in a book, a family guide to moving to Luxembourg, but the descriptions of nearby forests and parks couldn't keep her thoughts from the darker themes already established.

Olivier eventually came to join her, placing his phone on the bedside cabinet and disappearing into the bathroom. She heard him lock the door, heard the cupboard opening and wondered how he decided which tablet to take. His prescriptions had looked random, prescribed by different doctors, and she couldn't see a set regime being followed.

She heard the water running and Olivier began to brush his teeth, a process that always took a full four minutes and was followed by careful flossing. On impulse she flung back the duvet and left the bedroom, walking swiftly to the lounge where his laptop sat, still open but with a black screen.

General padded over to her, sitting at her feet and gazing up as if asking what she thought she was doing. Then whining, head on paws, as a rumble of thunder preceded a crack of light in the sky. Cate went to the balcony to watch the start of the storm.

'Dogs die on days like this,' Eva had said that morning, when the August heat was stifling, but it was the fox that was suffering now. Cate saw him, a long red animal, seeking hither and thither, as if disorientated by the storm, his body damp and low to the ground, as if his wet fur made him sink. He was by the entrance to the carport, then up on the path, crossing the road a few times before jumping into the undergrowth. Cate watched with sympathy, she knew how it was to have the weather make you lose your sense of place. Her weather was Olivier, was Ellie's disappearance. In England she knew the route, but in Luxembourg she was confused, unsure of the rules that operated here.

She turned back, considered the computer again, but realised that she hadn't the time to start scrolling through emails, she didn't even know his passwords to access them. But then she remembered the phone.

Quickly, she returned to the bedroom. She told herself that if he would only talk to her, she wouldn't need to do this, he was giving her no choice. She unlocked Olivier's phone, wincing at the guilty beeping as she scrolled to his messages.

The water stopped running and she froze, listening. She heard a click, then a gargle. She still had time.

She opened the most recent text. It simply said *Beauty Asiatique*.

She wanted to read the preceding messages,

but they were in French and she didn't have time to translate, she wasn't even sure this text pertained to Ellie's disappearance — but it must, surely; there was only one case that Olivier would be actively working on. She could hear him in the bathroom, the sound of clothes being dropped, and she knew he would soon be finished. Cate had only just placed the phone back on his side of the bed when the bathroom door opened.

Amina

Amina is woken by their voices, muffled and low at first, but becoming increasingly louder, as though whatever control was there has now gone: Auntie and Uncle Jak are arguing.

She can hear Fahran's name, again and again. At one point the shouting stops and all she can hear are the sobs, the crying sound a grown woman makes when she has succumbed to despair, it was a sound she heard after a martyr had been named, though always from behind a closed door. Wondering why Auntie was grieving, Amina can't stop herself from listening. Jodie is seemingly oblivious, as she begins to get dressed, readying herself for the day ahead.

'It won't do any good, Amina,' Jodie says, as she combs her hair. 'We just here to learn and get some money, we shouldn't get involved.'

'I'm not doing anything,' Amina answers, irritated that Jodie was once again telling her what to do.

'Yes, you are. You are caring, and that could be a big problem for you. There is nothing to be done but to get dressed. Auntie will be expecting us downstairs very soon.'

Amina moves closer to her and snatches the comb from the other girl's hands.

'You know something,' Amina accuses, surprised at her own anger.

Fleetingly, Jodie looks like she is deciding whether to slap Amina for snatching the comb, but then she softens. 'These few days I have come to know Uncle Jak, just a little. Often he is silent, and he disappears sometimes without saying. But sometimes he is very thoughtful and if I make myself stay very quiet, I can listen when he talks to Malik. He tells Malik most things.'

'So you do know what's wrong with Fahran?'

'Mmm.' Jodie begins to clean her face with some of her oil, using a cloth she brought from her home. She crosses her legs, sitting so that the window can be used as a mirror.

'Tell me, then.'

She can see that Amina won't give her any peace until she does.

'The boy had cancer. A tumour in his head. You know what that means, village girl?'

Of course she knows cancer, people in the commune had it too, in all sorts of places. The elders can't cure it with their herbs, and the body is eaten away from the inside. But she knows they can cure everything in Europe.

'If the eye is gone, then so is the cancer,' says Amina, sensibly. 'Why do they not get him a false eye?'

140

'I ask Malik this. He told me that Fahran needs to heal where the tumour was before they can put one in. But that is not the big problem, it is not why they are shouting. It is because though the tumour has gone, Fahran needs other treatment. To stop the cancer returning.'

'Then why don't they go to the hospital and see a doctor?' she asks for the second time that day. 'Is it because they are illegal?'

'This is Europe, village girl. Here, even illegal people can get medicine. It is why they came. The tumour was removed in Algiers, and they came to Europe because here is better treatment. But it is expensive, and must be paid for in advance. For those with papers it would be refunded, but that is not the case for the likes of us. It is more expensive than they dreamed, and so now they are shouting.'

Amina is now more confused than ever, that Uncle and Auntie are in Luxembourg for health care, but getting none. She asks Jodie, again and again, but she says she knows nothing more.

'Uncle Jak gets upset, talking about Fahran,' she explains. 'I have no wish to make it worse.'

And then Amina begs her. 'Please, Jodie,' she says. 'Ask Malik. Please find out why they are not getting this help from the hospital, how much it is they should pay. If you do I'll steal you a nail polish from the shop.'

Jodie looks at her nails, which are strong and long but not very pretty.

'We have gold and purple. We have pink with white stars, and we have red like film star lips. We have . . . '

'Okay, Amina,' Jodie says, desperate to stop the flow of tantalising beauty treats. 'I'll find out what I can. And then I'll take the pink. And you better not be lying when you say it has white stars. Now, we must go downstairs or Auntie will be angry.'

★　★　★

The white van leaves soon after, this time driven by Malik, with Uncle Jak sitting beside him and Jodie again in her red dress, on the wooden bench in the back. Amina busies herself about the kitchen, and has already been upstairs to check on Fahran who is watching his cartoons. Satisfied that all is straight in the house, Amina goes into the shop. She wants to get the nail polish for Jodie, before anyone else is around. Also, she had noticed the day before that the cotton wool was low in the dispensers and Auntie had told her that it was very important to keep the cotton wool stocked. Without cotton wool, nails cannot be cleaned and made ready for the gel, which is what all the Americans and British want so much. Nail polish that will last for as long as possible. It is a mystery to Amina who does not know why they think it is so hard, to paint their nails every few days. For her it would be a pleasure, especially if she could choose a different colour each time and these rich ladies could have as many as they liked, the salon prices are nothing to them.

Amina had noticed yesterday how new customers looked around at the salon, sniffing

142

with a sour expression that said it was beneath them to even be inside such a place and not nearly so fancy as they deserve, but when they handed over their money from fat designer wallets they checked they heard right. The fee the salon charges is small compared to the local and French salons, Auntie had told her, so the customers return.

'You will see, Amina, they are less sniffy on the second visit.'

★ ★ ★

Amina was going to the stock room, but when she opened the door she let out a small scream because a person was there, in the dark. It scared her.

'It's me.'

So small, these words. Spoken in such a sad voice.

Amina started to back away with a hundred apologies, but Auntie said, 'What is it you need?'

'Cotton wool pads, Auntie.'

And then she put the light on and said, 'Well, there they are.'

But Amina hesitated to take the packet because she was staring at Auntie, at her tiny eyes and the puffy skin around them.

Auntie started to cry again, but she didn't push the girl away and shut the door, she pulled her forward, Amina's face was pressed against her bosom so she could barely breathe.

Eventually she seemed to stop, though she still held Amina tightly.

'I'm sorry, Auntie.'

'Why, Amina? What have you done?' Despite the tears and the puffy eyes, the woman's tone was fierce.

'N . . . nothing. I mean I am sorry that you are so sad. Is it because of Fahran?' Although she had not said his name before it seemed wrong to say 'your son' when she had been thinking about him so much. It was as though he had only existed as an attachment to Auntie before, but now Amina knew about his brain tumour, he seemed more real to her.

Auntie didn't know she was thinking all of these things, but even so her face widened when she heard his name, as if it would once again melt into hot tears.

'I am always thinking about my sweet boy,' she said. 'Tell me, Amina, when your mother sent you here, was she frightened?'

'I was frightened, but I don't think Omi was. She was sad to say goodbye. But why should she be frightened?'

'She was sending you to another country, many miles away. With people you did not know.'

'We know Uncle Jak,' Amina protested. 'He has been to my town before. We all know that he saved a baby once, who would have perished. He is a good man.'

'Maybe,' the older woman conceded. 'But you don't know me and I may not be a good woman.'

'Omi doesn't know you,' Amina agreed, 'but she knows me. And she knows I am a good girl, and so the world will be good to me. If you want an object to be solid, make it from your own clay. This was a favourite saying of hers. And I am of her clay.'

'And so it goes,' said Auntie, nodding as if the girl had spoken a great truth.

★　★　★

Just before nightfall the white van returns. Amina is impatient to see Jodie and to hear what more she knows. All day Fahran has been in his room, playing but also sleeping, and Amina has had no chance to speak with him. But she will, once an opportunity arises. She is resolved to befriend him.

Jodie waits until all is quiet in the house below, and still she whispers, serious over all that she has learned.

'Uncle told me that Fahran started falling over,' she tells her. 'He told Auntie that the boy, he say that his world was spinning and Malik said this was the same thing he said before the tumour was discovered two years ago. The elders tried many things and finally Auntie took him to see a doctor, then to a hospital in Algiers. That is when they were told that Fahran has brain cancer and they took out his eye. As soon as he was well enough, they decided to travel to Europe, to get medical help.'

Amina thinks about how desperate they must have felt, to make that terrible journey with a sick child.

'And now?' she presses.

'Wait, Amina, I have not finish with this part

of the story. After they arrive here, Uncle saw that he need money to live and that is when he returned to Algeria, started the collections, of girls like us,' Jodie says. 'It was supposed to pay for the medicine, the special treatment that Fahran need, to stop the cancer from coming back.'

Amina smiles. 'That makes me feel good, that my mother's money will be helping this little boy get better. So, then.'

'You fool, child,' says Jodie. 'By the time that boy got here, the hospital say he is too sick for a big treatment. They give him radiotherapy, but that makes him weak and very ill. They cannot give him anything else. The illness is in him, deep in his blood. There is nothing else for it.'

Amina shakes her head, thinking, *How, if the tumour has been cut out, can he still be dying?*

But Jodie isn't a doctor, she doesn't know the answer to this any more than Amina.

'Auntie was in the stock cupboard today,' Amina whispers to Jodie, glad that she has some information of her own. 'She was crying.'

'Why are you whispering? No-one can hear us, we're too high up.'

Amina moves closer to her, so that even if she didn't whisper she could speak quietly. 'Auntie has been very upset today. How was Uncle Jak?'

'Strange too.' Jodie frowned, as if thinking back to something that had taken place earlier. 'He left me for a long time again. I was just with Malik, which I didn't mind.' Here she giggled, and Amina feared she would change the subject, but mercifully she didn't. 'I do not know where he went, but when he returned he was sweating as though he had run a great distance, or been in a fight. I've seen men like this, Amina, and it is never a good thing. We were at the Schueber-fouer.'

'What's that?'

'A fair. A big one, more colourful than anything you've ever seen, louder than anything you've ever heard. I tell you, Amina, this is a better kind of religion.' Jodie sat taller, her eyes lit with energy. 'It's a huge place with rides and food stands and so many people. More than you could ever imagine here in Luxembourg, or even in the whole of Europe. It was so exciting.'

'And what were you doing?' Amina asked, trying to hide her jealousy because all that she had yet seen of Luxembourg was the beauty salon and the storage cupboard and the small square of concrete Auntie called the yard.

'Malik and I had lots of different jobs. One was to stand around a circle, while Uncle did a card trick, and to pretend to be customers. I had to say which cup a ball was under, and when I got it right he gave me one hundred euros. Then Malik would do the same.'

'A hundred euros,' Amina marvelled. 'But that's a fortune!'

'Yes, but we had to give it back, silly. It was to make the customers have a go, and once they did we would move to another corner of the fair and pretend to be a customers again.'

'But why? If it was only you, Uncle was not winning or losing.'

'Oh, Amina, you are so simple! The plan is

that others at the fair saw me win money, and so like fools they would decide to play. But then they would guess wrong, and lose their money. You see?'

She didn't really see. If Jodie could see which cup the ball was under, then why would the real customers get it wrong? It seemed a very easy thing to know.

'And Uncle was strange today?'

'It is hard to say for sure, because he is never exactly chatty. But he was much quieter than normal and he went off alone. Me and Malik went on the big wheel. Malik flirted with a girl. Her skin was as pale as Reza and Safiyya's, but her hair was like their blonde hair had got dirty. She had a yellow t-shirt, but I think this is a bad colour for a white girl. With the hair and the clothes she looked like a yellow weed, those weeds that are everywhere here, and not pretty. Malik told me they are called dandelion.'

Amina thought it was a beautiful word, and she tried it on her tongue, wishing she could see these yellow weeds for herself. 'And what did Malik do?'

'He went and spoke with her. He asked her to join us, and Uncle Jak was pleased.'

Jodie began to nibble her thumbnail and Amina could see that even if Uncle was pleased, Jodie wasn't. 'A non-Muslim! And Uncle seemed so happy that Malik was with this girl.' She half laughs, partly scandalised, disappointed in Malik, but also thrilled. 'Imagine, Amina! Luxembourg could be a place where the rules of home no longer exist.'

Amina thought that this could be a good thing, but it scared her too.

'So what happened to the dandelion girl?'

'She rode the ferris wheel with us. And then Malik took her for a walk.'

'What is a ferris wheel?'

And Jodie told her then of the massive wheel and Amina tried to let her tellings transport her to the great height, and to imagine what it must be like to see out over the whole of Luxembourg. She wished that she would see it for herself one day.

There seemed to be so much to ask, so much Amina didn't know.

'And I have one more thing to tell you, about Fahran. Something that may make you happy. But first, do you have my prize?'

Amina lifted her pillow and under it was the bottle of nail polish that she had eventually managed to steal, as an exchange for the information. Jodie snatched it, held it up to see the tiny white stars floating in the delicate pink.

'But don't let anyone see,' begged Amina. 'Please, it must be our secret.'

Day 4

Ellie

'Please let me go home.'

She stumbled, her head was pounding and her words came out slurred. Shock made her weak, as she was walked to the white van, Malik holding her right arm the bulldog gripping her left.

It was clear that there was no escape, yet still a part of Ellie refused to believe this and she began to beg. 'I won't say anything, I swear. Just let me go. Please, my mum will be so worried.'

She wondered, somewhere back in the cold storage of her calculating brain, where she had learned this script. She must have been taught it from so many films where girls begged to be freed even as the audience knew it wasn't going to happen; and the logical part of Ellie's brain was of the same mind as that audience, calmly stating through the shock and fear: *They have you. You just need to survive, find the time for escape. But this isn't it.*

Not now she was on the bench in the back of the white van, her arms restrained at her side by Malik, being driven by the bulldog to God knows where.

'If you fight me, I'll have to use the rope,' Malik told her, though she felt he was saying this for the bulldog's benefit. The rope was on the dusty floor of the van, coiled like a snake, but as he spoke, Malik pushed it away with his foot and gave her a look that seemed to be begging her to cooperate. He gripped her arm as if he was keeping her safe, and his body was supporting her.

She still felt odd, woozy, and she wouldn't fight anymore, she was so compliant now it sickened her, but the headache was powerful, a grip all of its own, and she knew that she wasn't ready to fight. Not yet.

Survive, Ellie. Live to see your mum and dad, to see Gaynor again.

And this thought was enough to still her, to sustain her.

Bridget

Bridget was also being driven somewhere she did not want to go.

Achim had got angry with Detective Massard, he was outraged that they wouldn't interview Bridget in her own home, why did they need her to go to a filthy police station? But the detective insisted, so Achim told the man he would drive his wife himself. They would follow the police car in his Land Rover. But in the passenger seat next to her husband, Bridget was wondering if she would have been better with the detective, who at least wouldn't be sulking over the steering wheel, banging it with his fist as the police car stopped at an amber light.

'Achim? They asked if I'd like a solicitor,'

Bridget said weakly.

'Fuck that. You've done nothing wrong, they're just trying to frighten us. If I speak to anyone it will be to the press. Or the British Ambassador.'

Bridget stared out of the window, to the rain-soaked pavements and homes of other people, people whose lives were untouched by Ellie's disappearance and wondered how life could continue when hers was falling apart.

'Bridget?' Achim was speaking to her in that tone she hated, like she was a child being told off. 'Don't tell them how bad your relationship with Ellie was. Don't give them any excuse not to search for our daughter.'

'I don't know what you mean,' she said, confused that her husband didn't understand how her heart was bursting for Ellie, how her head was full of her. 'I love Ellie.'

'I know that,' Achim snapped, frustrated as a car cut in front of him just as he was indicating to turn into the police station. 'But don't say you hit her. Don't mention her cheekbone. Okay?' He pulled in, parked, and stopped the engine. Then he turned to her, his bloodshot eyes fixed on her own. 'Okay?'

'I never hit our daughter,' Bridget said, confused and hurt. The bruised cheekbone had been an accident. 'I love her. I just want her to come home.'

★ ★ ★

As it happened, the police didn't just want to speak with Bridget, they wanted Achim to be interviewed too. Bridget thought that he was the one who needed a warning, he was already close to losing his temper.

Bridget found herself in a cool room with no windows, sitting at a desk, across from Detective Massard, who had visited the house just two days before brandishing a business card and empty promises to find her daughter, and who was now asking about her treatment of Ellie, recording every word that she said. Did he not see, that by bringing her to the police station he was sabotaging everything? Ellie would be home, should be home, by now. Bridget should be back there, waiting for her daughter to return.

The police room offered no comfort. The only thing that soothed Bridget was to speak to Ellie, to mentally continue the letter that she had started to write to her girl on the night she went missing.

Dear Ellie,

Your father and I, we are very different. It is not just that we are from different countries, different cultures, it is in our very personalities. He knew that when he met me, all those years ago in Durham, but he's never accepted it. I am sick of him trying to change me.

When I was nursing in the field, my behaviour would have shocked him. As well as the smoking and the drugs there was sex too. With doctors, mainly, but also some of the local volunteers. Every day I saw five or six deaths and each night I craved life. Sex is life.

I wonder what you will say to this. You see me

as being so stiff, so serious. Maybe you prefer that, to thinking about your mother as a slut, but I promised you a full disclosure. I should have told you this, maybe when I found out you were no longer a virgin. But I got angry and I'm sorry. I made you go to the doctors for a morning-after pill even though you tried to tell me there was no need, as if I was naïve enough to believe that. It wasn't disgust, though, or disappointment. It was fear.

Because you have so many choices to make, so many places to see, and sex can be a trap.

I don't want you to think I mean getting pregnant with you was a trap, because I swear that, once I decided to keep you, I never for a second saw it that way. I love you, and I've loved you since the moment I knew that I couldn't go ahead with the abortion, that my life path was changed. And all because a soldier had placed a baby in my arms and taught me something about my own needs.

But what if I had refused to leave MSF, and continued nursing in Algeria? I could have placed you in the care of a local woman while I worked, or found a school that was still functioning and maybe, much later, have married one of those doctors, or one of the other workers I met in the field. Brave and unconventional and terrifyingly moral; a morality that was higher than the laws of the country, we often made decisions that other people would question.

It would have been a different life for us, certainly, and you would have been a different girl. I don't think you'd fight me so hard, if you respected my work. You wouldn't demand so much, if you knew how others have so little. I blame myself for giving up on nursing, for not being able to show you these truths.

I have done us both a great disservice.

Even though I worked when we were in Heidelberg I never took you into the hospital, where I could have shown you children who were dying, who were being eaten away by cancer. I thought about it, but Achim stopped me. He said it would ruin your innocence, but what would be wrong with that? I would prefer you to be wiser, and kinder. We all have to lose our innocence at some point.

Achim persuaded me that what you needed was security and stability. It was what I always strived to give you, everything those poor children lacked.

Oh Ellie, I am ready for you to come home.

I am ready to talk to you, honestly this time. To try again to be a better mother if only you will be a better daughter.

But I fear that when you do come home, I won't be there. And outside of the house will be a police car.

What will happen to you then?

Cate

Cate woke to see that the storm had passed, but the sky was still dark and ominous. The sun was half-hidden behind a cloud, as if unsure whether to bother trying to warm the world today.

Despite this, she felt invigorated, and all because she had read Olivier's phone message. She wondered about calling Eva at the school, but decided against raising the woman's hopes when the text could mean anything or nothing and besides, Eva would be teaching.

It had started raining again by the time she pulled up at Bridget's house, all the blinds were down but one; in the downstairs lounge a figure was standing at the window. It was Bridget, looking out into the road. Their Land Rover was parked in the drive, so Cate guessed that Achim was also in the house, but she simply couldn't face knocking on the door and seeing Bridget's face raise then fall.

'Run and get Gaynor, love,' she said, holding General back by his collar from pouncing out as Amelia opened the door.

Amelia didn't need to wait long at the door as Gaynor was ready, her rucksack on her back, and both girls sprinted to the car to avoid getting wet, looking every bit like normal kids on a regular day. But when Gaynor was buckling herself in, Cate couldn't help herself from asking, 'Any news, Gaynor?'

'No,' Gaynor said, forcing Cate to say that she was sure there would be some soon. The young girl gave a tiny smile of hope then buried her face in General's fur.

★   ★   ★

Back at the flat, Cate succumbed to the power of the Internet. If Olivier wasn't willing to talk, she

156

would do her own detective work. She started by googling *kidnapping in Luxembourg*, and up popped the information given by the Ministry of Education, the advice that no child should attend school unaccompanied. The report said:

These steps come after police reported two attempted kidnappings in Steinfort and Kleinbettingen and three attempted kidnappings in the Arlon area in Belgium in recent weeks.
Last week, an 11-year-old girl was approached by a man in Esch-sur-Alzette, prompting a police investigation.

No mention of Ellie Scheen. Also, frustratingly, the report answered none of her questions, such as why did the kidnapping fail? Just how serious were the attempts and did the victim have to struggle? Or was it enough that they refused to get in the car? Also, what was the kidnapper saying to try to get the victim into the car, and in what language, did they use a threat or coercion? Were all the potential victims the same age and gender . . . ? Cate realised she was approaching this like a probation officer, wanting more case information than a journalist here would receive. Olivier would know the answers to her many questions, he would have direct access to all of this information, but he wouldn't talk.

Okay, then. If he won't tell me, I'll just have to find out for myself.

She typed *Beauty Asiatique* and it came up

straight away, with a simple website and a map. Without thinking too hard about what she was doing, Cate called to General, 'Come on, boy. Walkies.'

★   ★   ★

Once she had the postcode her sat nav did the rest, directing her there in perfect Received Pronunciation that irritated Cate only slightly less than the alternative Irish brogue.

She found herself in three-lane traffic, her windscreen wipers doing the best they could as she slowly navigated the area around the train station. Through the rain-splattered windows was a part of Luxembourg she hadn't yet witnessed: run down properties, boarded-up buildings next to occupied flats, sad curtains hung limply at dirty windows, a child's mangled scooter leaned against a graffitied wall. She stopped at a red light and looked to the car park next to her, empty but for a couple of abandoned shopping trolleys and a white van. In the front seat was a man in his fifties, and beside him a too-pretty girl of about sixteen. They seemed to be arguing and then the girl leaned forward and kissed him, full on the lips. This was not the Luxembourg of the tourist books, nor even the place she now thought of as home. It was an even farther cry from the ice-cream sweetness and gloss of Ellie's home.

The lights changed to green and Cate drove on, seeing how some of the houses had made a valiant effort with ornaments at the windows and cheerful floral displays on the steps. It didn't faze Cate, in fact, it felt very familiar and in many ways she would have preferred to live somewhere like this. Sometimes broken things can feel more human.

*   *   *

Cate parked on the opposite side of the street to Beauty Asiatique, which was wedged in the middle of a line of shops on rue de Strasbourg, a notorious street off the main road with an odd assortment of shops and businesses: a Chinese herbal dispensary and high-end Italian delicatessen were cheek-by-jowl with bars with curtained windows; alongside a brightly painted crèche was a narrow passageway littered with discarded beer cans and used syringes.

Though the sun was now making a weak promise from behind a ghostly cloud, the rain persisted, huge splodges hammering on her car roof. In theory she was parked where she could see the comings and goings at Beauty Asiatique, but the rain was obscuring her view. Beside her, on the passenger seat under General's paws, was the free paper. It was in Luxembourgish, so she usually just flicked to the cinema listings, but today the front page drew her attention: *Fraen dei op den Dapp Gin.*

The picture showed a woman leaning into a car, and the backdrop was clearly the car park near the station that she had just passed. Cate could work out the gist of the article, explaining how prostitution was a growing problem, and the police were enacting a night curfew.

The car felt humid, so Cate cracked the window open just as a line of lightning snagged the sky, with a grumble of thunder following on its heels. The storm would soon be on top of her and she would see nothing if she remained in the car.

⋆   ⋆   ⋆

Beauty Asiatique had purple orchids in the window, and there were opened fans in rainbow colours taped to the glass. Alongside the lilies were plastic banks of nail varnishes in ruby colours, cherry and damson. Before she could give herself time to think twice, Cate pushed the door open, with General on a short lead at her side, and it sent a wind chime tingling in rapid chorus, announcing her arrival. Near the window were two tables, both set up for nail work, and at the furthest one a pretty girl with a ponytail of black hair was bent over a large brassy woman's curled talons. The girl only looked about fifteen.

'And it's so expensive here,' the customer was saying to her in an Australian accent. 'How do people even eat out? I mean, it's two hundred dollars just for a decent meal. And that's not including wine.'

The girl kept politely nodding, but was otherwise fixated on the woman's nails that she was painting deep purple, her shiny hair falling forward over her exquisitely shaped face, so tiny that the Australian seemed huge and vulgar across from her.

160

It didn't look like a beauty parlour. Not that Cate's experience of such things was extensive but, of the few salons she had graced, they shared a medical feel, were bright and clean and the walls tastefully decorated with silver mirrors and with posters showing clear-faced young women.

Beauty Asiatique had red painted walls and the air was scented with cooking spices. At the back of the room a bamboo curtain bloomed and out stepped an older woman, short but making up for it with girth, older and less submissive than the girl. She had the weary expression of a woman who had seen something of the world and no longer expected it to give her any hand-outs.

'*Bonjour, Madame. Je peux vous aider?*'

Cate thought hard then said, '*Je voudrais prendre un rendezvous, sil vous plait.*'

The woman pinched her lips upwards in what may have been a smile and said sympathetically, 'Of course, Madame. For which service?'

The whiney Australian was still chattering, but her nails looked perfect. The older woman followed Cate's glance.

'You would like a gel colour?'

'Yes, please.'

Cate was guided to the nail bar to choose a colour. 'Please, wait here. Tina will be with you shortly.' Pulling General to sit by her side, Cate took the free seat facing the back of the Australian who was now regaling the young beautician with a monologue on her opinion of Luxembourg, thrilling at the closeness of Ikea

161

but complaining about her Portuguese cleaner's tardiness. General was more alert than usual, and despite Cate telling him to sit, he whined and tried to pull towards the bamboo curtain.

'Lay down, General. Or I'll have to put you in the car.'

Whilst seeming to be studying the colour options of nail varnishes, Cate assessed her surroundings and wondered why it had featured in Olivier's phone. She picked up a leaflet from a pile on the window ledge. It was advertising a swimming pool in Saarburg and there was a picture of water cascading into several circular pools. She folded it and put it in her bag, thinking Amelia might like to go, then turned her attention back to the salon.

When Cate was in training her practice teacher had said once that everyone who worked with crime, be they probation or police, got a thrill from it. 'We're closer to the criminals than to other civilians,' he'd said. 'We prefer a life with crime because it's more interesting.'

At the time, young and earnest, she had disagreed. 'I want to do this job because I'd prefer a world without crime,' she'd insisted. 'Not for any sort of kick.'

But now she wasn't so sure. She could have taken a different path in Luxembourg, and remained oblivious to the darker side of life going on around her, but instead she was delving into her lover's secrets, sniffing out crime like a well-trained spaniel. After all, she wasn't really that interested in having buffed nails.

Finally, the Australian woman paid, peeling off

five euro notes with the pads of her fingers, keeping her nails up so as not to mark the gleaming surface. The young girl held the door for the customer, and when she was gone came over to where Cate waited. Cate saw now that the girl really was young, she seemed little more than a child and she revised her earlier guess to fourteen. The beautician, though surely she'd had little training, at her age, smiled shyly, her head bowed submissively, and then she took the seat opposite and reaching for Cate's hand before she had even engaged eye contact. The girl's small hand was damp with nerves, and Cate allowed her to dip her nails into a bowl of warm water, not wishing to make the girl more anxious than she already was.

'You choose colour, Madame?' the girl asked, and Cate selected a neutral shade, thinking that Amelia would have told her off for being so pedestrian. It was a simple pink, barely a shade above the natural colour of her nails.

As the girl worked, Cate wondered what she was doing and how this was helping Ellie. She wasn't a detective, she should just have her nails done and go home. Olivier was taking them out for dinner, to a restaurant over the border in Belgium, and that was all she should be thinking about.

Her mobile sprung to life, beeping out a jocular ringtone until she silenced it by accepting the call. It was Eva.

'Where are you?' she demanded, and Cate could picture Eva's pretty but serious face as she spoke.

'Having my nails done.'

There was a pause and then Eva said, 'Well, you need to come here now, things have escalated.'

'What's happened? Has Ellie come home?'

There was a pause. 'No.'

Cate felt dread creep up her spine. 'Is she . . . ?'

Eva cut her off. 'Bridget has just called me, she's in a terrible state. She's just left the police station. They just told her they no longer think Ellie has run away.'

'Well, that's good,' Cate said, aware that Tina appeared to be listening to her call. 'They are finally taking it seriously.'

'They're taking it seriously alright,' said Eva. 'They interviewed Bridget in a police cell, for god's sake. They think she's responsible, Cate. They've let her go home, but I just know they're investigating her. It's easier for them, to blame the family. It means the sickness is domestic, an isolated case. It's not the whole city that is diseased.'

★ ★ ★

'One thing the *Belges* have got totally right, is their beer.'

Cate watched Olivier sip at his Orval in its matching glass, wondering if he was going to tell her that he had interviewed Bridget. Wondering also why he had suggested this drive out for tea, to Bastogne. It was a summer evening, warm and light now the rain had stopped, but forty minutes still seemed a long way to drive on a school night.

The beer was dark as chocolate with a creamy head and she took a sip too, then pushed it back to him. It looked nicer than it tasted. 'Wow, that's strong.'

Olivier grinned. 'Exactly.'

'I don't like this much,' Amelia said, picking apart her *croque madame*, opening up the toast and scraping off the thick ham slices, then nibbling on what was basically cheese on toast, leaving the rest untouched.

'We'll order you some frites,' Olivier told her. 'You'll like those, another thing the Belges have got down to perfection.'

They had the window table and directly across the road from the bistro was a nail bar. Cate noticed it was similar to Beauty Asiatique in its red colour scheme, also the same purple orchids along the upper window. Olivier kept glancing across at it, and Cate had a feeling they were not simply here for the Belgian specialities.

'And the chocolates, they're good at those,' she added, an afterthought to prove she was not thinking about Ellie, but Olivier wasn't listening. He was watching the door of the nail bar, and the young man who had just walked out. He was stocky, not tall, but held himself with a certain confidence as he walked towards a white van, and climbed up next to a man who was in the driving seat. The van did not pull away, and Cate saw it was advertising a swimming pool. The picture seemed familiar, but she couldn't think why.

Amelia pushed away her plate. 'Chips and chocolate it is then. Anything is better than that.'

Cate finished her salad and Olivier's attention returned to them.

'Mum, Isabella was showing me her tracker yesterday. Most of the girls in my class have got one now. Can I get one?'

Olivier snapped to attention. 'What nonsense! Those parents have more money than sense. There is no need for you to be tracked, Amelia, Luxembourg is the safest city in the world.'

Amelia shook her head stubbornly. 'But my German teacher, Madame Schroeder, is telling us about self-defence, so she can't think so.'

'That Madame Schroeder needs to watch it. She's overstepping her remit. The police may need to speak to her about causing unrest.'

Olivier was angry and Cate had a flash view of what he must be like in an interview room, of how scary he must be if you were on the wrong side of the desk. Had Bridget experienced this, when she was questioned today?

Cate had headed straight to the school after leaving the beauty salon, and returned Gaynor to her home. Achim had opened the door. She had asked after Bridget, who she had seen standing at the lounge window, looking out. Achim hadn't gone into any detail, simply said that the police had needed to speak with them. But why at the police station? Cate knew enough to think this was odd, and would have liked to ask Olivier. Wondering whether, if the police had no leads, they were instead focusing on the family.

166

Now Cate felt a pressing need to defend her new friend. 'I think Eva,' she quickly corrected herself, 'Madame Schroeder, simply wants to protect the girls she looks after, because of Ellie going missing. Parents are worried for their children, Olivier. It's natural.'

'Maybe so. But not all parents are the same, Cate. You must know that, with all you have seen. We must keep an open mind.'

'What are you saying, Olivier?'

There was a silence and his face was serious, but he said nothing more, as always.

She knew she was pushing Olivier, but she couldn't stop. 'I don't believe Bridget has anything to do with Ellie's disappearance.'

'Cate, you do not know this woman. By all means take her daughter to school, assist her if you must, but please do not make the mistake of thinking that you know what has happened with Ellie.'

But it was too late, Cate was unable to remain silent. 'I heard that Bridget was questioned at the police station today. Isn't the poor woman going through enough stress, without that?'

Olivier's shoulders were tense and his eyes seemed very dark. 'That is not for you to judge, Cate. It is for the police to investigate, and it does not help with hysterical teachers scaring the children. There is always danger in a city.' Then, noticing Amelia's alarmed face, he reached forward to touch her wrist. 'But Luxembourg is a very safe city. The safest in Europe. And you have me to protect you.'

Then he lifted a euro coin from his pocket,

and hid it in the linen napkin, making it reappear from behind Amelia's ear so she laughed and begged him to do it again.

Cate returned her gaze to the window and the nail bar opposite. The van had pulled away and the young man was returning to the beauty salon. She could see him better from this angle, and noticed his distinctive yellow-blonde hair and skin as pale as alabaster. His clothes, she now saw, were old-fashioned and formal, a shirt and suit trousers, too hot for the weather. *An unlikely customer at a nail bar*, she thought. And judging by Olivier's keen interest, she could see that he thought so too.

* * *

After their meal they caught the last opening hour of the Bastogne War Museum, and Cate was distracted from recent events by the tourism of remembrance. They sat inside the mini-theatre that was created to look like a forest, on seats made to replicate logs. A snowy landscape was set around them, above them was the projected image of planes, and they could see mannequins dressed as soldiers. For several minutes Cate was absorbed, but then she became aware that Olivier was not concentrating on the presentation, but was once again tapping a text message into his phone. Amelia pressed close to her mother, unsettled by the noise of gunfire around her.

'It's okay,' Cate told her daughter. 'Nothing's going to happen to you.'

★ ★ ★

The final part of the tour was a short walk outside, with a view towards the Mardasson Memorial, the monument to fallen American soldiers. The evening sun gave Cate warmth and she tried to take in the breath-taking majesty of the monument, but Cate was blind to the view, lost despite knowing exactly where she stood, and wanted nothing more than to go home. Her real home, in England.

At that moment, Olivier had taken her wrist, waited until she was looking fully at him and said, 'If you ask me again to breach confidentiality on this case, if you say any more about some danger you imagine exists in Luxembourg, then I will have to reconsider.'

He did not elaborate on what, nor did she ask, struck dumb by the cold tone of his command.

Olivier shifted his hold from her wrist to her hand, firm and controlling, but also the same hand that had been so gentle just last night, playing her body with ease so she made sounds, felt things, she had never allowed herself to before.

His threat was a moment, and it was gone. The beauty around them remained, Amelia was oblivious to what had just happened. 'It's like a fairy tale forest. Do you think there are any deer?' she asked, running off to look.

'She's so happy here, Cate,' Olivier said. 'Just relax, and you could be too.'

'I think I saw something!' Amelia ran back to the dusty path, her legs covered with dirt but

169

also kissed by the sun, her hair blonder than since they arrived. She looked so pretty, so happy. Cate hated herself for ruining it.

Olivier squeezed Cate's hand, and she felt him watching her anxiously, worried he had gone too far. 'You know, I love you, Cate,' he said.

Cate turned back to him, in shock. He had not said this before. He pulled her forward, so they were again walking side by side.

'I may be a difficult man, with strong views,' he said. 'But I think we are a good match. We just have to learn how to be with each other, and I think you are finding it hard to not be a probation officer. You are imagining worse crimes, something domestic becomes a kidnapping, to keep your brain busy. Perhaps you should start some voluntary work, would this help?'

Cate felt her anger soften and turn against herself. She too was in love, and Olivier had given both her and Amelia a chance to be happy. He was right. He was in the best place to judge if Ellie's case was domestic or something wider. She should let it go.

'What kind of voluntary work?'

'At the prison, maybe. There are many inmates who have no visitors, and who prefer to speak English. Would you like me to arrange something for you?'

Just then Amelia gasped, and the three of them watched as a deer crossed their path, just a few yards away. It stopped, gazed at them, as from behind its young offspring darted, coming level with its mother and waiting until by some secret signal she indicated that they must leave. Mother and young ran into the protection of the trees. Only then did they hear a crack in the air. Men, following. Evening hunters.

★   ★   ★

Later, back at their flat, Cate stood in the bathroom brushing her teeth. It was a moment of solitude, just her and the mirror, the sound of the brushing, the thoughts in her head. She found that away from Olivier her thoughts ran differently, in a straight line: Eva's advice on self-defence during German class, the leaflets at school and the texts on Olivier's phone. Suddenly she had the creeping suspicion that his anger towards her was because she was onto something.

Their relationship, her first chance at love since her divorce from Tim, and she was risking it all.

She spat out her toothpaste, leaned over the sink and gazed at her own reflection. She wasn't young anymore, her hair was turning more brown than red at the roots, her skin was less taut, though her eyes still gleamed brightly and she knew she was lucky. A handsome man, a life abroad, and she was jeopardising it. Better to be right and single or in love? She couldn't fix anything anyway. So long as she kept Amelia safe did it matter what else might be going on in the city?

Compromise and silence. This might be what it took to have a successful relationship, a feat her parents failed at, as she had with Tim. Olivier's parents seemed happily married, he didn't have any divorce behind him. Maybe he knew more about what was required to keep a relationship healthy. She should stop rocking the boat.

'Mum?' Amelia called out from her bedroom. 'Can you read to me?'

Cate splashed cold water on her face, gave herself one last look and then she went to read to Amelia.

Amina

'Malik say he wants to find a wife,' Jodie tells Amina that morning. They are sitting cross-legged on the thin mattress, both combing through their hair, yawning.

Amina listens to Jodie with growing anxiety. She is very pretty and Amina fears for her friend.

'Does he mean you?'

Jodie snorts, so hard she has to swallow. 'I say to him a wife would want nice house, sparkling jewels. He just wants the nasty thing! If there's no house, no garden, no ring, then there's no wife and no nasty either.'

Amina doesn't see why this is so funny, she wonders at Jodie who always seems to know so much more than her, yet she isn't worried about ridiculing Malik in this way. Omi would say that such talk was disrespectful, and Samir would say it was sacrilegious. But Amina isn't thinking either of these things, she is just worried for her friend, that her big dreams will come to nothing and she'll end up as trapped in Luxembourg as she would have been in Algeria.

She wonders if Samir has returned from Paris, if he knows she has left. If the Algerian police are still visiting Omi, all the time, demanding to know where he is. He may be dead.

Fighting back tears, Amina wants to hold Jodie, and tell her she's only a girl and not ready to be a wife yet, that they have their whole futures ahead of them. If they work and learn. But Jodie is too interested in boys as the ticket to a better future, to that house with the swimming pool she wants so badly. Amina has only met Malik a few times, but he always works with Uncle Jak, and so Jodie has seen him plenty. Amina fears for her friend, she fears for Omi too. She wishes more than anything to be free from this. All of this.

'You know, Amina. When Malik said 'wife' he looked at me like I was a delicious treat, so he could swallow me whole. He said my titties look like pieces of okra for him to chew.'

Amina reaches forward to grasp her friend's leg. 'Jodie, you mustn't let him say these things to you. He is Uncle's son, so like a brother to us. He is supposed to look after us.'

Jodie waved her hand dismissively. 'Auntie won't let him do anything bad! She was there and shooed him away, kicking his backside as he left. He's frightened of her.'

Amina felt calmer, knowing that. Auntie wasn't easy to like but Amina felt safe with her and that was more important.

'I don't think he's Uncle's son, anyway. Malik does not call him father.'

Then Amina remembered that for once she had some news to share.

'Auntie put me to work in the front of the shop, where the customers are, but with a warning: 'Nosy customers ask questions, so you no speak to them. Remember, you '*non parlez anglaise*', okay? Once they know you do it will be, you so pretty, how old you are and then why you not in school. Next thing we in trouble. Nosy pushy, should just shut up and let us paint them nails, they so rich they can't paint them on they own. Probably have maid at home cleaning up they shit while we file and polish.''

Amina mimics Auntie's voice and likes it that Jodie can't stop laughing. She could always make Pizzie laugh. Never with words like this though; she can feel herself changing, becoming braver. More Western.

When Jodie caught her breath she put her hand over Amina's knee. 'Auntie is right about that, though. We, all of us, just seem the same to those Western types. They don't see where we come from, our long history, our different stories. All they see is our brown skin. You and me, we speak Arabic differently, we follow different customs because our homes are far apart. But not to them.'

Amina didn't tell her, but all the whites she had met so far looked similar. Sounded it too, loud booming voices, fleshy legs and arms, straight long hair. No wrinkles but shiny skin where the wrinkles belonged. Auntie had told

Amina that these white women inject poison into their faces to freeze the lines, but she thought this must be a joke, as surely no-one would be so stupid. Wrinkles are pretty, Amina's mother had many and they showed she's had a good life, that she's laughed a lot, at least until a few years ago. Amina hoped to get many wrinkles, to have things to smile about. She was waiting for this to happen.

'Come now, Amina.' Jodie pulled on her red dress. 'I am ready for my breakfast.'

* * *

The day began as the others had before. Both girls had bread with jam, and the white tablet medicine that Auntie said was herbal and would help them relax, washed down with black tea. After breakfast, Jodie left with Malik and Jak and Amina opened up the salon to begin her work.

Though Amina had been told not to get into conversation with the white women while she was working, she allowed herself to look. And she was diligent, doing as she was told. Auntie had shown her how to clean the equipment with a blue solution so powerful she had to wear latex gloves that felt loose on her hands, so her fingers wiggled inside like the gloves are a plastic bag and she was reminded of their goat and how it felt to milk her. As she worked, Amina wondered if Pizzie was doing this very thing, right now. She often occupied herself with that thought, of what Omi or Piz may be doing, but sometimes she was too homesick and tried not to think of them at all. Amina used a tiny brush for the cleaning, and did a good job in making the tweezers and nail files gleam.

Amina likes work, and she finds the tasks she has to do in the salon are easy, the tools begin to shine and the muck comes away much easier than it lifted from Pizzie's clothes. She works slower than she could, not wanting her morning to end as she's happy in the shop, and wants to see and hear as much as she can before Auntie sends her back into the house, to prepare for lunch. The brush on the steel reminds her of the sound of the broom, when her mother cleaned inside their home, corner to corner, so every scrap of the floor was fit to eat a meal from.

Amina's favourite place in the salon is the nail bar. It's a colourful stall, like she saw in town when Omi took her there on market days, only in the salon, customers choose between pots of nail paint, not piles of figs and grapes in baskets, bundles of herbs and spices. The polishes are all the colours of the market, though: the green of a leaf on an olive branch, the yellow of the flowers, pink as fragile as the inside of Pizzie's mouth when she laughed, black as her hair after she washed it in the rain. With all the world to choose from, how can anyone select just one colour? After her morning shift, Amina closes the salon for lunchtime and goes through the bamboo curtain as usual, looking first for Fahran to see if he will smile for her today, but instead she hears men's voices in the kitchen, talking to Auntie, quick and hushed. As she edges closer she realises it is Uncle Jak and Malik, and she wonders what they are doing home at this time. Usually, she does not see them until the evening.

She hears Uncle say, 'It was not what we agreed.' He sounds sad, angry too. 'She will think I betrayed her.'

'And you bring this trouble here, under my roof?' Auntie's voice is shrill. 'What a stupid risk!'

'Where else should I take her? This is the safest place.'

'Safe? Ha! And we all go to prison for you, because of your guilt, your stupid promise.'

Amina freezes. Who will go to prison?

'She saved my life. I owe her this.'

Auntie's voice answers, louder and defiant now. 'She will be fine! Rich woman like her, what does she know of trouble? But this is our chance. Our boy's chance. If you go to prison, we all lose.'

Just on this last sentence her voice falters, and Amina put her fists to her mouth. Was there a way to save Fahran? A sound escapes, she is so happy, and there is silence in the kitchen.

'Is that you, Amina?' Auntie calls out.

She has no choice but to show herself. She steps forward, into the kitchen, with her head bowed.

In the kitchen, Malik is seated, turned away from Amina. He is twenty, Jodie told her, and handsome too despite the green woollen hat that he always wears. Jodie tells Amina it is the fashion, but Amina doesn't understand why any man would want to cover his dark curly hair, which would make all the girls look. Seeing

Amina in the doorway Uncle stops shouting, he looks annoyed to have been interrupted. Malik continues to gaze down at his hands, and she sees that there is a bruise around his eye. Amina has the sickening feeling that she has walked in on something she would rather not know about.

'This here's Amina, and she's a good girl. I want to keep her here with me,' Auntie says, her face is flushed and she is speaking loudly.

Uncle nods. 'As you wish.'

Amina felt happy that Auntie valued her. Omi would be proud. But part of her was curious too, to know had happened to Safiyya and Reza, and what really happened when Jodie went outside of the house to work. Jodie had described the card tricks and cup game that they played at the fair to fool the tourists, and Amina thought she would like to try to do that work, if only she was brave enough. But she was never good at playing tricks on people, and was not sure that Omi would approve of this work, so she said nothing, just, 'I am happy to help in any way, Auntie. Thank you for having me in your home.'

Auntie looked pleased with that and Uncle gave a tiny smile too. 'Go now, Amina. Go and check on Fahran.'

She was glad to leave the kitchen, but the feeling did not last. Fahran was not in his bedroom.

Instead of Fahran, another person is laying awkwardly on his bed. A girl, older than Amina by the length of her, but not by very much. Amina studies her, wondering what this has to do with the conversation she just overheard. The girl lays on her stomach so Amina cannot see her face but her arms are exposed and it is enough to see that this girl has not travelled like she did, her skin is not bruised with dirt and her blonde hair isn't greasy from days without care. Her clothes are crumpled but they are modern, jeans and a yellow t-shirt. A t-shirt as yellow as the weeds that Jodie described, the ones with the beautiful name. Dandelions.

Amina steps closer, daring to enter the bedroom, gingerly checking the girl is actually breathing. The part of her face that Amina can see is pale and though she seems to be asleep her eye is half open, but blank and empty. A string of dribble hangs from her open mouth.

Amina is not stupid. She has seen men in the village like this, when they have had too much drink. But this is only a young girl, only sixteen or seventeen, so why has she been drinking? And where are her family?

Amina hears feet behind her and turns to see Uncle, coming quickly up the stairs, head down so he hasn't yet noticed her. Behind him is Malik. He notices Amina, and makes a quick sideways motion with his head, warning her away.

She feels it, deep inside, just like when Samir first suddenly left home. Something bad is happening, it has already started. Amina does not wait but walks swiftly to Auntie's room, where she finds Fahran. She tries to tell herself that she is safe and that whatever is happening to the blonde girl in the other room is none of her concern.

Later, when Jodie arrives home from the fair, Amina listens patiently to her account. Today she was allowed to work on a stand, a darts game, and she had to count the numbers each customer got and then give them a prize. 'These prizes, they so cheap,' she told Amina, 'that even if a customer gets the highest number possible we still make lots of money. It's a good trick, yes?'

Amina wasn't so sure, it sounded mean to her. But she didn't want to prolong conversation about the fair, she wanted to tell Jodie about the girl in the downstairs bedroom.

'You were with Uncle all day, then?'

'Not all day, no. He left me to work with another group around lunchtime. Why?'

'I think he has done something bad. I think he has taken a girl who did not choose *harraga*. Do you think it is the dandelion girl from the fair?' Amina asked, after she had described the yellow t-shirt.

Jodie thinks. 'It sounds like her.' They are both whispering now. 'She was with Malik, they disappeared together. Maybe she's his girl-friend?'

Amina thinks about this, and wonders if that was why Uncle seems so involved. Had Malik got his girlfriend drunk, and Uncle is looking after her until she is well enough to go home? Had she lashed out and given Malik his black eye?

The two girls whisper long into the night,

180

wondering who the girl was and why she had arrived. If she is not Malik's girlfriend, then maybe she has travelled to Luxembourg just like them. But Amina thinks she is American, or at least rich, so she cannot need to travel to work because her family already has money. The two girls cannot understand why she is here, even Jodie cannot make sense of it.

★ ★ ★

The following morning, Amina makes her way downstairs as usual, thinking through the jobs she must do to ready the salon for the first customers. But as she passes Fahran's bedroom door she pauses. She puts her hand on the handle and dares herself to open it.

The girl is gone, but Amina can hear movement in the bathroom along the corridor, a scuffle. Perhaps Auntie has taken the girl to get cleaned up.

In the room, everything was as if she had never been, except for a dark patch on the mattress, which may be urine or vomit. Amina is embarrassed for the girl, but does not blame her because she seemed drunk, and certainly not happy. This confirms it, she thinks; the girl was indeed Malik's girlfriend. She sobered up, and now Auntie is helping her to freshen.

But she cannot see how this has anything to do with Fahran, or what Uncle said about betraying someone. She decides that she is best not to know, something she learned eight months ago when Samir travelled to Paris. 'I am

181

just the first drop,' he told her, 'but soon there will be a flood.'

Sometimes it is best not to understand what such things mean.

Day 5

Ellie

It was the drink he gave her in the back of the van. As soon as Ellie swallowed it, having snatched the plastic bottle of Rosport from Malik, so desperate was her thirst, she began to feel unsteady. This fizzy water hardly had time to hit her stomach before her vision seemed to close in, as if curtains were being drawn across her eyes, and she had enough time to see Malik, his look of fear, and she lunged at him, her fist landing in his eye socket.

Then she remembered nothing.

Whatever the drug was, it was the same as the one that had been slipped into her beer on the night of the fair, because she woke knowing nothing with a pounding head. They had moved her, she was no longer in the van or back in the caravan, but in a house now. A child's bedroom, not like her own bedroom at home.

This child, a boy judging by the crumpled shorts and checked shirt on the chair, slept on a mattress with faded but clean blue sheets, and the few toys he had looked old, his brown bear had lost an eye and the battery operated robot was armless. Ellie doubted that the batteries in it worked, though she didn't care to try. That was the most overwhelming thing about waking up after drinking the water: the heaviness she felt, the way she could actually remain lying in her own urine and fall back into a coma-like sleep.

What roused her was her own resolve, but also voices. Men's voices in the corridor, she recognised as Malik and his father, the bulldog, but a woman's voice too. In her disorientated state she thought it was Bridget, and she tried to call out.

'Mum?'

Her voice was broken and weak, no-one could hear her. She crawled to the door to listen.

The door was ajar, and when Ellie managed to peel open her eyes she saw a young girl, a skinny thing. She thought at first it was the girl from the fair, the beautiful one in the red dress, but then she saw that this girl was younger. Ellie didn't know if she would help her or if she too had been taken. Fear bloomed on the girl's face, she darted away from the door and rushed along the corridor, as if afraid of the voices. Though the skinny girl was gone, Ellie tried to call her back, 'Please . . . ' She lifted her arm to reach out, but now the bulldog was in the room and he was almost upon her, saying something in an angry tone.

'Shut up! You must be quiet while you are a guest in my house.'

Ellie heard light feet going up stairs, pitter-pattering, and then movement above her. If she could get to the girl, ask her to take a message to her mum . . .

Or maybe the girl knew a way out.

The woman arrived, and then Malik, closing the door to the room so Ellie was locked in with her three guards. She gazed up at Malik, who had tricked her.

'Please. I want to go home,' she said, more bravely than she felt. Pushing herself to sit up, trying to focus her eyes. 'If you let me go now, nothing bad will happen to you.'

Malik's eyes looked wide with anxiety and Ellie could see the bruise where she had punched him. He looked like he might want to set her free, but he was cowed by the other adults beside him. The woman took charge, taking Ellie by the top of the arm and pushing her back to the bed. Sitting beside her, as if she was an over anxious nurse and not her prison guard.

'You rest here, you aren't feeling so good,' the woman said, almost kindly, as if she were doing Ellie a favour. But even so, it was true that Ellie's head was spinning. She was thirsty, so parched her throat felt like sandpaper, and though her stomach was empty her bowels were twisting and full.

'I need the loo,' Ellie said, and felt the truth of it. 'If you don't let me go now I'll shit myself.' She was beyond caring what they thought of her.

The woman, who still had a firm grip on Ellie, propelled into action, yanking her up and into the hallway, then along to the toilet.

It was almost too late, but Ellie was glad to sit and open herself, glad to empty out all the badness, the blackness and urgency that must have been caused by drugs and stress and fear.

She sat with her head in her hands, her body straining, and moaned.

But once she was done the woman returned her to the boy's room. She left her there, alone. The door was locked.

Still desperately thirsty though glad that the drug seemed to be wearing off, Ellie looked about her for a way to be free, a weapon, a place to escape. The window was small, she could see it was painted shut but she still tried to prise it open. She could break it and scream but they would hear her before she could even make the risk worthwhile.

There was nothing to be done, not now anyway. Ellie closed her eyes and tried to order her thoughts through the haze.

When she was in the caravan she had tried to run, tried to scream, and that had failed. Her next move would have to be cleverer.

Bridget

Across the city, Bridget was back at home, standing once again by the window. There was an unmarked police car parked along the road. In it sat a man in a suit, watching the house, recording everything. Bridget shivered, though it was stuffy in the lounge. She rubbed her arms, knowing that the detective was watching her.

Achim was upstairs, showering. She hadn't showered, still hadn't changed her clothes.

Dear Ellie,

This was not what we planned. Not that I planned any of it, how could I have ever known that our trip to Schueberfouer would go so badly wrong? If only you hadn't run off, if only you'd been a good girl. If Jak hadn't found me.

It was a moment, that was all. I was angry, I was drunk. Was it such a bad thing?

'Take her,' I said. 'Give her a scare.'

Jak and I, we have both seen real danger. We know what the world is, how people can hurt each other. I wanted you to know this.

You are not in real danger. I trust Jak. I saved his life, he told me so. I saved the baby and in doing so I saved Jak from his fate. Not everyone wants to be a martyr.

And so he will not harm my child. Because he is in my debt.

It was only supposed to be for a short time.

So why aren't you home?

Cate

Cate woke feeling unrefreshed, as though sleep had passed her by. She had been disturbed in the night by Olivier's groans, by him moving around in the kitchen, making a hot water bottle.

She entered the bathroom, just as Olivier was swallowing a tablet, the blister pack still in his hand. He quickly replaced the packet inside his drawer, turning his back to her as he did, though his face was plainly exposed in the bathroom mirror, flushed red either from shame or anger.

187

She touched his shoulder, moved to his side, so they could both see each other in the mirror.

'What's wrong, Olivier? Aren't you feeling well?'

'You've already worked out the answer to that, Cate. You've been snooping, I can tell from where my packets have been placed.'

She didn't deny it. 'You have five different types of drugs in that drawer for stomach ulcers, so I'm guessing you aren't on top of it?'

'It hurts.' He winced as he spoke, touched his stomach. 'Like a twist, right down inside.'

'What does the doctor say?'

Olivier pulled away from her. 'No time to find out, not just yet.'

'Because you're busy with Ellie Scheen's case?'

He walked from the bathroom to the bedroom and sat down heavily on the end of the bed, rubbing his face. His armour was gone; Cate saw him as a defeated and poorly man. Whom she loved, now more than ever.

He nodded his head, exhausted. She sat below him, on the wooden floor, her chin resting on his knee, arms either side of his body.

'How long have you been unwell, Olivier?'

His eyes showed the quick calculation that was happening in his brain. 'Since before we met in Ipswich. I've tried to ignore it, but it seems that isn't working.'

'More than a year?' Her voice rose with concern. 'And you haven't sought help.'

'You have seen from my medicines that I have been many times to the doctors, both in Ipswich and back here. But they want me to go to hospital for a scan, and I simply can't spare a whole morning. I will, though. Once Ellie is found.'

Cate's breath caught on that promise. 'So you will find her?'

Again he rubbed his face. 'I hope so.' His eyes were shadowed with fatigue, weary with worry.

'You really think Bridget would hurt Ellie? That she knows where she is?'

Olivier's voice was cold and steady. 'I can't divulge what we know, Cate. You just have to trust that I am doing my job, and that I know more about this case than you do.'

'Oh, Olivier . . . ' He looked so defenceless, Cate knew that if ever she was going to tell him, about her meetings with Eva, about visiting Bridget and her certainty of the woman's innocence, about the beauty salon named on his phone that she had visited, then it was now. Time to be honest, to lay her cards on the table and forget her own investigations, but to support her man. Instead she sat taller, so their faces were close, and sealed his mouth with a kiss, which deepened, and would have become something more had his mobile phone not begun to ring. He took the call, his breathing quickening as he listened to what the caller told him.

'Cate, I have to go.' His face was flushed, his eyes were now alight.

'What's happened? Is it Ellie?'

'I can't say. But it's an interesting development.'

Just minutes later, Olivier left the house.

Trying not to think about what was happening down at the police station, Cate made herself coffee, and poured cereal into Amelia's bowl as her daughter rubbed her eyes and took her seat.

Cate yawned, but when the telephone rang she snapped alert. Bypassing Amelia, now munching cornflakes and gazing out at Merl park, Cate picked up the phone.

'Hello?'

There was a pause. 'I'm sorry to bother you so early, Madame. I am Achim Scheen. I think you are friends with my wife?'

Cate's chest tightened and she glanced to where Amelia sat, tensing herself for bad news. 'Yes, that's right. Has something happened?'

'My wife is at the police station.'

Cate's heart sank, thinking of Olivier leaving the house, the pleased look on his face. 'They took her in for questioning again?'

'No,' Achim said. Even in this one word, Cate could detect his barely concealed rage, whether at her assumption or the police she could not tell. 'She has gone in of her own volition.'

Cate hadn't expected to hear this. She grappled with what to say next. 'Is there anything I can do?'

Now he spoke quickly, efficiently. 'Yes, please. If you pick Gaynor up from our house, and take her to school, that would be helpful. And maybe if you could also collect her at the end of the day. I know this is a lot to ask, but my wife suggested you would want to help.'

190

Cate wanted to ask what Bridget was saying to the police, but even if Achim knew, he was unlikely to tell her.

'Of course I want to help. I'll be there in ten minutes.'

'Gaynor will be waiting.'

'Well, I'll see you then.'

'Ah, Gaynor will be waiting alone. I am at the police station already, I have been here since six, to support my wife.'

Cate was surprised that a man with one daughter missing would leave another in the house alone for two hours, but said nothing. Who was she to judge what was acceptable in such a strange and awful situation?

★   ★   ★

Amelia was forced to leave half her cereal, and Cate yanked a brush through her hair briskly, telling her they must go. 'Gaynor's waiting.'

She drove as quickly as she dared to collect Gaynor, who was perched nervously on the doorstep, the door to her home open behind her, when they pulled up. The poor child looked relieved to see them and ran down the driveway, forgetting to close the door. As she sat beside Amelia, Cate walked up the path to the house to close the front door, hesitating just a moment to look within. She could only see the kitchen, directly ahead as it was, and the counter was splashed with milk. She then saw there was a broken mug on the floor, and pieces of it lay across the tiles.

As she turned, pulling the front door closed behind her, Cate saw a white van parked further up the road. The driver seemed to be looking her way, but maybe she just imagined this. Then she saw the picture on the side of the van of a swimming pool.

Again, she had that feeling of seeing it before. She shook her head, and concentrated on the task of getting the girls to school.

★   ★   ★

In the back seat, Amelia tried chatting to her friend, but Gaynor was not responding. She was chewing her nail and staring at her lap. Cate got into the driver's seat and turned to face her, saying gently, 'Gaynor, did you just break something, love? In the kitchen?'

Gaynor's eyes narrowed, then looked teary. 'Dad did it.'

'When the police came?' asked Cate.

Gaynor frowned, she shook her head as if confused. 'No police came. I heard Dad throw a coffee cup when my mum said she was going to the police station, on her own. But then he went with her and left me.' She began to sniff, and looked down at her knees.

Cate thought it wiser not to ask any questions, and Gaynor wouldn't know anyway what it was that Bridget wanted to say to the police. She turned to face the front and put the car into drive. Amelia continued to try and engage with her friend, telling her about the deer they had seen yesterday at Bastogne, but Gaynor was distracted and could barely lift her head to listen.

Cate wondered why Bridget could not speak with the police in the comfort of her own home. To be at the police station at six in the morning, this was not how a victim was treated, not in England anyway. It was how the police treated a suspect.

Cate shivered as it dawned on her that this was indeed what the police thought. It matched Olivier's response to the case, his determination that this was not the work of a kidnapping. Cate realised that she now knew why Olivier had been so excited when he was called in to work that morning: Bridget was the main suspect, and she had come into the station to make a statement. He thought she was about to confess.

Cate had known women who had harmed their own children, and she knew they didn't have horns, but she had seen Bridget straight after Ellie had gone missing at the fair, she had been at her home just two days later. Cate had seen a mother in distress, a mother who loved her girl.

If Olivier arrested Bridget, if she was charged with Ellie's disappearance, than that would mean that his search for her would be confined to places that Bridget may have hidden her body; their home, nearby wooded areas, the family's regular haunts. The police's energy and focus would be directed inwards, not out to the borders with France, Belgium and Germany, or onwards to the known routes for human trafficking.

Whatever had happened to Ellie wouldn't be

solved by arresting Bridget, Cate knew it in her bones. How was it that Olivier couldn't see that too?

★ ★ ★

Cate stopped at the lay-by, promising Amelia and Gaynor that she'd be waiting for them when school finished, and then she drove home. She padded around the flat, then opened the sliding door and stepped onto the balcony, followed by General who was panting heavily and seemed glad of the breeze. He lay down and Cate gave him a stroke. 'What's going on, General?' she asked. He lifted his head and gave a whine. 'Do you know?'

Cate could see the Belair church spire, pointing up, and across to the green field where she knew the fox family lived, the same foxes who had been disturbed by the storm a few nights ago. But today the sun was shining, everything looked perfect, and it gave her the sensation of being in the movie of her own life, where everything looked colourful, but none of it was real. The sky above that spire wasn't helping, it was so blue, fading with the white of the clouds that scudded like boats over its canvas, one huge and shaped like a whale. Sun rays edged the corner of the balcony where she stood, warming her shoulders, then hid behind a cloud leaving her shivering in the shade. If only it was a totally clear sky with no clouds, then she would be warm enough. But the return of the warmth kept her hoping. Olivier was like the clouds. No, that wasn't right, he was like the sun, sometimes warming her, sometimes leaving her cold. But when the warmth came, Cate felt it as so total, so complete, she couldn't imagine it getting cold again. Like feeling full after a meal, and not even being able to imagine hunger. But still, eventually it comes.

She knew that her best option was to steal enough good memories to sustain her through the chill.

How much of her emotion was connected to Liz, to the trial back in England, she couldn't begin to fathom. All she knew was that it was time to phone home, to find out if Liz had been proved to be a liar or if their father would soon be starting a prison term.

She picked up her phone and pressed the contact for her sister, checking her watch and realising that court may still be in session. She was just about to hang up when a voice answered. 'Cate?'

'Hi.' Just hearing Liz's voice made a lump come to her throat, so she was unable to speak for a moment. 'How are things going?'

'We're on a coffee break. The judge is good. She lets us take lots of pauses.'

Cate could hear the tiredness in her sister's voice. She could also hear, in the background, other voices. Talking in the corridor or waiting room, wherever Liz was now standing.

Cate was aware that Liz hadn't actually answered her question, so she tried again. 'So, what's happened?'

Liz breathed out. Cate heard a car's horn and

realised she must be outside the court house, taking a five-minute smoke break. 'What do you expect, Cate? My childhood is being cracked open like a ribcage and everything that happened is being poked about, bloody and sick though it is. I feel raped, all over again, and I haven't even stepped foot in the court yet, I still have the witness box to come.'

She breathed heavily into the earpiece and Cate could see her, forehead against the cold brick of the court house, eyes closed. Cate closed her own eyes and placed an arm around herself, wishing she was there to comfort her sister.

'How's Mum?'

'Drunk.'

A single word, a damning one. If their mother was drunk in the witness stand, as Liz's only witness, her credibility would suffer.

'God, I'm so sorry, Liz.'

Her breath was sharp, cutting through the line. 'Then come home! Come and stand in the witness box and say I'm not a liar. If you don't he'll get away with it, Cate. Just like he always did.'

'I . . . I can't . . . Amelia needs me and . . . '

'I get it,' Liz said, quickly. 'Your daughter needs you, your new boyfriend needs you. I understand.'

And then she hung up.

Amina

Auntie is trusting me more, and best of all she is trusting me with Fahran. Because the dandelion girl is in his room he has been sleeping with her and Uncle Jak, in the big bedroom along the hallway where they have the TV. I have to collect him from their room and bring him down for breakfast. Auntie is so busy, getting herself ready each morning and opening the salon, and I am so quick at getting myself dressed, that it is good sense for me to look after the boy.

He takes many minutes to get dressed, and I understand now that his slowness is part of the cancer. He has to wear the clothes he wore yesterday as the door to his bedroom is locked so I can't get him anything, even though there are clean shorts and a shirt on the chair by his bed. He is a good boy, though, he holds his arms up so I can pull on his t-shirt, and he puts a hand on my shoulder as he wobbles into his pants and shorts, doing the zip up himself and frowning with the effort. His fingers will not do what his brain wants, so he fumbles with buttons and zips, but I am very patient and let him take his time. I think this is better than me doing it for him, as that way he would never learn. I can feel his slight frame, how unsteady he is. Even though his tumour was removed, something is still not right, and he is shaky on his feet. It makes me want to hold him tight, to steady him. It makes me want to help.

'Fahran, would you like some breakfast?'

He nods, shy but also happy at the prospect of food. I take his little hand in mine and we go down to the kitchen, slowly because he is shaky on the steps and I don't want him to slip.

As we walk past his bedroom, with the closed

door, I do not pause. It is best he does not know about the girl.

In the kitchen I don't ask him what he wants, as I know that all children like sweet things and also milk, so I get him a glass and put some jam on bread. Pizzie would have enjoyed this meal, and Fahran likes the jam so much that it gets smeared all around his lips which makes me laugh.

'Do you want some more?'

It is then that I realise his muteness is not simply shyness. He is struggling to speak, he has a stammer and the words come out in a gust of exertion. 'No thanks.'

I take a piece of kitchen paper, lick it so it's softer for his cheek, and wipe the jam from his chin, careful not to graze his bandaged eye with my hand. The bandage is looking dirty, but I would never dare to try and change it. That is Auntie's job, though by the look of it, she forgot yesterday, or was too busy.

'You like jam, young man. It will make you have a fat tummy, like your father!' I place my hand on his tummy and tickle him until he laughs, properly losing his shyness for the first time, and my heart sings for Pizzie and home and for this little boy.

'Fahran, from now on, you may call me sister.'

*　★　★*

I don't want to leave Fahran, but there is work to do, and I am just settling him on Auntie's bed, in front of a cartoon, when she comes to fetch me.

198

The first customer is already parked outside, waiting for the shop to be opened. She will look after Fahran now, it is usual that she changes his bandage as he watches the cartoons on the screen. I will not see him, or her, until later when we close for an hour over the lunch period and often he is sleeping then, and has to be woken to have his lunch.

★ ★ ★

As I turn the lock in the front door I see that Auntie is right. There is a car parked directly opposite the salon and, sitting in what should be the driver's seat, is a black dog. Next to it, behind the steering wheel, is a woman and it is then that I know that this is a British car, and I see that she is the English woman from Tuesday. Back to have her nails done again, so soon.

I turn the sign to signify we're open to the outside world, and see the woman leave her car, tugging her dog along with her. I am not so fond of dogs, as the ones we had in the village were often diseased and besides, they would steal food, so I was never encouraged to make friends with them. This dog seems friendly, though.

The English woman greets me, and gestures to the empty seat, the same one she sat in last time. I know Auntie told me not to speak English, but this woman seems to want to speak with me.

'*Oui*, Madame. I shall be with you. Would you like *café*, Madame?'

She says she would, and I fetch some from the

filter machine that I switched on earlier. By lunchtime the pot of coffee will be gone, and I will make a second. These Europeans like their coffee.

I give the English woman her drink and take her hand to study her nails. They are still perfect. I am not sure what she can want me to do, and I ask if she wants me to change the colour. She seems uninterested in picking a different colour, so I start to give her a simple hand and arm massage, like Auntie taught me.

'Madame, your nails do not need any work. Maybe another treatment?'

She stares at me, as if it had not occurred to her that we do other things. It is true that there are not many other options.

'We have a tanning booth. You could look like you have turned golden in the sun.'

She laughs at this. I think she says something like, 'Well, that would be a first!' which I understand to be a yes.

As I prepare the tanning treatment she tries to speak to me, but I keep my head low, simply nodding at her words. I prepare the lightest shade, a creamy colour just a shade darker than her own. She has pale skin and hair the colour trees turn between summer and winter, just before the leaves fall, when they are most full of fire. It was the best time in Tizi Ouzou, when the heat was not so strong, but we had not yet entered winter, which could be so cold and so long that it felt like summer would never arrive. When Samir first left to live in the mountains, I was worried, as each winter he would get ill with asthma and who would care for him if he had an attack in the hills? But he would not hear of such concerns, he told Omi that he may have a short life but it would be the noble path of jihad. He stopped noticing the leaves or flowers, then, and thought only of the path to God. He said that he hoped to arrive soon, in Allah's house, and then he left. And it seemed he was not in the hills anyway, but in Paris.

The English woman sips her drink, and seems more interested in looking around than in making a start with the tanning. But it is just she and I in the room, there is no real hurry, so I relax. She smiles back, though she looks tired.

Finally, she steps towards the tanning room, which is just a curtained off side area with white paper on the floor and a pop-up plastic tent. She stands within it, and I wait until she is wearing only her underwear, and then I begin to spray her.

'This will not take long, Madame. Ten minutes.'

She is shaking slightly, there is some tension running through her body that I can see as surely as a charge of electricity. I work carefully but also quickly as Auntie told me to, and soon her skin is turning a shade darker.

Often customers watch my every move, inspecting my work as I spray, but she looks behind me, towards the back of the salon where the bamboo curtain is pulled back and the door is ajar, though as far as I can tell there is not much to see beyond. Just the flowers on the hallway table, Auntie's scarves tacked to the wall.

It is a simple place.

As we are not talking we can hear the television coming from the room above, the cartoons, and she lifts her head to listen.

'My brother is watching his favourite show,' I say, though I know Auntie wouldn't approve of me divulging this, or of calling Fahran my brother. But the woman looks like she needs some conversation.

She smiles. 'That's nice. How old is he?'

I don't know how old Fahran is, so I guess. 'Five.'

I think that I've made a mistake, a five-year-old should be in school, wouldn't they?

'He's off school because he's not well.'

'Oh,' she says. 'I'm sorry to hear that. What's wrong with him?'

She seems to shiver again, so I reassure her. 'Nothing catching, Madame. And now, we are finished.'

'Thank you.'

Two minutes later she is dressed once again, she takes her purse to pay me, turning to pat her dog, patiently waiting.

'How old are you, Tina?'

She has remembered my new name from last time, and this alarms me, but pleases me too. It is a strange feeling, to want a thing that you know you shouldn't have.

'Sixteen, thank you Madame.'

She looks closer at me, and I see she doesn't believe this. She is about to ask me something else, and Auntie will get mad if she hears. If she sees me talking too much English she might send me back into the house. I try not to think about the girl in Fahran's bedroom, curled on the mattress, sad and lonely. I'd rather be down here, with the bright polishes and scarves, the smell of remover and glue.

The woman's hands still shake as I take her credit card, though I don't know why they should.

'Are you okay, Madame?'

She looks at me. I give her my best smile, glad that Auntie is not here. She wouldn't like that I asked a customer if she was okay.

'I'm thinking about a girl. She's older than you, though not by very much. She's missing and it makes me feel very sad. She was last seen at the fair. Perhaps you've heard about it?'

'No, Madame,' I say in my best voice. 'Where has she gone?'

'No-one knows. But everyone is very worried about her.'

I put my head down, so she can't see my face. The dandelion girl upstairs is the same one she is talking about, she must be.

'So, what is wrong with your little brother?'

The abrupt change of subject surprises me, and I realise that this woman has been listening to every word I say, making connections, even though she appeared distracted.

'He is poorly, Madame. With cancer.'

Her face falls and her free hand rises to touch her throat. 'Oh, but that's awful. Where?'

'In the head, Madame. The doctors, they took the tumour away, but he is still not as a boy his age should be. He is too tired to play.' We are silent, both listening to the cartoon jingles above our head.

'Is he having chemotherapy? Radiotherapy?'

I shake my head. I think I might cry.

'There are some excellent treatments available now,' she says. 'There was a case in England, recently. A boy travelled to Prague for a special procedure, maybe you heard about it? It's been in the news.'

'No, Madame. I do not know about this boy.'

'Well, they were saying on the news that he's now cured. Proton therapy, that's it. I think it's easier to get here in Europe. What has the doctor said about your brother?'

'I am not sure, Madame. But I will ask about this new treatment.' I repeat the words in my head. I have not heard them before.

I worry about Fahran. I worry about Jodie too. Last night she hardly spoke when she came back to our room, and when she sat on the bucket to pee she took a long time, wincing like it hurt her. I don't know if there is a new job she is doing or if she is still fooling people at the fair, but she talks about it less than she did and I have the feeling that although she is going out into the city and seeing Luxembourg, while I have not left the house, I may have been the lucky one.

Something has changed with Jodie, and now the other girl is here too, both these things make me frightened.

These thoughts run through me as I finish my work. I have forgotten the English woman is still watching me.

Before she leaves she slides a piece of paper

into the palm of my hand so that I understand it is just for me. I see it is a twenty euro note. 'Thank you, Madame.'

I slip the note into my sleeve before Auntie can see. Because this is for me, a tip for my work, and I will send it home to my mother.

★   ★   ★

Once the salon is closed for lunch and I have cleaned all of the surfaces, I mop the floor. Auntie will be in the kitchen, starting to heat up the soup we will all have for our lunch. I slide the note from my sleeve to study. I haven't had any money of my own, I don't know when I will get paid. But this money is mine, given to me by the kind English woman. Then I see that she has written on the note, or someone has. Six numbers. A phone number.

I don't have a phone, but there is one in the salon. I've used it, to call clients who have left messages, or to take calls and book appointments. My language skills have got much better since being here. But to use the phone now, when the salon is closed, is risky.

Still, I call the number, watching the door for Auntie who may appear at any moment.

'Hello?'

It is the same woman's voice, I recognise it. It is enough, to know that she has given me her phone number. She is offering me her help, if I should need it.

I replace the phone quietly and leave the salon, the note safely hidden in my sleeve. It makes me feel safer, to have some money of my own in this world that I hardly understand. To have the phone number of a woman who looks kind.

I go back into the house, eager to go upstairs to see Fahran. I pass his bedroom but the door is still closed, and I imagine the dandelion girl. It makes my heart beat fast with fear and not knowing, and I touch the money for luck.

And then I hear the girl calling: *Please*, she says, and I know she is desperately calling out to me. *Please help me*. I feel unable to walk away, even though my brain tells me this is the sensible thing to do.

I reach for the door handle, and to my surprise I find that the room is unlocked.

Inside, Auntie is bent over the girl and I see then that she is crying for help because Auntie is roughly trying to pull her up. I move closer, coming up behind Auntie, and can see that the girl is frightened.

'Auntie, let me help her.'

I offer the girl my hand, which she doesn't take, so I kneel down beside the bed. I can smell her, the sweet urine and something stronger and foul too. The smell of fear. Her body is curled away, she is twisting from Auntie, and seems unaware that someone is now trying to help her. When I touch her on the shoulder she flinches.

'She thinks she is the queen of England, acting like this?' Auntie says, and I don't reply because I think the reason is something different to this. Jodie and me, we are also away from our homes and families, but the dandelion girl looks broken by it. I think her story is not our story.

'I can look after her, Auntie. Why not go and sit with Fahran? I can help the girl.'

Auntie is so mad at the girl, so relieved to have an escape offered to her, that she agrees.

'Make her clean, Amina. It is not decent, the way she is carrying on. But don't talk to her. I am trusting you to be a good girl. You understand?'

And then she leaves.

★　★　★

I begin by fetching a wet flannel from the bathroom, and I give it to the girl, urging her to get up and sit on the wooden stool chair, which is painted blue and Fahran-sized, but at least means I can set about stripping the mattress so I can scrub it.

'We could make a life, you know. This isn't such a bad place to be.'

She doesn't seem to understand what I am saying, and first I think that maybe I am wrong and she doesn't speak English, but then she says, 'What is your name?'

I hesitate, and then decide there can be no harm in telling her. 'Amina.'

'Where is this place, Amina?'

I am surprised she doesn't know. 'It's a beauty salon. At the front, anyway. This is where we live.'

'No,' she says, shaking her head, looking the wet sheet and soiled mattress. 'It's a prison.' She leans back in the stool, so her back is supported by the wall, holding her stomach as if it pains her.

'Is something wrong? Can I get you some . . .' I falter, wondering if Auntie has given her some medicine to calm her, the white tablets that Jodie and I take. I think she must have, because the girl is acting strange and her eyes aren't in focus. I wonder what else I can give her that may help. 'Would you like some mint water, to soothe your stomach?'

The girl looks bitter and shakes her head.

I finish with the bed. I'd like to open the window, but it has also been painted shut, so I settle for opening the door wider, though not so wide that Auntie may hear.

'We must make the best of this situation.'

'For how long?' she asks. 'When will they let me go home?'

This dandelion girl, she is frightened and it makes me think I should be too. Because I don't know when I will go home any more than I can answer her question.

Ellie

After the girl has gone, Ellie finds herself being tugged back into sleep.

She has been falling in and out of sleep for hours, or is it days? How many days since she last saw Gaynor stepping up to pay at the booth of the ferris wheel, as Ellie walked away, quickly, towards Malik? Because she wanted to have fun and she was angry. She was stupid and selfish, and now she is here, wherever here is. She can't grasp her thoughts, has lost precious days.

When she wakes again it feels like morning, though she has no idea which one, or how long has passed since the girl cleaned her. How many days and nights have passed since she tried to run from the caravan? Using the fence around the fair as her guide, searching for a spot to climb, before being trapped and returned to the van? Sometimes when she wakes she is back in the moment when she was first found by Gaynor, watching Malik cling on to the bar with all his strength. The moment when their mother slapped her for running off, called her a bitch.

That she is being drugged is obvious, but her alternative is to not eat or drink and she has received precious little of either, her stomach feels hollow and the hunger gnaws away in the pit of her stomach, but it is the thirst that is the worst thing. Rasping, dry-throated, she would do anything for water.

Malik came on the first day with food and drink and wouldn't look at her or even speak. It gave her some satisfaction to see the bruise around his eye, dark and rosy. She realises he isn't the one with control of the situation, that he is under the orders of the bulldog, but he's still a part of it and she hates him as purely and strongly as her drugged brain will allow. Mostly she feels sleepy and sick. She hates herself, even though there are other people hating her and she should be strong. She needs to get out of here. She gathers her thoughts:

I'm in a house. It's near a road, I can hear the

cars, though I haven't the strength to go to the window and see if I recognise where I am. I could be anywhere, I could still be in Luxembourg.

There are other people in the house, people above me too because I've heard feet and voices, though I can't make out words. There is the girl, who cleaned me. And the older woman, who was rough.

No-one has told me why I'm here, or what they want from me. But I've seen films, I've read the papers. If the bulldog was a psychopath I'd be dead by now, this is something more business-like, less personal. The suffering will be longer.

The door must be locked, or maybe not because she is too weak to escape anyway.

She can hear footsteps, light ones. Ellie hopes it's the girl, the skinny one with black hair and wide eyes. If she could only make her come again, speak to her for longer this time. The girl would know why Ellie was here, she may help her.

'Please?' she calls out. She can only call weakly, but she fears it is too soft to be heard, too loud and it would attract others. She can't risk that.

The feet stop, she can hear breathing. The girl has heard her, she's outside the door.

Ellie dare not speak again, but she lifts her head, desperately waiting and aware that the door handle is moving down. The door slowly opens, catching on the rough wood of the flooring, a narrow gap. And then a face, small and pretty, brown skin and dark hair. It is her.

'Please,' Ellie says, almost a mime the words are so weak. 'Please will you help me?'

Bridget

Bridget was once again standing at the window, but this time her eyes were dull. There were no passing cars, it was too early for that, so the road outside was of no interest. Hope had left her.

It had been so clear to her, what she must do. In the early dawn she had watched the sun rise and realised that, whatever happened to her, she must tell the police the truth. Jak had betrayed her, he had Ellie, but she had no idea where.

She had been leaving the house, the car keys already clutched in her hand, when Achim called from the top of the stairs, 'Bridget? Where are you going? It's half past five.'

He would find out, of course, what she had done but she couldn't be the one to deliver the news, to see his disbelief turn to rage. This would be the end of their marriage, but all that mattered was Ellie.

She returned to the kitchen, Achim following close behind, and made herself a small coffee. She needed a kick of caffeine. 'I want to talk to the police. I want to tell them about something I saw at the fair. Something I remember.'

'What?'

'A man.' She would say no more. She wouldn't tell Achim that the man was Jak, a soldier she had known from before. All this she could tell the police, but not her husband.

'And you've just remembered this now? What about him, why do you think it's connected?'

She backed against the kitchen worktop, so it dug into her spine, and sipped her bitter and hot drink, avoiding Achim's eyes. 'It may be nothing.'

'But you think you should go to the police station now?' he asked. 'You have a strong feeling about this. Why?'

Again, she didn't explain but felt his eyes boring into her. 'I can't wait, that's all.'

He ran a hand through his greasy hair. His face was haggard. He may have been in bed but he hadn't slept.

Bridget finished her drink and put the empty cup on the counter top, then turned her back on her husband and began to walk away. She felt a rush of movement behind her as he grabbed the hem of her jacket.

'I'm coming too,' he said. 'If you think it's this important, then I want to hear it.'

'No, Achim.' She shrugged herself free of his grasp, and was turning, moving away, when he reached to grab her a second time, his arm reaching across the kitchen counter knocking the coffee cup to the floor. They both watched as the pieces shattered, the coffee dregs splattered black flecks on the white floor tiles, brown watery drips down the cupboard doors.

'Now look,' he said, bitterly, 'at the mess you've caused.'

* * *

212

At the police station in Hamm the woman on reception looked like she had been dozing at her desk. Her eyes widened, she hadn't expected visitors.

'We need to speak to Detective Olivier Massard,' said Achim, taking charge of the situation. 'I assume you know who we are?'

She looked from Achim to Bridget, to the pink rabbit she was clutching. 'I'll message him now.'

★　★　★

They waited. The sun began to rise and people arrived, early morning shift workers desensitised or too polite to stare at the couple waiting, hands clasped, for the detective to arrive. Bridget took Achim's hand and raised it to her face, rubbing the back of his hand against her cheek then opening it and kissing his palm. She knew it would be the last time he would let her.

★　★　★

Detective Massard arrived in a rush, his face was freshly shaved and his hair still wet from a shower, his eyes bore bruises of fatigue. Bridget was glad to see this. It was evidence that he cared about Ellie. He would find her daughter, she only had to tell him in which direction to look.

She wouldn't speak, not until she was in a private room with the detective. Not until Achim was out of hearing. He led her to an interview room. Finally, before her courage failed, she

213

turned and said, 'I need to tell you something.'

The detective's face was blank, he was wearing a mask of professionalism, but his lip curled slightly as if anticipating delicious news. 'Go on.'

He wasn't going to smooth-talk her.

'At Schueberfouer, I saw a man. He was hanging around the ferris wheel. I thought I recognised him.'

'Recognised him from where?'

Bridget breathed deeply, willing herself over the edge. For Ellie. 'From when I was working in Algeria. He was with the Brotherhood.'

The detective leaned forward. 'Go on.'

She took a deep breath. *Say it*, she told herself. *Tell him what you did.* 'A fundamentalist, he killed many people. He killed many but he saved one.'

'Oh?' The detective was skilled at appearing noncommittal, but she could feel his attention, as though he too were on a precipice waiting to jump.

The room was too hot, stuffy. She could smell his aftershave, the minty scent of his shampoo. She hadn't eaten and her stomach rumbled, though the thought of food sickened her.

'I just want my girl back,' she said.

'Then tell us where to look.' He was leaning forward, scrutinising her.

Bridget felt herself about to be swallowed whole.

They were eye to eye, unblinking. It was clear now, there was no pretence.

'I don't know,' said Bridget, truthfully. 'I don't know where he took her. It was only supposed to

214

be for a few hours.'

'What is it exactly that you are telling me, Madame Scheen?'

'I asked him to take my daughter. I wanted to teach her a lesson. It was supposed to be for a very short time.'

Stillness. Detective Massard rubbed his dry lips together, though she saw the gleam of his tongue, the dilation of his pupils, and hated him for it. He thought he had won, that this was success.

'Detective, please understand, Jak is an Algerian soldier, he knows how to hide. I will tell you what I know, but we must find my daughter.' She could feel it, loosening inside like water, the sudden fear that she had given away all of her power. That she had made a mistake. 'We must work together,' she begged. 'I'll tell you all I know, everything I did. But we have to find Ellie.'

Detective Massard's expression became one of barely controlled pleasure. His mouth twitched, and she saw he was longing to smile but trying his best to control it.

'Bridget Scheen, I am arresting you for the murder of Ellie Scheen . . . '

Bridget's attention began to swim in and out of focus. *Murder? Ellie? My girl is dead?*

' . . . You do not have to say anything. But it may harm your defence if you do not mention when questioned something you may later rely on in court. Anything you do say may be given in evidence . . . '

Bridget felt numb. Her breath caught in her chest. Her girl was gone.

Day 6

Ellie

Since waking I have laid on the mattress and stared at the stain on the ceiling, watching the golden line of sunlight move across the cracked surface, and I know I have to try something new today. If I don't, this despair will grip me so tight that I won't care anymore and the fight will leave me. If that happens I'm as good as dead.

So when the door finally opens I make myself sit up, though my back aches with stiffness. It's the older lady, and she's so surprised to see me upright that she almost drops the cup, which is plastic and has a blue rabbit painted on it. It's a child's cup.

I'm thirsty, but I won't take it from her. 'Is it drugged?'

'What rubbish you talk, girl. It's milk.' But her face is red with shame, and I won't look away.

'I don't want you to drug me anymore. I won't try to escape, I'll be good. But I can't take the nausea and the headaches. Please. I promise I won't try and run.'

She leaves, taking the drink with her.

★ ★ ★

When the door opens again it's the girl, the skinny one who has smiled before, and instead of the rabbit cup she is holding a glass, with a Bofferding logo on the side. She also has a plate of food.

'Auntie says here is your breakfast. She wishes you *bon appetit*.'

I take the glass from her and sip. The milk tastes good, normal, and I know I have had a small victory. Today, at least, the old woman will not drug me. I bite into the bread and it tastes almost fresh. The crumbs trigger my hunger and I eat quickly, hardly tasting the butter or jam that have already been spread for me. Finishing it and longing for more.

The young girl is gaping at me.

'You feel better today?' she asks. 'You are up.'

She can't know what it has taken for me to rise from the filthy mattress.

'Amina?' I think I remember her name right. 'Tell me who the woman is. And the man.'

'She is Auntie, and he is Jak, her husband. They have a young son. This is his room.'

I look around, at what I've seen again and again during the hours and days of my captivity. 'So where is the boy?'

'He's downstairs, breaking his fast. He sleeps with Auntie as you are here.' And I can see that Amina is upset, talking about the boy. She looks like she may cry. 'He is missing an eye. The doctors had no choice. They did what they could, but it is no good. He had the cancer, and when it was cut from his brain it took his eye. He is still very poorly.'

217

I think about my mum then, I can't help it. The work she did in Heidelberg. 'What about chemotherapy? What about radiotherapy? Proton treatment.'

She gasps at this last suggestion, staring at me with wonder.

'You know about this?'

I lick my fingers, hoping for crumbs. My stomach growls. 'I heard it on the news. Can't the boy have that?'

I don't know why I'm having this conversation, why I should care about the child of my captors. But Amina is hanging on my every word.

'We don't have papers so we are not legal. It is not so easy,' she says, as if repeating a script.

And then I understand something. 'Would money make it easy?'

Amina looks worried, she reaches for my cup, eager to leave, but I don't want her to go yet.

'Is that why I'm here, Amina? Are my parents to pay a ransom?'

Amina's eyes narrow, and I can see that she is close to tears again. 'You are our guest,' she says.

I laugh, short and harsh but I can't help myself. 'Your guest! Are you fucking kidding me?'

Then we both jump as the old woman yells, from just outside the door, 'Amina! Come out now. And lock the door behind you.'

But before she leaves I take hold of Amina's hands in both of mine. I whisper, 'Please, Amina. My parents have money and they will pay. Oh God, please help me to get out of here.'

And even though I have to watch her go, and I hear the key turn in the lock, she leaves something behind that has a whiff of hope; if a ransom has been requested then everything will be alright. Because my parents will pay. Of course they will.

Bridget

In her locked cell, Bridget is staring at the grey, scarred wall and wishing it was a window. She is listening to the loud male voices beyond the cell door, the police officers and others talking and moving, and wondering how it came to this. Why she is not home, with her daughters in school, and the world as it should be.

The world, she says to herself, to Ellie whom she is always talking to now in her head, *is never as we think it should be.*

Dear Ellie. Oh, dear Ellie, how has it taken all of this for me to understand that though the world is not as we would wish, we cannot change it? How is it I didn't know that, after all I saw in Algeria?

Did I tell you about the teachers? Of course not, I told you nothing. I am forty years old and it is more of a mystery now than back then, when I was younger and closer to the rebel soldiers. I thought I understood their passion, their conviction, even if their methods were barbarous and cruel.

The teachers were good women. Local

219

women, educated in France, but returned to Tizi Ouzou to teach at the village school. They were devout too, but not as devout as the men in the mountains wanted. And it was a small thing, a simple thing, just words. A girl, fifteen, had spoken to one of them because she had a crush on a boy in the class. She was worried that it was a sin, she was full of self-loathing. But the teachers, who were kind and also worldly, said it was no sin. That love and desire were natural, and that the young girl would experience it many times in her life. They had laughed, maybe. No-one told me this, but I like to think of them that way. Smiling and laughing with the girl, and each other, as they remembered their own first loves.

It was the girl's brother who informed the soldiers. He had been going to the mosque, where the radicals recruited, and he told about the teachers and their advice that love was normal, that desire was allowed.

That night, as they lay sleeping, the teachers had their throats slit, as though they were calves being strung up for meat. At least I hope they were sleeping. After, the school no longer had teachers and no-one spoke of love anymore.

So you see, Ellie, I have known the worst of the world. And I was so scared for you, before, because you hadn't. That you argued for more freedom, that you slept with boys and pierced your nose and forgot that the world is not always on your side.

But I am. Everything I did, was for your own good.

Even if my methods now look barbarous and cruel.

Bridget called through the cell door for the police officer to come. She had made a decision. 'I want a solicitor,' she said. 'And I want to make an official complaint against Detective Massard. He has lied about me. He has falsified statements and I won't stand for it. I am a British national and I demand my rights.'

Cate

The morning was almost spent and Cate was padding barefooted around the flat, collecting stray glasses, sticky with last night's bourbon, and balled up socks. General was panting by the window, his tongue dripping onto the wooden floor, happily fatigued after their morning walk and now enjoying the sunshine. His ears lifted when he heard the key in the lock, he pushed his muzzle into the air, sniffed once, and let out a single warning bark.

'What, boy?' Cate asked, but then she too heard the door to the flat opening. 'Is that you, Olivier?'

'Well, I hope no-one else is coming to see my girlfriend at noon with his own key!'

And there he was, grinning like a fool, quickly taking her in his arms and lifting her slightly as he kissed her lips. She felt his happiness, his lightness, a stark contrast to the weight that he'd been carrying around for days now.

'Is it Ellie? You've found her, haven't you?'

Olivier placed Cate back on solid ground, his mouth momentarily pulled down, but his humour undiminished. 'Not yet, but we will. Bridget has told us everything. It's over, Cate.'

'What do you mean it's over? What did she say?'

'You know I can't tell you. But enough for her to be detained in a cell. Enough for me to take a few hours to relax.'

He stretched his arms high and let out a long sigh of contentment, almost touching the ceiling with the tips of his fingers, then he winced, his face crumpled in pain.

'What's wrong? Is it your stomach ulcer?'

He nodded. 'Just a twinge, *ce n'est rien*. Now, I would like to take you to lunch, Cate! We have not had a moment when our time has not been heavy with my work, and I want this to change. And then later, after Amelia has finished school, we will drive to Nancy, to see my parents.' He placed his hands on her shoulders. 'I have neglected you, I know. And my family. I'm sorry. I want us to be happy.'

His kiss was warm and it felt like a gift, a fresh start. Cate closed her eyes, trying to enjoy the moment.

'Instead of going to lunch, Olivier, I want you to make good on your promise. You said you'd see a doctor about your ulcer. Do that first and then what we do for the rest of the day is up to you.'

★ ★ ★

Hospitals, same the world over, Cate guessed. That antiseptic smell, the grey linoleum squeaking underfoot. The waiting.

Olivier sat beside her, his laptop balanced on his knees, typing quickly but humming as he did. Bridget's arrest had lightened him, and Cate wished she could share some of this pleasure. Olivier felt he'd solved the case, but she didn't see how this could be true when Ellie was still not found. He said that it was now just a matter of time, that the uniformed officers were pursuing Bridget's leads. In what way Bridget was responsible, he had not explained.

Cate remembered how Bridget had looked, standing at the window clutching the pink rabbit, desperately waiting. Whatever she had done, whatever she had confessed to, Bridget was devastated. There was no denying that.

In the waiting room, dull voices rumbled, no-one spoke at full volume as if sickness was less dangerous when talked about in whispers. An elderly woman shuffled along, chaperoned by her middle-aged daughter, a ball of cotton wool taped into the crook of her arm. Several patients made muted requests to the administrator, officious and dark-suited behind a high desk, for the whereabouts of the toilet, a mother tried to distract her child with a magazine aimed at octogenarians. Finally, the nurse called Olivier's name.

'Monsieur Massard?'

Cate made to stand too, but the brisk nurse held up a hand, and said in perfect English, 'First the examination, then I call you to discuss the results in a few minutes, okay?'

How the nurse had ascertained at a glance that Cate was a foreigner she had no idea, but she took her seat meekly, catching the gaze of the child, whose interest had wandered from the magazine. She smiled at him, then looked towards the closed door behind which Olivier had just disappeared.

She had made him do this, and his agreement felt like a validation of her role, but being left outside the examination room negated her. Would she have been allowed in if they were married, or was it just because the space was too small? She assumed they would be doing an ultrasound and her only experience of this had been when she was pregnant with Amelia and Tim had always been there, both of them gazing at the screen in a rare moment of unified delight, a moment when they had been a happy family. Thinking of this, Cate felt herself tense, the years that had passed since her divorce were not quite the emotional barrier she would have liked.

Relationships had always been a changeable thing for her, an unfixed point. The only family that had been constant was her mother, and that relationship was as unpredictable as the British weather. Just thinking of her mum made Cate feel edgy, and she began to run a thumb over her nail, itching to peel a cuticle but finding nothing on the glossy gelled surface. Her mother was possessive, demanding. Often drunk. But at least she hadn't left. Unlike Tim. Unlike Liz, and their father.

She thought again of the trial back home.

Totally unsurprised that her mother had arrived at court drunk. Unsurprised but sad.

Her hand had found her phone, deep in her pocket. *Fuck it*, she thought. And texted a quick message:

Hi Mum. I spoke with Liz yesterday. Sorry things aren't going well in court. And I'm really sorry I'm not there with you.

This time, she actually meant it, and she pressed SEND.

She waited, staring at the phone, but there was no response. Her mum could be in court, her phone switched off in her bag. Or she could be ignoring her.

The door to the examination room opened and Cate sat taller, alert, but it wasn't Olivier. The nurse did not see Cate, or opted not to, and walked quickly the other way with efficient little steps. The door opened again and this time Olivier appeared, striding towards her.

'Well, that's over,' he said. 'And I have done as you ask.'

She had thought the nurse was going to invite her into the room, to share whatever they had found, but clearly that was not going to happen.

'What did they say?' she asked, anxiously. He had been groaning in the night, and since last weekend the pain had registered on his face, a pallor that showed his anxiety. Something was wrong, that was certain.

'*Rien.*' He began searching for his keys, then his phone. 'Just that I should rest.' Olivier chortled at the amusing idea. 'Okay, *on y va.*' He began to walk out of the hospital, and Cate followed, though not satisfied.

'Maybe we should stay at home tonight, then,' Cate suggested, rather fraudulently. 'Your parents would understand, you just need to explain that you're not feeling great, and things are busy with your work.'

She knew it wasn't entirely true that she was thinking of Olivier. Meetings with his parents stirred her anxiety, she hadn't seen them enough times to have overcome this yet.

'Nonsense, Cate! I feel better than I have in a long time and my parents already know we are coming. They will have a meal waiting. And, for me, this is a moment to enjoy. For you as well.'

★　★　★

It was an hour and a half to Nancy and Cate drove, in theory so Olivier could relax, but in reality so he could take the calls that continued to come in.

'She's asked for a solicitor,' he said, smiling, as he ended one call. 'Maybe a full confession will come quicker than I hoped.'

He remained upbeat through the journey, though whatever his colleagues were telling him, it wasn't the big news he was now hoping for: Ellie was still not found. He ended each call and looked out of the window. At one point he said, 'We'll find her,' though more to himself rather than Cate, who kept driving, staring at the road ahead. Wondering how he could be so sure.

She was thinking of Liz, poor Liz, going through a trial in which though she was not the accused, she may as well be. *I should be there. I'm a coward.*

Amelia slouched in the back seat, with General beside her, distracted, at least for a while, playing Minecraft on Cate's iPad. Cate had tried to understand the game, but as far as she could tell, Amelia was building a farm that consisted of square sheep and lots of green blocks. Still, it kept her quiet.

As they drove beyond Luxembourg the landscape opened out and Cate noted that the large sky could almost rival Suffolk's bucolic plains.

'Look, Amelia. Cows!'

Amelia glanced up, but soon returned her attention to the computerised animals on the screen.

★ ★ ★

Driving into the French city of Nancy, Cate could appreciate the old grandeur of the houses and Art Nouveau buildings, the intricate details of stained windows and stonework, but there was a feeling of neglect to the place too. The city belonged to a golden age, and often the stonework was chipped, the coloured glass in the doors was cracked, the heavy curtains at the windows were faded. This was not true of Olivier's parents' home, which was perfect with its square lawn, its grey stone brickwork, and its heavy wooden door with shapes of sensual but symmetrical curves.

As if they had been waiting directly behind it,

the door opened as the car drove over the white gravel, revealing two perfectly presented people, unmistakably French, who to Cate's regret, were then able to watch her park clumsily in the narrow space beside their new bronze Citroën. She breathed in, as if to make her own car smaller, and prayed she wouldn't scratch the perfect paintwork.

★ ★ ★

Josephine Massard greeted Cate with three dry kisses on alternate cheeks, during which Cate endured a sharp blast of heady perfume. Like the house, Josephine was aging well. She had the air of a woman who would think nothing of spending a hundred euros on a lipstick but would object to leaving a tip in a restaurant if service was poor. Josephine wore black pleated trousers, a fitted black silk blouse, and a single strand of pearls. Her hair, also black, was cut into a sharp bob that Cate envied for its sleekness. She put a hand to her own auburn locks, and wished she'd thought to use straighteners before they set off, tugging at her blouse so it sat flatter against her stomach, though the crinkled fabric was meant for comfort rather than elegance. Thank God she had thought to put on heels, a pair of patent designer stilettos that Olivier had bought for her. They were a nice gift, though Cate couldn't help thinking of them as a comment on the rest of her wardrobe.

'You look very well, my dear. Very fine shoes.

And have you done something different with your hair?' asked Josephine, scrutinising her. Cate felt quietly pleased that her skin was slightly tanned, that her nails were freshly polished. But Josephine could not guess why Cate had had these treatments, she would simply think that Cate had a new interest in grooming, not that she had been trying to find a missing teenager. All along it had been futile anyway. Bridget was responsible, so Olivier said. *It's over.*

Olivier's father, Roland, was less severe than his wife and his rosy cheeks and pot belly made Cate like him even more. His grey hair was unruly and Cate had before seen Josephine running her fingers through it, trying to smooth it down. She liked that it sprang back up regardless. A man who enjoyed his wine, who enjoyed the ladies too from the lingering way he appraised Cate. 'Welcome, welcome,' he said, turning to give Amelia a kiss on each cheek, something Josephine had not done, and delivering General a vigorous rub on the chest. 'A handsome dog, aren't you, General?' The dog wagged his tail, his mouth wide and almost smiling, as if to say that he was indeed very handsome.

They all entered the house, and Cate felt as she had the other two times they'd visited, that it wasn't so much a home, more a museum, that she should hold her breath and be careful not to touch. To be a child growing up here, to be Olivier at just ten or eleven, must have been stifling. Every object was so perfectly positioned, she couldn't imagine a boy's muddy football boots ever being allowed. Maybe that was why he could be intolerant of Amelia's mess, going into a frenzy of tidying that Cate realised he must have inherited from his mother.

Amelia had finally switched off the iPad and her green eyes widened as she gazed around, the house was still a novelty to her. And there was plenty to be captivated by: the gramophone player and thick black records, each the size of a side plate; the green-brown marble figurine of a woman dancing; the framed butterflies that were dotted around the room. 'Are they real, Mum?' she whispered, as if they might wake and fly away.

'Well, they were.' Real corpses, now. But for Amelia it added to the mystery of the strange house.

'Aperitif,' announced Josephine briskly, tapping her fingers to her palm. 'But quickly, if we are to make evening Mass. And when we return from church the food will be ready.'

Cate stared at Olivier, he had not told her that they would be going to church. He avoided her look, and busied himself with filling small delicate glasses with Pastis, handing one first to his mother, then to Cate. She downed it, swallowing aniseed with her words. If it made Olivier happy, that was good enough.

Thirty minutes later they were walking to the Catholic church which was just around the corner, the evening sun cast an antique bronze hue over the boulevard and Josephine linked arms with her son, leading the way in an efficient tapping of high heels on paved streets. The bells rang as they walked, guiding them closer. Roland ambled behind his wife, chatting genially with Amelia, asking how she was liking her new school, what she thought of Luxembourg, and Cate was gratified that Amelia didn't mention Ellie, but spoke instead about how much harder the homework was and how glad she was to finally have a dog. 'I wasn't allowed a pet in England,' she told him, 'but General was already here so Mum couldn't say anything.'

Soon they arrived at the church. It was small but beautiful, and inside were rich paintings in flaked gold and reds. The air was heavily scented and along with the darkness it felt strangely comforting to Cate, the effigy of Jesus, the bowed heads of the congregation. She could smell perfume and incense, hear the slow breathing of contented souls finding solace in God. As if he had been waiting on their arrival, the priest promptly began his service. His voice was incomprehensible to Cate, yet so familiar, deep and steady, the tone of someone who knew he was right, who deigned to share a little of what he knew with other, lesser beings.

In the stiff wooden pew, Amelia pressed against her, awed by the vaulted church and also by the strangeness of the language of the devout, the slow serenity of the people who smiled hello. Cate took her hand and together they stood, sat, prayed, all following Josephine's cue. Afterwards, Cate tugged at the hem of Amelia's dress so she remained seated as the congregation moved forward into neat lines, waiting to receive the

231

bread and the wine. Olivier stood at the altar with his mother, one hand lightly on her elbow as if going simply to support her, but he too opened his mouth for the sacrifice.

'What are they doing, Mum?' asked Amelia.

'Drinking Jesus' blood,' she couldn't help but tell her, smiling when Amelia's eyes went wide.

'But not really!'

'They think so,' Cate said, silencing herself as Josephine returned to the pew, her mouth closed on a wafer and her face as serene as a sleeping baby. Cate saw, as she had seen before, how religion could do this and for a moment envied the faithful.

Service over, the groups broke away and approached the Massard clan, kissing Josephine and Roland, as well as Olivier. Some also glanced at Cate and Amelia. She initially gave a tight smile, but when no-one introduced them she focused instead on straightening her blouse and tidying Amelia's ruffled hair.

$$\star \quad \star \quad \star$$

Back at the house, the evening meal was quickly served, and Cate realised that Josephine had help, seeing for the first time the elderly woman in a black dress who bustled to and fro with dishes of steaming vegetables. In the dark, oak-panelled dining room, Roland sliced the meat, which to Cate's dismay was venison, and Olivier poured the wine, which was red and heavy, like a bowl of winter fruits left to rot in the sun. Cate drank hers too quickly.

'And how is work?' Roland asked Olivier.

'Fine, no problems at all.' Olivier winked at Cate.

If Olivier's parents knew that he was dealing with a kidnapping, they did not say. The meal was eaten politely, the wine bottle soon emptied. Amelia talked about the dance class she wanted to join, she fed a slice of meat to General, who had positioned himself under the table at her feet, and was only lightly chastised.

Cate was just thinking that they had got through the evening unscathed when Olivier reached for her hand, surprising her with his urgency.

'Everything is wonderful, now Cate and Amelia are part of my life. And I would like to make this more official, if she will agree.'

He lifted her hand to his lips and kissed her fingers, making Amelia groan with embarrassment. Cate's heart lurched.

From the pocket of his jacket, Olivier produced a small velvet box. Even before she opened it her heart thumped uncomfortably. *Oh, no, not like this* . . .

Inside the box was a beautiful antique solitaire ring. When Cate looked up to the head of the table, Josephine was dabbing her eyes.

'It was my mother's ring,' she said. 'She wore it until the day she died, and then we put it away until this moment. When her only grandson . . . ' Josephine would not allow herself to cry, but she stopped speaking, sipping at the last of her wine, blinking quickly at Olivier. Cate realised then that this had all been planned. Olivier had choreographed the proposal with his mother's blessing.

Amelia clapped her hands excitedly, grabbed the box to better see the ring and slid it on her own finger. Olivier and Roland laughed, but Josephine looked less than happy. 'That is not a toy, Amelia.'

Cate gently took the ring from her daughter, gave her a smile, and slid it onto her wedding finger. It fit perfectly.

It was only later that she realised she had never actually said yes.

★　★　★

There was champagne, two bottles that were already sweating in coolers when they arrived, and Josephine insisted they stay the night. She was enjoying having this impromptu party, if indeed it was, and a small buffet of finger food was produced as the evening drew in.

Roland placed his hand on Cate's shoulder, in a quiet moment when mother and son were talking in French within the curtained seclusion of the window seat. 'Welcome to the family,' he said, and Cate could have kissed the old man on his rumpled cheek for his kindness. But Amelia was yawning, her eyes were narrow with fatigue and she needed to go to bed. Taking her upstairs, Cate bade her future mother-in-law and husband a goodnight.

Cate was not allowed to sleep with Olivier under his parent's roof, good Catholics that they were, and so Amelia and Cate went straight to their own bedroom at the front of the house, with a generous bay window shrouded in dusky pink curtains. The room was beautiful, heavily flowered drapes hung around a four-poster bed and in the bathroom, thick towels had been placed alongside toiletries. Amelia was delighted, a princess in a castle.

The four-poster bed had a wooden canopy and creaked painfully when Amelia got in, having tossed her dress on the floor and wearing just her underwear. 'We should have packed pyjamas,' she said, but Cate pointed out this stay hadn't been planned. Someone, however, had thought to equip the en-suite bathroom with new toothbrushes, a tube of paste and wrapped soap.

Cate felt uneasy amid the fine fabrics, the antique furniture. Olivier's family home was laden with wealth and tradition and she knew instinctively that any discussion they might have on religion or politics would end badly. She would have to keep her mouth shut.

'So. How do you feel about me marrying Olivier?' Cate asked Amelia, snuggling next to her. She knew her daughter was tired, but she needed to ask this one question.

Amelia's eyes glittered. 'Can I be bridesmaid? I know what to do, it would be my second time. But I'll need a different dress.'

'Of course,' said Cate, not wanting to be reminded of Tim's wedding to Sally, 'but more importantly, Amelia, do you want Olivier to be your stepdad?'

Amelia paused, as if considering the matter,

though her broad smile said she was still dreaming of dresses and shoes. 'Will you have a baby? I'd like another sister. Not a brother though.'

Cate smiled and pulled Amelia close. She and Olivier had never talked about having children. There seemed to be so much that they hadn't discussed, so much about him she didn't know, but did that really matter? What mattered was that it worked, or seemed to. It would work better, she thought, now she could stop thinking about Ellie's case, meddling in something that wasn't her concern.

Amelia's breathing levelled out and she drifted to sleep. Cate realised that she should return downstairs to her fiancé and his family, that they were probably expecting she would, but instead she continued to lie on the bed and stare at the canopied ceiling. She lifted her left hand and examined her ring, which sparkled like a star in the night sky and felt heavy on her finger. Then she closed her eyes, realising that she was slightly drunk and very sleepy, and she allowed herself to drift.

Amina

I am alone in the beauty salon, it is not yet time to unlock the front door, and I touch the screen of the laptop and see that beyond the page for emails, which Auntie checks often during the day, there is a section that says 'search'.

It is not a fancy computer, which is good

because I am not very clever at such things, but I know that there is information that can be gained through it, that just by asking one question, a million answers will pop up.

Why does Auntie not do this for Fahran? Surely something can be done to make him better. But I am afraid, and have to tell myself to be brave. I know it is forbidden, that my job is tanning and painting and waxing, not trying to cure the boy. I may answer the phone, if I am polite and careful, but Auntie is the one who deals with any enquiries that come from the website. Twice now she has taken photos of the nail work I have done, to post onto our page, and it is through this that we get our email appointments. But there is more to know, more things to search, and the computer has answers.

Hoping I am spelling correctly, I type the words the British woman said, the cure she mentioned, the words Ellie said too. It must be so easy, so common, yet to me it is a strange and frightening: *proton therapy*.

The answers pop up, the hospitals where it happens. There is a picture, too, of the little boy treated in Prague, the one the British woman told me about. He is smiling, in the arms of his father, and the headline simply says *Cured* and below is a quote, *It justifies everything we went through*. Inside I am sinking, thinking that this boy is lucky. This boy is not Fahran. We can't afford to buy medicine and we have no papers. Knowing that a cure is possible just makes it worse.

I hear a scuffling behind me and know that it

is Fahran. He has taken to me now, and will often seek me out in the house, though he still says very little. Something stops him knowing the words, just like something makes him trip up every now and again. I think it is the cancer.

I spin quickly, as if surprised, my hands up to my mouth in a clownish show of shock that makes him laugh so hard he stumbles and I have to grab him before he falls to the floor. And touching him like that, it feels so like hugging Pizzie, that I pull him closer and he hugs me back, still laughing with delight.

When I look up, Auntie is standing in the doorway, watching me with her boy. I see she has been crying again, the sadness never completely leaves her, and it is hard to bear when the solution has just been at my fingertips, is even now on the screen behind me.

'Fahran doesn't have to be sick,' I tell her, impulsively, believing it so strongly I can no longer keep the thought inside.

Auntie's mouth becomes smaller and she blinks, so I know she is holding the tears inside. Fahran wriggles in my arms and pulls away from me, running to his mother. He may not speak, but he knows that she is upset and that we are talking about him.

When she is kneeling on the floor, her boy in her arms, I tell her, 'There is a boy here who had the cancer, but now he has been cured. Look, Auntie.'

When she looks at the photo on the computer screen I see her aging by ten years in seconds. She looks so tired that I think of Omi, and for a moment I hate myself for causing her such sadness.

'You think I haven't thought of this treatment, Amina? You think I don't know that there are clever people, close by, who could help us? But we are illegal here. You know this.'

'Yes,' I agree, she is only saying what I had been thinking, not ten minutes ago. 'But there must be other ways to get help.'

Auntie frowns.

'The girl upstairs,' I whisper. 'Her family. She said they would pay to have her home.'

I realise I am holding my breath, because my plan is so perfect. I want to help Fahran, and I want to help the girl. If Auntie agrees to this, then both will end up happy.

But Auntie is angry, her voice is a ragged flag of war. 'Never speak of this again,' she says, gripping my hand like a vice. 'She is our guest. Be careful, Amina. To think we can change our path is a way to madness. Madness and jail.'

Day 7

Ellie

Amina brings my lunch and this time I am ready. I have pulled my fingers through my hair, and though it is greasy at least there are no tangles. I am sitting up, my back to the cold radiator. I make myself smile at her before she has time to put the bowl on the floor and leave, as she has done before.

In the caravan I was angry, and that did me no good. The last few days I felt sick, but the drugs have cleared my system and what is left is a sharp need to escape. By any means.

'Will you sit with me while I eat? Please?'

She looks towards the door, and I know she's frightened to stay.

'Please? It's so lonely, being here all day.'

She stops, turns. She isn't a monster like the bulldog or the old woman. She doesn't want to be part of this, I can see that. I greedily take a spoonful of soup. 'Mmm, this is nice. Did your mum cook it?'

She looks at me suspiciously. 'My mother is not here . . . '

I lean forward, desperate to hear what she has to say. But her sentence tails off and she is once again looking out into the hallway. If I don't persuade her right now to stay with me, I'll have lost my chance.

I cough, as if a piece of bread is caught in my throat, and then my coughing is so violent that it actually happens, my mouth is a funnel but no air comes. I clutch my throat.

Amina moves swiftly, she crouches beside me and bangs my back, hard and frequent, more slaps than it takes to clear my throat until I say, 'Okay, I'm good. Thanks.'

She's sweating, beads of moisture dot her hairline.

I daren't eat any more, and am so glad she's close that I don't move from where I'm sitting. Grateful for the kind human interaction.

'Amina, what's going to happen to me?'

'You're going to be alright,' she says, in a low whisper. 'Nobody is going to harm you.'

I don't believe her, but I see that she wants this to be true.

'Am I being ransomed? Have you asked for money from my mum and dad?'

She bites her lip. 'No money will be exchanged. It is not to be that way.'

This makes me frightened.

I remember now, I've heard my mother, talking to the television, when journalists or human rights workers are taken hostage in the Middle East. 'Only an idiot would give in to a tactic like that.' She says that to pay a ransom would only encourage more kidnappings. But for her own daughter, surely such opinions would change.

'Has my mum refused to pay?' I ask, terrified, suddenly convinced that this is what has happened, why I am still here.

'No, truly,' Amina says quickly. 'You are our guest.'

'I don't think so.' My mother believes that principles are everything, would rather suffer and do the right thing than take an alternative route. And whatever she believes is right, is always right. I learned that years ago. I may not agree with my dad a lot of the time, but he's usually working so it doesn't bother me too much. Thinking about Mum and her strong beliefs is much harder. I feel guilty about the last few months, for shouting at her, for staying out with Joe just to spite her. For not taking Gaynor on the ferris wheel.

'I haven't been getting on with my mum lately. I was planning on leaving, going back to England to live with my grandmother. She found out.'

And I want to cry then, for the part of me that was so sick of her, so sick of Luxembourg that I wanted to leave. She was so mad when Grandma told her that I'd asked if I could move to England, because I wanted to study sixth form in Durham. We argued so badly that I went to Joe's, and stayed the night. I was frightened of her, but all I want now is to hug her tight and tell her I love her. Because my mum may be controlling, not an easy person to live with, but I always knew she could make things right. And right now I need, more than ever, for her to do just that.

Bridget

In another part of Luxembourg, Bridget sits on the bed frame fixed to the wall of the police cell. She sits primly, neatly, waiting. The solicitor is on her way and so is Achim. She knows now, what she has to say. She was a fool to trust the police, to think that the truth would help her to find Ellie. She cannot do that from inside a prison.

Whatever she has to say, whatever it takes, Bridget has made up her mind. She will be free.

Dear Ellie,

You should be home by now. You should never have left.

The police have questioned me, my darling, but I made a grave error. I told the detective what I have not yet told you. You deserved to hear it first. The man who took you, I know him.

I imagine you hearing me say this, the shock you must feel, the anger. So I wait a moment, let this sink in, before I continue. Because continue I must, there is no going back now.

He was a man who hid in the mountains, a radical. We were warned about such men, as early as my induction training in Brussels, when Algeria's bloody history was explained, we were told that for those men, killing was a way to serve God, their own deaths a way to become a martyr. I didn't know much about religious fanaticism. My only encounter with religion was RE classes. I regretted not paying attention when

I received my posting, though, trying to dredge up what I remembered about the Muslim faith.

Algeria was in a state of emergency and all volunteers sent to Tizi Ouzou were under no illusions: this was a nasty place. The Islamic Salvation Front and other off-shoot groups were killing civilians, journalists and children. The fury in the country, the bloodlust, was uncontainable. There seemed to be no end to it, and we would be called to villages where whole families had been attacked, trying to find one person who might still be breathing. It was a desperate time, a desperate place, and I have never felt closer to death nor so very much alive.

You will not have heard of this, Ellie, and I wish I'd told you about it sooner. There was a massacre. Actually, there were many, but this one especially, shocked the world. In a village not twenty miles away, fifty-three people lived and on one terrible day, the year you were born, fifty-two of them were killed, their throats slit as their souls fled.

Only one villager lived.

I think you may be guessing that the man who survived was the man who is your kidnapper, but that is not the case. The soul that lived is still a young man, and was just a baby then. And the person that saved him is your kidnapper. The person that saved him is me. I was the nurse to whom the boy was brought, wrapped in the uniform of the man who had been ordered to leave no-one alive.

One more death, that was all it amounted to,

what is one baby when fifty-two have died? But the soldier brought me that baby, he begged me to save it. The baby wasn't unwell, just hungry. A baby would die without a family, we had no way to care for the child longer-term, and in a war-torn country there is no such thing as adoption or care homes. As I cared for the baby, I wondered why the soldier had saved him. A baby is defenceless, it can't protect itself, and you were already inside me. I had already decided on the abortion though, that my fate was to work and help others. I thought then that all the soldier had done was prolong the agony, as the baby would surely die anyway.

But the following day the soldier returned. He was dressed differently and his gun was gone. He had a backpack and had cut his beard shorter. He took the child and promised me he would raise him as his son. He called him Malik.

And that was the moment, Ellie, that snapshot of a moment, when I chose to be a mother.

Our fate was changed by Jak. And he is changing it once again.

Jak owes me his son's life; he said that moment saved his own too. I thought I would never see him again, but there he was at Schueberfouer, and I asked him to help me as I had once helped him. I asked him to take you, for one day. To show you a different life, to shock you into goodness. To teach you a valuable lesson.

I thought I was being a good mother, doing a wise thing.

But it has all gone so terribly wrong.

Sleep did not last long enough and Cate woke before the day had really begun. Beside her, Amelia was lost in the dark alleyways of dreamland, her mouth open and her eyes blinking under thin blue lids. Cate turned slowly so she wasn't disturbed, though the wooden bedstead creaked. Through the gap in the pink damask curtains the sun cast a flame and birds were chattering noisily, their day already old although it was not yet six thirty. Suddenly longing to see Olivier, Cate could not stop herself from quietly padding along the hallway to his room. Josephine and Roland wouldn't be awake for an hour or so and she wanted to see her fiancé, she wanted to hold him. Had they even kissed since his proposal? She didn't think so. She didn't knock, not wanting to make any noise that would disturb his parents, opening the door quietly as she entered.

The bedroom was a young boy's paradise, air fix planes hung on string from the ceiling, and a pair of child's skis was balanced against the wall along with ski poles. The bed was another antique, with a high wooden base and decked with a patchwork quilt in red, white and blue checks, which Cate imagined was made by hand, but not by any that still lived. On the dresser was a wooden yacht, neatly held in its wooden stand, and next to it a neat pile of faded comics. It was a child's room from another era, with no posters of pop bands, no topless women, a child who had not grown up. It was a time capsule.

Olivier was not in the room, but the blue-and-white wool rug was awash with papers and his laptop was balanced on a square footstool covered in the same checked fabric as the quilt. The screen was alive with light, and it was open at his email page.

Cate should have made herself stop, realising that Olivier must be downstairs. She should have left, backed away, returned to her own room, or gone downstairs to the kitchen to join him, but her feet continued on and she crouched down on the rug, feeling every bit the young child for whom this room was designed. Every piece of paper spread there, every printed email, related to the disappearance of Ellie Scheen. Cate could no longer stop herself, even if she wanted to. Her fingers grabbed the reports and file pictures, she pulled at the laptop and scrolled through emails, gorging herself on new information.

Some of the police papers were in French, so she missed the meaning of most words, but the Scheen statements were in English and Cate began to read.

Bridget had told Cate that she had watched Gaynor and Ellie board at the ferris wheel, that she had remained below as the wheel turned, that she didn't understand how Ellie had vanished. Yet Cate read that one witness had seen her drinking heavily at a pop-up bar, had seen her talking with someone, whom they described as a *well-built Arabic male in his fifties*. Bridget had lied about her whereabouts.

An even more damning statement came next. A customer at the fair, a parent from the school who recognised Bridget, had come forward when she heard about Ellie's disappearance, to say she had seen Bridget slap Ellie, hard on the face. The woman speculated that Ellie had run away to escape her violent mother. Paper-clipped along with this, as though they were connected, was a statement from the school nurse. She acknowledged that Ellie could be very difficult with teachers but when she spoke with Bridget she had been dismissive and defensive.

More damning was the short, cryptic statement from the family doctor, saying that Ellie had attended the surgery with a fractured cheekbone. Bridget had claimed that she had fallen from a zip-wire in Merl park. The doctor had last seen Ellie two weeks ago, when Bridget took her for a morning-after pill. The doctor had asked to see Ellie alone and when Bridget had left the room Ellie had insisted there was no need for the pill, that she was in fact still a virgin, and her mum was just trying to teach her a lesson for staying out. The doctor made no comment on either fact, the fractured cheekbone or the seemingly baseless demand for emergency contraception.

The last statement in the pile was from the European director of Médicins Sans Frontières, and was in French. Cate stumbled over the words but gathered that Bridget had worked for them, in several countries over a period of a few years, but they had let her go. She had become political, she had got involved in something forbidden, assisting a criminal in some way. Cate re-read the paragraph but no indication seemed to have been given as to what Bridget had actually done. They had no choice but to terminate her contract.

Frustrated, fascinated, unable to stop, Cate sifted again through all of the information that Olivier had, every scrap of the police case, not hearing the door open or Olivier come in behind her.

'What the fuck do you think you are doing?'

She turned to him, and before she had time to fully register his ashen face, that his eyes that were puffy, she shot back, 'This case has become a witch-hunt, hasn't it? All of this, it's about accusing Bridget, not finding Ellie. Is it all you have?'

Olivier lifted his chin and Cate saw then, that he was angry. Angry and upset, but not with her. His face was already mottled, his eyes were bloodshot.

'Yes, it's all I have. That and what Bridget admitted to me, that she knows who took Ellie, that she asked the Arab man to do it. She is now denying that the conversation ever took place, but I have a witness who saw her talking with him. She is adamant that I have lied, that I am mistaken in my understanding. Bridget has just been released.'

'What?' To digest this, when she had just learned of the arrest, was hard.

'She got a clever solicitor, and said many clever words, and now she is free. And this morning she is giving a press conference at the British Embassy. So we need to return to Luxembourg. Now.'

Olivier gathered the paperwork from the rug, and Cate left his bedroom in a flurry of confusion to wake Amelia. Josephine and Roland had just begun to surface as they were making their way downstairs, and Olivier explained to his mother that they had no time for breakfast.

Cate drove at speed back to Luxembourg, Amelia was yawning in the back seat and General whined plaintively, desperate for his morning walk. Olivier sent texts and spoke in rapid French to colleagues, about the woman who was now free, about the accusations she had made against him, and what they were going to do about it.

★　★　★

The British Embassy was close to the city centre, down a tree-lined street. The residence itself was quietly grand, with an iron fence and an imposing stone face that suggested wealth and importance, but not glitz. It seemed the perfect place for a British Ambassador to work, though Cate's knowledge of what such a job might involve was limited. Two vans were parked on the kerb outside, one from the Luxembourg television network, RTL, and the second from the BBC.

Olivier saw the van too. He paused, sucking in his cheeks, then leaned over and kissed her cheek drily, and simply said, 'See you tonight.' That was all. Not an idyllic start to their engagement.

★　★　★

The next stop was the school, despite Amelia complaining that she was wearing the same clothes as yesterday and wanted to go home and change. But there wasn't time. Not for Cate. Because she had somewhere else she wanted to be.

Without thinking about possible consequences, only knowing that she needed to do so, she drove back into the city, and parked underground, just around the corner from the Embassy. She hadn't thought through what she was doing, and hadn't stopped to ask herself if she'd even be allowed in to the press conference, but walked determinedly to the building, knowing only that she had to hear what Bridget was going to say.

There was a bustling crowd in the corridor and Cate found herself pressing against the backs of journalists holding notepads. She followed them, trying to look like she belonged, as they edged their way into a grand room, where a marble fireplace dominated, and cornicing on the ceiling matched its elegance. Wooden folding chairs had been placed in straight lines for the meeting.

The room was already packed and Cate was lucky to get a seat, albeit at the back. Around her journalists checked the batteries on their microphones or fiddled with camcorders. All lenses, all faces, were directed towards the raised platform, upon which was a table with a white cloth, a bank of microphones. No-one was seated at the table yet, but glasses of water waited, as did a box of tissues.

Cate felt someone watching her and looked up to see Eva, five rows ahead. Eva nodded and gave a tight smile that looked slightly triumphant. Cate didn't know how she herself felt about Bridget being released, and she was glad of the distance from Eva, so she didn't have to hear her opinion. Not yet, at least. Olivier believed Bridget was guilty, and if he was right then this press conference was a travesty.

A side door opens and camera bulbs flash as Bridget, flanked by a smart-looking woman in a navy suit and Achim looking sombre and serious, makes her way to the central chair. *God, how different she looks from the woman who gazed out of the window clutching the pink rabbit*, thought Cate. Bridget walks tall and she looks determined not to cry. Her outfit is loose, not a stiff suit but a cotton dress in yellow with intricate beading around the neck and cuffs. But what Cate notices most is that her hair has been washed and dried smooth, so it falls to her shoulders which are pulled back, her chin raised, her eyes taking in the crowd. She looks every inch like her daughter, like the pictures of the rebellious teen Cate had seen on the leaflets. Cate can see for the first time how Bridget would have conducted herself in her previous professional life; there was a toughness to her that Cate hasn't seen before. Bridget's dress dazzles, the beads flashing turquoise and red like an exotic form of Morse code, and she looks as if from another world to everyone else here. She must have chosen this dress deliberately, as if to say that she has travelled, has seen things. She is a woman who knows the world and should be taken seriously.

In contrast, the woman in the navy suit beside her looks conservative and solid. She speaks first, introducing herself in accented English as Bridget's solicitor and saying they had called the press conference as a direct response to the feeling that the police were not taking Ellie's disappearance seriously. Cate hears the words but it is Bridget she watches, her face is fixed as if she is detached from the information that the journalists are frantically scribbling down. She seems to be staring at a fixed point at the back of the room, but when Cate turns to see if someone is standing there it is only a picture, an old-fashioned painting of a young girl in a yellow dress, sitting in an idyllic garden.

The solicitor begins by thanking the British Ambassador for her support, and turns to gesture to a woman who is standing discreetly to one side. She takes a step forward and turns to the audience, the cameras around the room follow her, the journalists lift their dictaphones higher. The British Ambassador is sombre in her appearance, professional, in a neatly cut maroon dress with simple gold jewellery. She gives a curt nod, her gaze seeming to assess everyone in the room. She slides a stray blonde lock of hair behind her ear and speaks without needing a microphone. 'I want to thank you all for coming. I also want to make it clear that this conference is not a reflection of any ill feeling between the British Embassy and the Luxembourg police. We know they are doing all they can to find Ellie

Scheen. However, I have a duty of care to al
British nationals and Ellie is still missing. I
hosting this event brings forward any information that leads to her coming home safely, then
that is our one and only goal.'

Eva turns again to look meaningfully at Cate
and though she is too far away to speak, Cate
can see from her expression that Eva thinks the
Ambassador is impressive.

Now the attention moves to the people sitting
at the table, where thanks are given to the
Ambassador and then the solicitor introduces
Ellie's mother to the crowd and invites Bridget
to say a few words. Bridget moves towards the
microphone, touches it and a sound rings ou
shrill enough to make the journalists in the fron
row flinch.

'I want to make a plea to Ellie. I want to say
please let someone know where you are. You car
come home now, it's okay. You aren't in any
trouble.'

Cate wonders if she has been told to say this
It's not what Bridget believes, that Ellie has
simply run away, so it must be some tactic.

Achim takes over from his wife, his voice is
steady and low, but she can hear the strain. He
says that if someone has got Ellie, or knows
where she is, that they should let her go.

Bridget interrupts. Her voice is high and
untethered. 'Just leave her somewhere safe, so
she can call home. Please. I don't want to see
anyone punished for this, it's not revenge I'm
after. It's my girl. Please return Ellie to me and
everything will be okay. I promise you, there wil

254

be no repercussions. You have my word.'

Cate thinks that whoever advised Bridget and Achim to say these things was a fool. No kidnapper would be naïve enough to think that simply by returning Ellie everything would be absolved. It was a lie, and Bridget was showing signs of not believing it herself, taking a tissue from the box and dabbing at her face though her eyes remained dry. Cate thinks then of the witness statement, the person at Schueberfouer who saw Bridget talking with a man in his fifties. Is that why Bridget's face is dry? Does she know where Ellie is?

The solicitor speaks again, telling those gathered that Ellie was last seen going on the ferris wheel at the fair, and that since her disappearance the police had failed to make a wide search or close down borders.

'In fact,' she adds pointedly, her voice rising with each accusation, 'the only person to have been interviewed for any length of time has been my client. The local police force is failing Ellie. They are failing Ellie's family. And they are failing Luxembourg. My client was kept in a police cell for almost twenty-four hours. Is that the way Luxembourg police treats victims? Perhaps Detective Massard would like to answer. Detective?'

The British Ambassador stands up, moving towards the panel, as though to silence this criticism, but it is too late; the words have been said and all three people on the stage are looking towards the back of the room where there is a movement. Heads turn and Cate sees that under the picture of the girl in the yellow dress is Olivier, standing with his back pressed to the wall, his arms folded defensively across his chest. Bridget is staring at him, had been staring at him all along, but Olivier is looking at Cate and he is far from happy.

Olivier shakes his head, he will not be forced into speaking publicly, and the Ambassador is hastily intervening, re-directing the conference away from accusations. Olivier tries to move towards Cate but no journalist is going to let him through at such a crucial moment.

'Please, Ellie,' Bridget says, and the journalists turn back to catch her final words, 'wherever you are, come home. Please, if you have her, let my daughter go.'

One of the BBC journalists calls out, 'Mrs Scheen! Ellie could be anywhere in Europe. Have Interpol been informed?'

'I believe my daughter is in Luxembourg,' Bridget replies. 'Someone has her, someone close. And it's time for her to come home.'

The perfectly quotable line appears spontaneous, and the journalists begin to speak at once, questions about Ellie, about the last time she was seen. Then one question, loud and clear, from a local RTL journalist seated just a few rows behind Cate.

'Mrs Scheen! Did you harm your daughter?'

Bridget looks to where the voice came from, then she looks at the back where Olivier is still standing, listening. Achim, too, seems to be leaning forward as if waiting on her answer. For a moment, Cate feels Bridget's eyes on her, as if

256

she is answering directly to her.

'I loved my daughter. I would never harm her. That is a lie that has been spread by the police, by that man . . . ' Bridget lifts her shaking hand and points again to the back of the room, to the man standing under the picture, but before she can finish her damning sentence the Ambassador places a hand over the microphone to cease the torrent of blame. The solicitor whispers to her client, and along with Achim, they simultaneously move Bridget so she is standing, then walking from the room. Cate can't judge if the solicitor is pleased with how things have gone or not, only one thing stays with her, something that feels wrong and important and that won't go away: Bridget had said, *I loved my daughter.* Loved, not love.

As the journalist's chatter rose around her, Cate felt she was drowning in accents, French and German and English, but that one word was the same in any language, repeated again and again: *Ellie.* Ellie Scheen. Cate wanted desperately to leave, but it was impossible. Journalists scribbled notes, technicians checked they had the film footage they required, when a tight pressure surrounded her elbow. She turned, hoping to escape, but Olivier had found her. For the second time that morning he said, 'What the fuck do you think you are doing?'

*   *   *

'Come, we'll leave by the back entrance. The Scheens will be giving more speeches at the front, it will be a fucking circus.' He guided her the opposite way, deeper into the Embassy, but he was wrong about the speeches. Bridget had not yet started; she was there in front of them in the dark narrow corridor, talking with her solicitor. As if sensing them, Bridget turned and saw Cate, with Olivier's hand on her elbow, the other on her shoulder. There was a moment, a frozen realisation when Bridget saw the woman she had trusted alongside the man who believed her to be guilty. The shock registered on Bridget's face, and Cate could do nothing, say nothing. She wanted to apologise, though she didn't know what for. She didn't know if Bridget really was wrongly accused, abandoned by the very police force who should be helping her, or if she was just a very good actress with an evil secret.

* * *

Outside, Cate breathed the fresh air. She felt as though she'd been underground for a very long time. A police car waited, the driver ready to speed Olivier away from the scene. He told her to go home, it wasn't a request, and she started to walk away with every intention of doing so. But when his car pulled away she realised she had a choice. Suddenly liberated, she turned around and walked smartly back to the Embassy, curious to see how Bridget would deal with the media when she made her exit.

* * *

She handled it with style. Not covering the yellow beaded dress with a jacket, but wearing it with pride and smiling sadly, now grasping the pink rabbit, which she told reporters, had been Ellie's when she was a baby. The journalists loved Bridget, and she obliged them, standing patiently as they snapped pictures and asked questions. She was wonderful, tough under fire, a world away from the woman Cate had come to know over the preceding days.

And then, as the journalists and cameramen finally began to disperse, Bridget's shoulders hunched and her smile faded. It was then that she looked close to collapse.

★   ★   ★

To escape the mélange, Cate took the same route that Olivier had shown her, only in reverse, and ended up back in the corridor. Bridget had said goodbye to her solicitor and was leaning against the wooden walls. Cate wondered where Achim was, why he wasn't supporting his wife. Her act was over, the mask had slipped and she looked tired.

Bridget looked up wearily. 'I can't do it anymore.'

'You need to sit down. Come on, we'll call Achim when I've found you somewhere to rest.'

Cate thought quickly, all the cafés she knew nearby would be busy now it was getting towards lunchtime and Bridget was fast becoming recognisable in Luxembourg. Instead, she led the now sluggish woman along the street and into the shrouded park. School had not finished, and there were only a few pre-schoolers climbing on the wooden pirate ship. Cate led Bridget to the bench furthest away from the few mothers sitting in the sun, enjoying some peace as their children played.

'I have to hand it to you, you were amazing in there,' Cate said, quietly, but Bridget shook her head.

'No, I'm not . . . '

'To speak like you did, to have that strength . . . ' Cate tailed off, suddenly uncertain. 'Should you text Achim, to say where we are?'

'In a minute. He's still inside the Embassy, speaking with the Ambassador. I need a moment away from him.' Bridget lifted Ellie's pink rabbit to her face, and appeared to be breathing it in. Her voice came out muffled, 'So Detective Massard is your husband?'

'Fiancé,' Cate corrected. How strange that the first person she should tell was Bridget. 'He proposed to me last night. I didn't expect it.' She didn't know why she felt the need to add this last sentence.

Bridget placed the rabbit on her lap, but her hands went back to her face, as though to warm them, though even in the shade of the tree the sun could be felt. 'He's told you that I'm guilty?'

Cate shifted in her seat. She watched a young boy hurtle down the slide, landing in his mother's arms at the base. 'He told me that he thinks that, yes.'

'It's true.' Her hands still half covered her face

and Cate realised it was shame.

The mother righted her son and off he ran, back to the steps to go again. Cate was silent, because she didn't want to hear. But she didn't walk away either.

'It's all my fault, Cate. I never meant it to be like this, Ellie should have been home the next morning. I don't know what went wrong. And I don't know where she is now.'

Cate believed her. She had seen that desperation when Bridget opened the door, the longed-for need for any news of Ellie. The way she held the hope just for a moment, before it was dashed, and she felt the loss of her daughter once again. Bridget was a husk of herself now, curled over, even her cheeks looked drawn. And now, in her colourful dress and with clean hair and makeup, the signs were still there.

'The police. Detective Massard. They aren't looking for Ellie.' Bridget looked across the park to where the mother was now preparing her child for home, dusting the dirt from his knees and buttoning up a cardigan. 'When I was in that police cell with him he was distracted. Tired. All of his energy is being put into interrogating me.'

The two women sat in silence, registering what this meant. Cate thought of the lost girl, wherever she was. Had she given up hope, or was she thinking that at any moment the door would burst open and she would be saved? Was she even alive?

'I mean, what are the police doing right now?' Bridget asked, the desperation making her voice shrill. 'I'm a victim of crime! What the hell are they doing? I have a meeting with my solicitor tomorrow, and all because we have to be ready for when they come and arrest me again. I should be looking for my daughter, and so should they. Instead they are building enough evidence so they can arrest me. Aren't they?'

Cate realised that Bridget was directing the question directly at her. 'How would I know?' Cate answered, hearing the snappiness in her voice. After what Bridget had admitted, she deserved it. 'I'm not a police officer.'

'You mean that your fiancé doesn't talk to you?'

Cate felt irritated, but also ashamed that Bridget could see the shabby state of her relationship.

'Olivier refuses to talk about work when he's home.'

Bridget was furious. 'Make him. You're a mother, can you even imagine how I feel? Please, Cate.'

'Look, Bridget, here's what I'll do, I'll pick up Gaynor, and look after her tomorrow so you can see your solicitor. And I'll do the school run next week.'

'I need more from you, Cate. I can tell you where to start looking.'

'Then tell the police!'

'I did!' Bridget hissed viciously, then seemed to get a hold of herself. 'I did, Cate. And he locked me up. I can't help my daughter from a prison cell.'

'So instead you lie. You say publicly that

Olivier made a false statement. Do you know what that could do to his career?'

Bridget shook her head, as if Cate was missing the point, and her fury became hotter.

'You need to work with the police, Bridget. Because they are the ones who should be searching for Ellie. And I simply can't help you. You're a liar and I don't trust you.'

And with that Cate stood and walked away.

Amina

Auntie hadn't left her room all morning, she'd just lain on the bed with Fahran, who was listlessly watching cartoons. He had been sick in the night, and had a seizure, so now he was sleepy and lethargic.

Amina had been up to the bedroom twice, once to ask if she should take Fahran for his breakfast, which was flatly refused, and the second time to take up a tray with juice and bread and jam. They had to eat, she reasoned, placing a white tablet on the tray for Auntie, knowing it will help calm her.

But Fahran was too sick to manage the food, the end of the baguette remained uneaten in his fist, the curtains in the room remained closed, the cartoon continued to play softly.

Amina stood on the threshold, not knowing what to do. Just then, Fahran began to cry, a pathetically weak whimpering that was more upsetting because he didn't even have the energy to make it heartfelt. Amina went to him, kneeling down on the floor so her face was level with his.

'Is it your head?' She touched the bandage, to check if it was securely in place, and he winced. 'What can I get him, Auntie?'

Auntie was on her side, and her tears were making up for Fahran's. Her hand was clutching his bare foot.

'Nothing. There is nothing we can get him now.' Her voice was heavy, like soil under vines, stiff and crumbling.

On the TV screen a cartoon cat was bashing a mouse with a large hammer. Fahran was watching through his fingers, his eyes wet with tears, and he flinched at each blow.

'At least turn this off.'

Amina picked up the remote and clicked through the channels hoping for something comforting, a programme to make Fahran smile, but what she turned to was the BBC news channel. She stopped, arrested by the sight of the white woman wearing a traditional Kabyle dress, bright yellow with and blue and red beading. It was something she had never seen outside of Tizi Ouzou, and the thought that someone on television should dress like her friends and family made her mouth drop open.

The woman in the Kabyle dress was speaking, her voice was strong and all around her people were writing and taking photos. This woman must be important, an actress maybe. Amina turned up the volume, and listened.

'I just want Ellie home. Please, if you have her. Let my daughter come home.'

Amina dropped the remote control as though

it was a hot piece of coal and stared at Auntie, who was struggling to sit up, propping herself so she could see the screen better. Her hand moved from Fahran's foot to his neck, she tugged him so his face was against her breast, as if hiding him from the woman on the screen. 'Amina! Turn it off!'

'Wait, Auntie. Look!'

The camera had panned the room and Amina spotted her, the British woman with red hair, sitting at the back, the customer who gave her a twenty euro tip.

'That woman, in the back row. She's been here twice in the last week.'

'What! Oh, no.' Auntie's face turned ashen. 'We'll go to prison for this, I know it. I told Jak, but he would not listen.'

'But she wants to help, Auntie. I know she does.'

'You don't understand, Amina.' Auntie was still stroking Fahran's head, lightly pressing his ear with her palm so he could not hear. 'Jak says he's can't return Ellie. The police are outside her house night and day. We are in big trouble, with a guest who cannot go home.'

She released her son, and he snuggled against her, too lost in his own misery to be concerned about what his mother was saying.

'But we have to return her home, Auntie. Her mother is on television, asking for us to do it. And the girl looks so sad.'

Auntie's face, usually so stern, was softened into lines of worry. She bit the inside of her cheek as though to stop any words that might be struggling to escape. Her eyes she kept fixed on her son.

'I don't know what we must do, Amina. Jak is the head of this family. We follow him.'

Amina smarted. *The head of the family*. It was a phrase she knew too well, and had never minded when it meant her own father. But his death had promoted Samir to this role, and that meant danger for Amina, and being forced to follow a way of life that was so severe it meant forgetting who she was entirely.

'We are in Europe now, Auntie, and we are important too. We can decide things on our own.'

Auntie made a sound like a chuckle and Fahran lifted his head at her amused tone. 'Just a few weeks in Luxembourg, and you are now a feminist, eh?'

'I just think this is something we must do and Jak doesn't need to know. We can get Ellie home, and save Fahran. Why should this be wrong?'

Auntie reached for Amina and grasped her face. She reached forward and kissed her forehead.

'Your words scare me, Amina, but also lift my spirits. What is it you think can be done?'

Amina was scared too. But she still knew what she had to do, for Ellie and for Fahran. She had a solution that would solve both problems.

* * *

Downstairs, in the beauty salon, she carefully uncurled the twenty euro note, to reveal the number. She said it in her head a few times before pressing the numbers into the phone, and then she felt afraid to press the dial button.

'Do it, Amina! Quickly.'

Auntie watched, with Fahran at her side, nestled into her body. Amina would do it for him.

The phone rang. And rang. Eventually, the woman picked up. 'Hello?'

Amina tried to find the right words, but failed. Into the silence the British woman said again, 'Hello? Can I help you?'

Help. For Amina, a magic word. 'Hello, Madame,' she said carefully. 'I saw you on the television.'

'Who is this?' she said, and Amina could hear she was not happy because her voice was higher, quick too.

'We have Ellie,' Amina said, slowly, so as to be fully understood. 'And we want to bring her home, but it is difficult. They will see our van. Can we meet somewhere, not Luxembourg? Do you know Saarburg?'

Auntie reached forward, she grabbed the phone from Amina, holding it in the air, her fingers wrapped around the buttons protectively. 'Not there!' she hissed, 'We cannot risk seeing Jak!'

Amina stared at Auntie, and realised her mistake. She took the phone from Auntie and drew a breath to speak, but it was making a single flat tone. In the fumble the connection had been lost, a button accidently pressed, and the line was dead.

Amina's courage had deserted her and she dared not try a second time.

Ellie

It was as though her spine was broken, the way she could no longer lift her head. She had lost track of the days. Why should they let her live? But why were they keeping her here?

Nothing was left to her, only the thin rags of childhood wishes: Father Christmas, the tooth fairy, the Easter bunny. She would sell her soul for something to believe in.

Ellie closed her eyes and prayed.

'*Our father, who art in heaven, hallowed be thy name . . .* '

She lost herself in the words.

'Ellie?'

Ellie stopped the muttered words from long ago and opened her eyes. It was the girl, Amina.

'I'm sorry. I don't want to disturb your worship, but the food is hot.'

It was the food that did it, a steaming bowl of soup. Soup, for comfort and sickness. Her mother would make it, when she was a child. *Oh, God, let me be a child again. Oh Mum, please find me.* And the tears came again, fierce and bitter now. Ellie could see no way of stopping them, as her body heaved and she felt the loss more keenly than she had in what felt like a long time.

Amina placed the tray on the chair that they used as a table and knelt down beside Ellie. She did not touch her, but Ellie could feel her closeness. 'I can get you something, if you like? To make you calm.'

Ellie looked through tear-soaked eyes at Amina. 'Drugs?'

Amina flinched. 'The tablets Auntie crumbled in your milk helped you relax. It is good medicine. I take it too, sometimes, and so does Jodie. Would you like some?'

'No. No more drugs.' Though Ellie realised that was why she was feeling so much worse than she had before, her feelings and emotions were no longer masked.

The two teenagers sat together silently. They could hear the road outside, a lorry thundering past.

'Where is the other girl?' Ellie asked, thinking back to when she first saw Jodie, at Schueber-fouer. How, later, she had smiled at Ellie and how that had made her wander over, as much as Malik it was the girl who interested her.

'Jodie does not work in the house. She is more useful to Jak.'

Ellie remembered seeing the girl walk away with the middle-aged businessman, the way she had led him into a dim alleyway. An unbearable sadness came over her, for Jodie and for Amina. Most of all for herself. Ellie couldn't imagine ever leaving, her only future was working the streets like Jodie or in domestic slavery like Amina. Or worse.

'Would you like me to go, Ellie, so you can pray to your god?'

Ellie sniffed, wiped her nose with the back of

her hand, and shook her head. 'I don't believe in that shit anyway. My dad used to take me to church in Heidelberg all the time, and when we first came here he took me to all of the cathedrals: Luxembourg, Nancy. Metz was the best. It was so nice in there, so cool and quiet. I was just trying to get that feeling back, that's all.'

Amina reached for the soup. She handed it to Ellie.

'Eat,' she gently instructed. 'And tell me about this cathedral. I have never been in one, and I should like to know what it is like.'

Ellie sipped the soup and considered Amina, who was leaning forward, her large brown eyes curious and attentive. Ellie knew that the girl was only trying to help, by distracting her from her plight, but it was also a moment of friendship. She forced herself to smile and began to speak.

Bridget

Now back at home, Bridget could not smile. The muscles of her mouth had shortened, it seemed, so the heaviness at the corners could not be fought. What was there to smile about anyway?

Achim was jubilant, still animated from the adrenalin high of the press conference. He kept rubbing his hands, pacing the hallway, and saying how it would change things. 'Did you see the BBC were there?' he asked, for the tenth time. 'They can't ignore media pressure. And that scene you caused will mean they'll have to put more effort into finding Ellie now.'

Bridget stared at him. 'Don't you get it, Achim? We've lost her.'

He grabbed her shoulders, shook her hard, just once. 'You are free. And now we have the international press on our side. So why are you giving up?'

Bridget hung her head low. 'My friend has abandoned me. Cate . . . '

'She supports you! She was at the conference.'

'No, she changed her mind, Achim. And somehow I thought she was the one who would find Ellie.'

She cried, then, and again he didn't comfort her. He hadn't asked why she had been arrested. He didn't know the details about Jak. And she couldn't tell him, couldn't talk to anyone but the daughter that lived in her mind, the one she spoke to constantly now. He didn't ask why it was that Cate Austin had stopped helping.

Bridget heard the front door slam, and went to the window to watch her husband walk away from the house.

Dear Ellie,

It is late. It is one week too late.

I have tried telling the police, and it got me locked up. I thought I had friends, but I have been abandoned. I can't say it any more loudly than I did today: I need you to come home.

I don't even think you can hear me anymore. I fear I am talking to myself, like the mad woman the police believe me to be.

I fear I won't see you again.

Cate was back in the flat, waiting for the phone to ring or someone to arrive. It was just a matter of time until one of three people she had let down that day arrived to berate her. No doubt Bridget would have called Eva, who would be furious that Cate had turned her back on Bridget. Bridget herself may come, beg her again to assist, but Cate was determined to refuse. The words Bridget had spoken, her confession in the park, *It's true, it's all my fault*, had shocked Cate to the core. She wanted nothing more to do with the woman.

The third candidate was Olivier.

What the fuck do you think you are doing?

His words reverberated around her head. She was thinking now of how to save her relationship. She would confess all of her meddling to Olivier, she would tell him that Bridget had confessed to her too, in the park, it might be enough to get her arrested again and put Ellie's safety in the hands of the police, where it belonged.

★ ★ ★

As it happened, the first caller at her door was none of those Cate had expected. When she opened the door to the flat she felt a jolt to see Achim Scheen standing before her.

His face was grey with fatigue and his eyes were flat, deeply depressed. Although he was wearing a suit jacket, the same one he wore earlier at the British Embassy, it was now crumpled and his shirt had a sweat mark around the neck.

'I'm sorry to bother you. I was hoping we could talk?'

Cate stood aside, letting him pass, noting his hunched shoulders and realising that everyone had somehow forgotten his loss.

'Can I get you a drink, Achim?'

He sat heavily on the sofa, his hands running through his hair, and shook his head. 'No, thank you.' The poor man looked like he didn't just need a drink, but food too. She could see he'd lost weight since she last saw him, and that was only a few days ago when she collected Gaynor for school.

Cate sat next to Achim on the sofa, wondering what he wanted but deciding that he had to find his own words. They sat in silence for several minutes and Cate found herself not uncomfortable, Achim was so engrossed in his own private nightmare that she simply felt invisible; they were sharing a physical space, but that was all.

Suddenly he coughed, struggled to clear his throat.

'I'll get you some water.'

Cate was glad to have a few moments, just while she ran a tap and filled a glass, to breathe. When she handed Achim the glass he drained the whole thing in one long gulp, as if suddenly realising that he was in fact very thirsty.

'More?'

'No.' He held the empty glass tight in his hands; she could see the moisture on the glass from his sweat.

'Achim?' She felt her hand rest on his arm.

'I don't know what she's told you,' he said, clearly trying hard to keep his voice even, 'but I have my suspicions. And I can see how devastated she is since you argued earlier today.'

Cate breathed deeply, she couldn't tell whether he knew that his wife had orchestrated his daughter's kidnapping.

'What I want to say to you,' he said, 'is that since Ellie went, I have come to think that Bridget has some information she is keeping from me, and this has given me hope that Ellie will come home. But whatever happened today, with you, it has taken that hope away. So I'm here to ask you, to beg you, that whatever it is you need to do to bring that hope back, then please do it. Please, Cate.'

'Achim,' Cate whispered, 'I don't know what you're asking me to do.'

'To be Bridget's friend,' he said, so plaintively that she felt the hairs along her arm bristle. 'I know that my wife is mentally unwell, and she may end up in prison, but if she loses your support then I'm frightened for her stability.'

'So *you* do it!' Cate said, suddenly angry. 'You support your mentally ill wife. I've said I'll look after Gaynor tomorrow, so she can see her solicitor, and I'll carry on doing the school run. But that's where my involvement ends. *You* have to help your wife.'

His response was quick, heightened with emotion. 'Don't you see, that's what I'm doing by coming here? Bridget won't tell *me* anything, but I think she's told you.'

'Maybe you're lucky not to know,' Cate said recklessly. But Achim didn't flinch. 'She's the prime suspect, Achim. I would be risking becoming an accomplice . . . '

Achim gazed at her, his eyes were intelligent and shrewd. Bridget may not have given him many details, but he knew that she was connected to the kidnapping.

'If there is something that you can do to bring my daughter back home, I swear to you, I will defend any action you take. I won't let the police blame you, Cate. I'll take the blame. Blame me. Blame Bridget. But please, save my daughter.'

★ ★ ★

After Achim had left, Cate went straight to her bathroom to run a hot bath, dropping in eucalyptus oil and lavender. She hadn't showered since yesterday morning, and a lot had happened since then. She undressed, dropping her creased floral blouse to the floor, tugging off her trousers, her designer shoes. Finally, she removed the engagement ring, placing its glittering self onto a smudge of foundation from a bottle that had been left upturned when she was getting ready, just yesterday. Just yesterday, and now she was engaged, with a fiancé who was not speaking to her.

And she'd so nearly pulled it off. Last night in Nancy she had been polite and attentive. Neither Josephine nor Roland could declare her unsuitable, and they adored Amelia. Well, Roland did anyway.

But what was that worth now that she had let Olivier down? He may be able to forgive her for reading his paperwork, for going to the press conference, but he would surely not forgive the fact that she had not been able to believe him. To simply let him do his job. All along, she had thought Bridget was innocent and she'd acted accordingly. And she'd been wrong.

And now Achim wanted her to help Bridget anyway. To continue on a wild-goose chase across the city.

In the steaming hot bath she saw that the fake tan, so flattering just forty-eight hours ago, now looked like a skin complaint, brown patches peeling away from mottled pink skin underneath. Her gel nails had started to grow out. *Beauty Asiatique*. She knew she couldn't go back there now. Not for Bridget, not for Achim.

Cate sank lower in the water, telling herself she would stop thinking about Ellie, her mouth would remain shut, just as etiquette demanded when a woman finally has a good man who wants to marry her, if he still did.

What the fuck do you think you are doing?

And the truth was that Cate didn't know anymore.

⋆　⋆　⋆

Bridget was involved in her daughter's kidnapping, but that didn't mean that love was entirely absent.

She thought then of her own parents, of the

court case. How abuse and love could co-exist.

Stop it, Cate. Stop thinking about it. Focus on this new life you have. Try not to ruin it all again.

Still submerged under the water, she heard the doorbell. Achim again? Or Bridget? *Don't move, ignore it.*

It rang again, as Cate knew it would. Sighing, Cate dried herself quickly, wrapped her dressing gown around her and went to open the door.

*   *   *

Seconds later, Eva was inside the flat.

'God, I really shouldn't be here. I told the school that I had a dentist appointment this morning, I couldn't miss the press conference. But I really don't have time for this!'

Cate refused to feel guilty. She hadn't asked Eva to call.

'Poor Bridget! She called me, from the park, where you left her. How could you, Cate? She was devastated.'

Cate tried to keep her voice as level as possible. 'She should be devastated, Eva. She asked a man to take Ellie that night at Schueberfouer. Did you know?'

Eva stood her ground. For a second Cate thought she was going to deny it, but then she gave a tense nod. Small and solid with dark beady eyes, she looked like a pug. 'It was a moment of madness.'

'A moment of madness,' Cate repeated, awed at Eva's delusion. 'Eva, she didn't just forget her purse, she organised the kidnapping of her daughter.'

The message seemed to get through, Eva looked mollified. 'Don't you think I realise that? It's a fucking mess. And only a matter of time before the police arrest her again.'

'Exactly.' Cate was thinking they were finally in agreement. 'Bridget is crazy.'

'Which is why she needs us more than ever,' Eva said, a quick turnaround that proved they were in fact miles apart in their thinking.

'What Bridget needs is her daughter back. And how can we help with that?'

Eva looked furious. She pursed her lips, fixed Cate with a stare of unbridled disappointment and waited. She looked like she would wait for ever if she needed too.

Cate stared back at Eva. 'This is for the police to investigate. I will help with Gaynor, I've already said I'll have her tomorrow, but that's where my assistance ends. Eva, I think you should be going now. The school will think something has gone wrong.'

Eva did not move, she remained fixed in the same pose, though her lips now relaxed into a contented smile. Despite the craziness, Cate felt a wave of affection for this earnest young woman, a recognition of herself a decade or so ago.

Eva's face loosened, her eyes no longer fierce but softened with pain. 'I told you once that I worked in Brussels, in the mayor's office?'

'Yes, I got the feeling that you weren't happy there.'

'Well, I was, at first. Before, as the Americans say, the shit hit the fan. When everything was smooth, it was a good place to work. But, Cate, do you know of Sabine Dardenne?'

Cate shook her head.

'Sabine was kidnapped when she was twelve years old. And she was not the first, or the last, victim of Marc Dutroux. Of him I think you most certainly know?'

'Was he the guy who had several girls held in his house? For years, and the authorities kept missing chances to catch him?'

'This, I think is an understatement. One man doing evil is horrible, but the police, the authorities, failing those girls is to me far worse. They had so many chances to save them, but the police failed. These were questions that could not be answered.'

'What happened to them?' asked Cate, hardly daring to hear the answer.

'A police officer called at the house where the girls were imprisoned to investigate another matter. Because information had not been shared, he did not know the address was under suspicion. He heard two girls, crying. Dutroux's wife said it was schoolchildren, playing outside, and he accepted that. He left, without doing anything.'

Eva paused, waiting for Cate to ask the inevitable question.

'Those girls, they starved to death. And he could have saved them.'

Cate's hand flew to her mouth.

Eva nodded solemnly. 'Dutroux was in prison

at the time. The wife, she fed the dog, but not the girls.'

'That was why you left the mayor's office?'

'It was why I was asked to leave. Because I said too much, I criticised the police. I asked too many questions.'

'And Sabine? Did she die too?'

Eva allowed herself the whisper of a smile. 'Sabine was very strong, she demanded things. She asked Dutroux for a friend, for company, and he took another girl. And this was his undoing. Both girls were saved and Sabine, she is a true survivor. The thing is, Cate, I know Ellie. And she is like Sabine. She is strong. And so I think that, wherever she is, she will be fighting.'

Cate was caught in her optimism, wanted to believe it so much.

Eva grabbed Cate's hands, covered them with her own. 'Whatever you think about Bridget, and she did a bad thing I know, we cannot let Ellie down. We cannot trust the police to find her. And I cannot be like that policeman, who heard the screaming and did nothing.'

★ ★ ★

Alone again in the flat, Cate felt like a boxer who has just been knocked out in two successive rounds. Punch-drunk she paced around the space, wondering how she had deserved this. Still, though, she might have been able to refuse Achim's request to help. She might even have been able to dismiss Eva's. But then the phone rang.

'We have Ellie,' the voice said. 'We could meet, though not in Luxembourg because our van may be seen. Do you know Saarburg?'

Cate was about to reply when the phone went dead.

The receiver, in her hand, emitted a single-note tone. Whoever it was, they were gone.

Our van may be seen, the caller had said. There had been a white van outside Bridget's house, with the swimming pool depicted on the side. She'd seen it at dinner in Bastogne that evening with Olivier as well.

Do you know Saarburg?

In the nail bar, she had picked up a leaflet for a swimming pool there.

And now she recognised the voice. It belonged to the girl who worked there.

DAY 8

Cate

Cate told Bridget that she would take the girls out for the day. What she didn't say was where she was taking them.

★   ★   ★

Saarburg is just beyond the Luxembourg border into Germany, a pretty town with a castle ruin perched over sloping vineyards. Because Cate didn't want to reveal the real destination of their trip, she took Amelia and Gaynor to the arctic slide first. Amelia's excitement evaporated when she saw just how steep the steel run was as it zigzagged through the trees.

'Can you come with me, Mum?'

Cate looked at Gaynor, who had still barely said a word since leaving home. 'Why don't you girls ride together? I can just watch from over there.' She pointed to a raised platform, which gave a view of the slide area. But also of the town, which Cate was far more interested in.

Gaynor shook her head. 'I don't want to do it.'

Cate felt she may have made a mistake.

'Okay, Gaynor, you don't need to slide if you don't want to. Why don't you go and get a Coke?

You can watch us from here. Just make sure you come back and don't leave this spot, okay?' She gave the girl a five euro note and turned to Amelia. 'Do you want to sit up front and control the brake?'

Amelia nodded vigorously.

Cate sat on the steel sledge, helping Amelia to find a comfortable seat between her legs, enjoying the warmth of their closeness, closing her eyes as the machine clicked into gear and the car began to climb.

'Look, Mum, *Paranormal!*'

Cate saw the massive sign, directly above the restaurant where Gaynor was now sat, sipping her Coke. 'It says panoramic,' she corrected her, laughing. 'Nothing to do with the film.'

The sledge began its long descent, Amelia screamed as Cate clung to her.

★   ★   ★

Relieved to be back on safe ground, all three were pleased to arrive at the swimming pool, and Cate explained to Gaynor that she had packed an extra swimsuit and towel. She wanted her to understand that it was alright to have some fun, that she shouldn't feel guilty, but she could see from Gaynor's expression that this was a big ask.

The water park was almost empty, which was surprising as it looked fantastic with three pools of turquoise waters, one with a flume, a bridge connecting them, and a whirlpool in the middle. Local teenagers should be crowded round, flirting and enjoying picnics, but the grass and benches dotted around the place were empty. It made no sense, especially when the entrance fee was only two euro.

The café-bar at the pool was closed, the chairs pulled up and leaning on the plastic tables, the umbrellas folded down. The few people who were there looked like visitors from the local campsite, families from other parts of Germany, red from the sun, smoking and sipping local beer in the heat.

Cate led the girls to a spot under a shady tree and Amelia and Gaynor pulled on swimsuits under their towels. After a generous slathering of suncream for them both, the girls slipped into the water like seals, not even testing the water first.

A drilling noise made Cate lift her head.

A man was beside the closed-up café, working on a block of wood at his feet and orange cans over his ears, a tan face with light blond hair escaping from under a woollen hat. Handsome, youngish, Cate thought she had seen him before somewhere and racked her brain. Had she seen him at the fair, or in the city? But then she remembered: he had been in Bastogne, coming out of the beauty salon, the one that Olivier had seemed so interested in. She saw a movement at the window above. It looked like a girl, gazing out. Cate held her breath, a desperate hope rocking her. Could it possibly be Ellie?

The young man switched off the drill and walked towards his van, which she saw was advertising the swimming pool, the same white van. Cate's ribcage tightened, and she realised her hunch was right: *I'm onto something, there's a link between this place and the nail bar and to Ellie.* Her heart surged with the ridiculous, terrifying, amazing realisation: *I could find her.*

The man had left the door to the café hanging open, a chance that Cate could not ignore, not now the forlorn hope of finding Ellie had entered her reasoning.

Amelia and Gaynor were fine, splashing around and riding the flume. They wouldn't even notice she'd gone, she would be so quick. If she alerted them, she'd alert the man with the van, and she couldn't risk that.

She pushed the café door wider and slipped through, her bare feet stung by the rough sawdust. Cate self-talked, an inner dialogue that was banal but soothing: *If anyone challenges me I'll say I'm looking for the loo, I'll speak rapid English and pretend not to understand that I shouldn't be here.*

That such an excuse would be tolerated, especially if Ellie was here, was crazy but Cate could not allow logic or good sense to intervene. If she did she would never be able to keep walking forward.

The room was large, presumably intended to be a restaurant one day soon, but right now it was full of rubble and half-finished projects, no way would any tourist think this was the way to the loos. Cate continued, ignoring the splinters catching in her soles. She could no longer hear the cascade of water from the flume, but instead she heard a voice. A woman's, no, a girl's. Then a man's, guttural and incomprehensible.

A movement, a door opening somewhere close, heavy boots approaching. Cate stepped into a side door, hoping it was a closet, not thinking but simply reacting, her pathetic 'looking for the loo' alibi tossed aside.

She was inside a bedroom. Small, with only a mattress on the floor. The blinds were closed but the window beyond must be open because she could hear that outside Amelia was calling for her.

'Mum! Mum, where are you?'

Amelia was too close, standing just under the window. *Go away*, Cate inwardly begged. *It's not safe here.*

'Mum?'

Cate was momentarily frozen by fear and stupidity. About to turn back she suddenly thought of the girl at the window.

There was a door, and she knew the answer was beyond it. With shaking hands she opened it. The room was empty. There were two thin mattresses side by side. Each was stained with something yellow.

The room held a memory, a sordid heaviness that Olivier would not understand but Cate could. Despair.

There was an odour, the salt of sex and the sweat of nightmares. The air was old, thick with the dust of shed skin. It was time to leave. But as she turned, something stopped her. Her eye saw it and then her brain caught up, and she moved forward, breath held. There was a mark on the skirting board, an etching in the wood. It was a heart, and inside the heart was a word. A name.

Cate ran her nail over the etching, saying the letters softly.

Safiyya.

A girl's name, but not the right girl.

She heard the voices again and strained to listen. French, quick words with such a strong accent that she couldn't get the meaning. And then a female voice, a teenager's youthful tone, but unhappy.

She knew now that she couldn't hide, she had to confront what was happening. She left the filthy room and realised the voices were further along the passageway now, walking away from her. She inched along the darkened corridor, hands feeling the way.

She heard the van, outside, its motor revving into action. Through the smeared glass of the nearest window she saw an older man was sitting in the driving seat, and a girl was getting in beside him. She was blonde, her skin was like milk.

Ellie?

Cate's heart was in her mouth or she would have screamed the word. She was so certain, in that moment, and then the girl turned.

But no, it was another girl's face. Not Ellie, this girl was younger. Fragile-looking, moving nervously.

Another girl needing help.

Cate pushed the window, so it opened just a few inches. 'Safiyya?' she called, shouting the name with a voice that had been hushed for too long, so the name came out ragged.

The girl looked up, her head on one side. She

had heard, at least a rough whisper of her name. Something was happening here, and Cate needed to know what.

She began to run, no longer caring for her own safety but needing to speak to the girl, Safiyya, her bare feet landing hard on a shard of glass, stopping her with a fall, a twist to the floor. When she righted herself and made it to the next window she saw that the van was pulling away. She had been close to something, she felt it, but it had sped away.

Cate's cut foot left a trail of bloody marks along the corridor marking her passage to freedom.

By the time she made it outside, the van was gone.

⋆　⋆　⋆

When Cate returned Gaynor back to her home, the front door wasn't opened by a police officer or by Achim, but by Bridget herself. The toll of the day showed; no longer glossy and strong as she had been yesterday at the press conference, Bridget's hair was tangled and limp with grease, her skin sallow to the point of jaundice. But worse of all her eyes had the flat dull focus of a woman in despair. She had given up.

She gazed at Cate with something like unsurprised disappointment. *When I tell her about Saarburg she'll react differently.*

A female voice called from somewhere inside the house, 'Who is it, Bridget?'

Thank God for Eva, who bustled forward to

see for herself, then beckoned Cate in with a look that went from surprise to a gloating relief, guiding Bridget back into the lounge, and into the soft embrace of a heavily padded sofa, and pointing Gaynor and Amelia upstairs. 'Go to Gaynor's room, girls. I can bring you up some juice and biscuits.'

Gaynor's bedroom door opened then closed, and in seconds pop music could be heard through the ceiling. It was as though all three women in the lounge had been waiting on this signal.

'Hi, Cate, we're glad to see you,' said Eva, as if she and Bridget were one being. 'I just arrived myself.'

Cate sat gingerly, she had not been in the lounge before and she was unable to ignore her surroundings. The room was impossibly neat considering Bridget had two daughters and Gaynor was Amelia's age. Where were the bunched up socks, the open books, the half-eaten tube of sweets? Not only neat, but oppressive because hung on every wall were photos. Pictures of Ellie and Gaynor and their mother, perfectly dressed, with backgrounds of famous places. The Eiffel Tower, Pyramids, Windsor Castle, the Golden Gate Bridge, a desert island somewhere. Cate couldn't see Achim's face in any of the photos, it was always just the three of them, smiling at the camera. Perhaps he was the photographer.

One wall, nearest the window, was solely dedicated to pictures of Bridget, her hair scraped back wearing a nursing tunic. Holding a child who is missing a hand, leaning over a woman with cataracts.

'Was that when you were with Médicins Sans Frontières?' asked Cate, wondering if she could find a way to ask why they had terminated her contract.

'My life's work,' said Bridget, pulling the words from somewhere deep. She looked at the picture that Cate had seen. 'That was in Africa, my first placement. That woman was looking after eight grandchildren and she'd lost her sight. All she needed was a simple operation, it took us fifteen minutes to change her life.' Bridget sounded proud, misty with remembrance. 'In some ways it was easier then. It was obvious what needed to be done.'

'Now,' said Eva, 'I'll go and make us coffee. Then, Bridget, you must tell us what happened today with your solicitor.'

Bridget's head lolled. 'What does it matter?'

Eva actually clicked her fingers under Bridget's nose. 'It is important! The police are treating you like a criminal. But first, I shall make coffee.'

She left, and Cate shared Bridget's dejected silence.

Cate admired Eva's drive but also marvelled at her naivety. To think that Bridget was in any position to galvanise support in that way; the woman was broken.

Cate moved seats, so she was next to Bridget, and took her hand. It felt dry and papery.

'Are you my friend?' Bridget asked Cate, a pathetic question that she could not answer.

'I think I've found something, Bridget. A place in Germany, with the same van that I saw here. I think it was your friend's van.'

Bridget made a loud sound, primal and shocked. 'Jak is no longer a friend of mine.'

Eva came running back into the room, a jar of coffee in her hand, a spoon in the other. 'What is it?'

Bridget was staring at Cate, grasping her hands together as if in prayer, 'Please, Cate. Oh God, please, tell me you found her.'

'I was following a hunch, it could have come to nothing. But at the swimming pool I saw a girl's name, etched into the skirting board.' Both women looked at Cate with such raw desperation that she added quickly, 'Another name, not Ellie's. But the van was there. I think it was where Ellie was taken, though she's not there now.'

The silence stung. A heartbeat of loss. Had they missed an opportunity? Were they too late to save her?

'There's something else,' she added, slowly. Knowing that her choice to tell this first to Bridget and Eva, rather than Olivier, would be her undoing. 'The reason I went to Saarburg was because I had a phone call.'

'Jak?' Bridget breathed.

'It was a young woman's voice. The call was cut short, but before they hung up on me they said they had Ellie and they wanted to meet. I thought I recognised the voice, I had a feeling it was a beauty salon I've visited.'

'So what do we do now?' Eva asked.

Cate said, 'I don't know why the call was cut short, but I feel certain they will call back. We should tell the police before we do anything else, now we know the beauty salon is involved, before they call a second time.'

'No!' Bridget jumped up, with more energy than Cate would have expected, and grabbed Cate by the wrist. She pulled her to the stairs.

'Where are we going?' Cate asked, following Bridget along the hallway, also covered in photos of huge buildings, impressive scenes from the Middle East.

'Here.' Bridget opened the door to a room that had a KEEP OUT sign on the door, handmade in some plastics class by the look of it. Inside was a teenager's room, obviously Ellie's bedroom, and Cate felt the absence of the girl. Here, too, was the mess she would have expected to see downstairs. But Bridget was impatient, placing firm hands on Cate's shoulders and moving her forwards, to the window.

'See?' she said, with arched triumph. 'There he is. Watching.'

Cate could just make out the nose of a car, its bulk blocked by an oak tree. But she knew the car. Olivier must know she was here.

'He's watching *me*, Cate, he's not out in Germany or wherever searching for my daughter. And Jak's people, they contacted you. We have to do this together. Anything we tell the police will just confirm my involvement. And yours. Please, Cate. We have to find Ellie first. If we involve the police I don't think I'll ever see her again.'

Amina

'I spoke to the girl again today.'

Jodie, who had been combing her hair free of tangles and tiny flecks that look like pieces of straw, stops and lifts her head. 'How did you manage that, Amina?'

'Auntie takes Fahran for a nap every day, when the salon is shut. Usually I clean. But today I went to see Ellie.'

'Not a good idea, Amina. That girl could mean trouble for us.' She pulls a blade of grass from her hair, and finally it seems free of debris.

'Why are you so dirty?'

Jodie holds her slick mane up for me to inspect. 'Not anymore. Dirt like this can be washed away.' Then she lets her hair drop and places her hands in her lap so I think for a second she is praying.

'Stay away from her,' Jodie says, which annoys me because why should she always be the one to give commands. She is examining her legs now, checking some scratches that have appeared on the shins, red and angry marks.

'How did you get those marks?'

'I tripped. It's nothing.'

I feel I am losing her, somehow.

'Jodie, what has Jak told you about this girl? Auntie says she is our guest, so when is she going home?'

'You think my job is to rescue everyone in this world?'

Jodie is mad at me. She places her mouth on her knee as if she is kissing it. Both her legs are pulled up now and I see that on her inner thigh is a purple bruise, as perfectly round as a coin and then I realise that she is not just angry, she is also upset. And this pain is not nothing.

'What is it you do with Uncle Jak when you go out each day?'

Jodie moves her head so her forehead is to her knee, her words almost lost inside the curve of her body, which looks so small and damaged, the first time I have thought of her this way. Where is my Jodie, who kept me strong on the journey here and dreams of a better life? And then I see not Jodie but Pizzie, and I take her in my arms. This time I will be the strong one.

'Jodie, what is it that happens to you when you leave this house?'

And when she speaks, streams from her nose are running in her mouth and her eyes are weeping. 'Don't you see, Amina? They didn't bring us here to help us better ourselves. We are here to be used up, our beauty and our bodies. What is happening to me now will soon be what happens to you, and to Ellie. *Harraga* is a factory, and we girls are what it produces. But we are broken goods, and I am the first to break. When I am all used up, you will be next, little one.' And I hug her harder then, comforting her but also myself, because I have never known Jodie to lie and it terrifies me.

I go to the mattress and lift it, checking the money from the English woman is still there. For a moment I don't feel it, but there it is, carefully placed in the folds of my yellow dress. I slide the dress free, smoothing the cotton and catching

Omi's scent. Inside the material is the twenty euro note.

Jodie sees me and starts to laugh, a laughter that is almost manic, scary because it is the very opposite of happy.

'That money is nothing. Nothing! You see this?' She points to a fresh bruise in the crook of her elbow. 'To put medicine in me, something to take away the pain, costs double what you now hold in your hand.'

The small violet bruise inside her arm, I know what it is now, it is a puncture. I shiver and my hand bunches the yellow fabric of my precious dress.

'You need this medicine?' I ask, wary. I know about medicine to take away pain, the kind that goes into the body in needles. Even in Tizi Ouzi we heard of this, and people would come back from the city longing for this medicine, shaking and crying. Omi would help them to sweat out the longing, and use herbs to take away the shaking. I must get Jodie herbs.

'You would too, if your job was to lie on your back. Now stop talking to me and let me be. I'm tired of thinking.'

So she curls up tight on her mattress and I move to hold her, my dress still in my arms. I lay behind her, half-covering her naked shoulder with the fabric of home. The act is a silent promise that I will fix this for all of us, if I am able. I can't let Ellie become like Jodie.

It will take a second phone call, and this time the line won't go dead. This time I will suggest a different meeting place, somewhere Auntie can get to easily by train, but somewhere Jak would never go.

And, after talking with Ellie, I know the perfect place.

Metz Cathedral.

Ellie

Ellie has been thinking about her mother often. The clarity of her mother's presence cuts through her thoughts. Sometimes she believes her mother is in the room with her, telling her that everything will be alright, that this is just a very bad dream and Ellie will soon wake.

At other times Ellie feels her mother behind her, is aware of a single knuckle placed into the centre of Ellie's back, nudging her spine, the way she does if Ellie slouches or isn't polite enough to adults. And feeling this nub of pressure, Ellie knows it is her fault that she is locked in this squalid room, away from her family and friends, scared and alone.

Gaynor she thinks of less, simply because it is too painful. Ellie keeps her thoughts about her sister simple: she hopes that Gaynor is borrowing that new H&M dress she coveted, she hopes Gaynor has taken her iPod nano as she used to do. It used to annoy Ellie, but now Gaynor can use it freely. Ellie promises her sister, in her head, that if she ever comes home she will never yell again. The iPod is hers, a gift. She will be different, if she is allowed home.

Who is in control here, who is even making

the decision to keep her locked up? The bulldog hasn't been back since she came to the house. Maybe the woman is the real boss.

The house is quiet, sleeping. It isn't always. Ellie sometimes hears the boy moving around, his mother speaking to him, or the sounds of feet in the room above. Where Amina told her that she and Jodie sleep. How is it that such normality can happen when she is here? Against her will? But she knows the door is locked and that screaming would only make it worse. She knows too, now, that no-one would come except the woman, or more often, Amina. She hasn't seen Malik since he brought her here. These are the people who exist in her world.

★   ★   ★

The door opens and Ellie expects Amina, so is surprised to see Jodie.

Jodie, beautiful Jodie from Schueberfouer. She holds a finger to her lips, and Ellie understands. Jodie comes closer and Ellie sees how ill she looks, that although she is wearing the same red dress it is now grubby and unravelling at the seams. Her eyes are dull and her cheeks are dry and flaky. The skin on her arms is bruised with finger marks and needle points.

'Your mum planned this,' Jodie whispers, into her ear. 'And Jak agreed, but now it is all fucked up. You have been here too long, I don't see how he is taking you back home now.'

Ellie moves backwards, crablike, until her back thumps against the wall. As if moving away from

Jodie will make her words disappear from where they worm their way, from ear canal to brain, gathering emotion as they go.

My mother planned this.

No. No it could not be, Ellie had never imagined she would be capable of this. This truth, so much worse than any other of the awful possibilities of her capture.

My mother.

Jodie stares at her, wide-eyed, and her voice stutters, 'I wanted to warn you. We could help each other. Before you end up like me.'

Ellie understands that Jodie is trying to save her from the same fate, from being sold like a piece of meat, from being a victim of abuse. But Ellie feels her own abuse as something far darker and devastating: her mother's neglect.

'How can I ever go home?' she asks Jodie.

The other girl does not answer. No-one could. But she slides a small kitchen knife from some hidden place in the fabric of her dress and presses it into Ellie's hands.

'Save yourself,' she tells Ellie. 'No-one is coming for you.'

She believes Jodie, believes her mother could do this. And as she curls her hand around the knife she knows that she can never go home, not now she knows just how deeply her mother despises her. But she could escape.

Day 9

Cate

Cate was in a court room, not as a probation officer or a victim, but as the judge. The wooden chair pressed against her spine, the black robes swamped her, the wig slid on her head. Cate knew herself to be an imposter but tried to hide it, though she couldn't remember what to do and everyone was staring up at her expectantly.

Then, a voice. Calling from the twelve-strong jury, which seemed to be made up of her family, old colleagues and faces from the school playground in Luxembourg. The woman who stood, Cate knew best, she realised that, but she couldn't remember how.

'How dare you pass judgement,' shrieked the woman. 'It should be us, judging you!'

'I'm not guilty,' Cate choked out, but she knew it wasn't true. The whole courtroom watched her stumble from the chair.

She woke, sitting bolt upright in the bed, sweat running down her back. Olivier was open-eyed, gazing up at her.

'What is it you are not guilty of?'

She wiped her eyes, fell back onto the mattress. 'It was nothing, just a dream.' She could see their faces. Eva, Bridget, Liz staring back at her.

Olivier reached to touch her. 'A bad one. Let me make it better.' He kissed her shoulder, her neck. Moved down to kiss her breast, but Cate pulled away.

She couldn't make love to Olivier, it felt dishonest. She had lied to him, and that was just one thing of which she was guilty.

★　★　★

Olivier left for work half an hour later, dropping Amelia at school on the way, and Cate found herself relieved to be alone in the house. They hadn't spoken properly. There was too much to say. He had seen her at the press conference, knew she had been to visit Bridget.

★　★　★

She stood on the balcony, leaning over the railing and breathing away tears, blinking sun rays and noticing the church, the tall Sofitel building in the distance, the white blocks of flats. How could the sun be so warm, Belair look so beautiful, when something so sordid, so disturbing had happened, right in the heart of the city? It all looked perfect. Maybe more so, because Cate knew she would soon be saying goodbye to Luxembourg.

She wouldn't be able to stay, not after she'd aided and abetted the main suspect in a kidnapping case that her lover was overseeing.

She could already imagine packing her and Amelia's bags. What it would be like to close the door on this place?

She had woken from her nightmare to find that it was true: she was guilty. She deserved the sentence.

★ ★ ★

As she pulled up in front of the house, Cate saw that Bridget was in her habitual position by the window. Achim's car was gone, and Cate was glad. He was one person who had been genuine throughout Ellie's disappearance and she couldn't stand to see him right now. Better to be with other liars.

As soon as Bridget opened the front door, Cate could feel her sick energy, her heightened arousal, the same that had worked so well in her favour at the press conference, but on this sad sunny morning it felt misplaced. Bridget's movements were jerky and unfixed, her face was rosy with heat, her eyes dark. Cate saw it clearly then, the obvious truth that she had only realised recently, which had really been evident from the start: Bridget was mentally unstable. A woman who orchestrated her own daughter's kidnapping had to be certifiable. Cate thought sagely that a mental illness might be the only thing that saved Bridget from prison when this was all over.

Cate was taking a lead role in this insane saga, without the same defence.

To be mad would be a blessing. To be sane on a day like today had to be far, far worse.

With Bridget beside her, Cate drove out of Luxembourg, past the Glacis car park where the Schueberfouer was still sleeping. Up to the Kirchberg plateau, past Mudam and the Philharmonie buildings, that Cate had not yet visited and doubted she ever would now. Onwards, looping the crazy interlocking motorways until she took the turning where they would meet Ellie's kidnappers.

★   ★   ★

As instructed during the second phone call, Cate was driving them to Metz, just over the French border and forty minutes from Luxembourg. Thinking it would be an industrial city, Eva had said as much, she was surprised to see grand facades of buildings, massive granite blocks towered into majestic homes that overlooked a pretty river, and all of it overseen by the sandstone cathedral.

Bridget was oblivious to all of Metz's charms, and simply stared straight ahead, leaning slightly forward, her hands clasped in her lap.

'I really believed Jak wanted to help me,' she said, for the hundredth time. 'How could I have been so stupid? I let her down. I let him take my little girl.'

Cate remained silent because she didn't trust herself to speak. The anger, which had erupted when Bridget had first told her that she orchestrated Ellie's kidnapping remained, but she also saw how broken Bridget was. What mattered most was finding Ellie and Cate knew that if Olivier arrested Bridget, then Ellie would never be found. Her goal was to find the girl, what happened to Bridget beyond that point was out of her control.

Cate's one hope was that the kidnapper would ask for money, a sum that Bridget could access easily, and that this part of the nightmare would be over.

★ ★ ★

They arrived in Metz city centre over an hour early for the designated meeting and Bridget wanted to go straight into the cathedral, but Cate persuaded her it would be a mistake. Two British women, one looking like she wanted to tear her hair out with grief, could hardly sit in a pew for an hour without drawing some attention.

'Let's get a drink,' Cate said, leading them to an Italian café within the shadow of the cathedral. Although empty, they took seats outside, at a cheerful red-and-white polka dot table under a red awning. Cate asked the waiter for a carafe of wine and even though Bridget said she couldn't eat, Cate ordered them both a bowl of risotto. It would pass the time, and Cate was hungry; she hadn't eaten properly since the evening meal with the Massards and Bridget looked like she was wasting away.

★ ★ ★

After Cate had finished her risotto, and Bridget had picked, moving stodgy grains around the bowl, they paid and made their way to Metz

Cathedral. It was oppressively beautiful, ancient stories glazed into over-bright windows, sealed between shapes cut from stone. *Religion teaches harsh truths.* Cate thought to herself. *Jesus, sacrificed by his own father for a greater good. Bridget, the mother willing to sacrifice her daughter to teach her a valuable lesson.*

In the nave, the only light came through the Old Testament images. Cate could not imagine God's mercy in such a place, though she could surely feel his judgement.

Shivering, Cate sat back in the pew and Bridget leaned against her shoulder for support. Even the square angles of the seat felt like a mild suffering. The woman beside her whispered, 'There she is.'

★ ★ ★

'Auntie will be waiting for you,' the girl had said on the phone.

The woman was shrouded in a lace veil, sitting in the side chapel, dedicated to Our Lady of Sorrows, designated for silent prayer and lit by banks of tea lights, their flames flickering specks of orange light.

Cate waited in the pew, watching as Bridget moved forward and took a seat beside the veiled woman.

She didn't want to watch the conversation unfold, she bowed her head and prayed that Ellie would soon be home. *Let this work out. Let it be soon,* she begged a god that she wasn't sure she believed in.

Amina

I want to tell Jodie about our trip to Metz, but when she arrives home she has a fever. She lies on her mattress, shaking as if she is cold, though she feels hot to the touch. She won't talk to me, but her bruises speak a language I am beginning to understand.

The only thing she asks about is Ellie. She is concerned, suddenly.

'Ellie will be fine,' I tell her, stroking her back, though gently as the slightest touch seems to be causing her pain.

Jodie shakes her head. 'I don't think so, Amina. Jak is talking about how to get rid of her. He is frightened of arrest.' I want to tell her then, that everything will be okay, that Auntie and I have sorted it all out with Ellie's mother, but Jodie closes her eyes. Her whole body shakes and I can see that nothing I say will reach her now, she is lost inside herself. Instead I hold her, and rock her slightly, until we both fall asleep.

★   ★   ★

We are woken in the middle of the night by Auntie's cries. In the moonlight Jodie and I face each other, both of us listening to the voices, the shouting coming from the bedroom below. Jodie looks startled. Though the words are not clear I know what Jak has been told.

Jodie is wide-eyed with fear. 'Jak sounds angry. He may be angry with me. I did not make good business yesterday, I was too sick.'

'Hush, Jodie.' I place my hand on her skin. It is still warm. I want to calm her, to make her see that he is not angry because of her. 'It is not what you think.'

Another yell from below, this time followed by a crash of something being thrown against the wall. Jodie begins to shake. 'He is very angry.'

'They aren't shouting about you, Jodie. Auntie is telling him about Ellie. That she is leaving here tomorrow.' I whisper as an afterthought but also as a prayer, 'Everything will be well, *inshallah*.'

Jodie's pupils are so dark they are like holes in her skull. She is really very sick, I cannot see how she will be able to go to work tomorrow.

'Where is Ellie going?' she demands, her teeth chattering after she speaks.

'Home. Once her mother has taken Fahran to the hospital to make him well again.'

She shakes her head, confused. 'Fahran is having treatment?'

'Yes,' I say, feeling how relieved the news makes me feel inside. 'It has all been arranged. *Alhamdulillah*.'

Jodie shivers and lays back on the mattress. She licks her lips so I know she is thirsty. 'I have fever,' she says, 'I must be delirious. I thought you said Ellie was going home to her mother. But her mother is to blame for this.'

'Shhh, hush Jodie, what you're saying makes no sense. Just rest,' I reply, carefully tipping some water through Jodie's cracked lips.

Finally, she sleeps. Despite the shouting downstairs that lasts until the first birds can be heard. Then there is silence, and I hope that Auntie has won, that Jak is silent because he has accepted our plan.

I get up and go downstairs. When I walk into the kitchen, Auntie is pulling Fahran's jumper over his head, and then she holds him close. She is crying silently. Fahran gazes at me and I see he is bewildered, unsure of what is going on. I reach a hand for his fingers and he grips me in his small fist.

'Is it okay, Auntie?' I ask, and she nods. She holds me close and I feel her heart beating against mine.

'We are doing this to save him,' I say, and she nods again. Pulling away from me, Auntie's eyes are swollen and her skin is blotchy. I have never seen anyone as upset as this. When I left Algeria, Omi cried for me but not like this, there is no glitter of hope in the water of her tears. But she has told Jak, and he must be in agreement. He will drive Fahran to the meeting place, and then all will soon be well.

★   ★   ★

Fahran is dressed to leave the house, clutching his favourite toy, a brown bear that is missing one eye.

Jodie is still feverish, unable to leave our bed, so Auntie is looking after her. I think she is afraid to leave the house, to be with Jak. He has not spoken yet, and as he moves around the kitchen collecting his keys and wallet his face is full of clouds. Finally, he is ready to go and he reaches

307

for his son, who seems to sense trouble and pulls back.

'Take me too,' I say to Jak, before I have had time to consider what I am saying. 'I will look after Fahran on the journey.'

It would be the first time I have left the house since the day I arrived in Luxembourg and I see Jak hesitate. He doesn't know me. I think of what happened to Jodie when she left the house, and wonder if I have made a mistake.

But then Auntie speaks to him, one hand rested on Jak's arm. 'Yes, this is a good plan. Take Amina with you. I trust her and it will give Fahran comfort.' Jak does not speak. He makes no sign that he agrees, but we all know that he does. And I see that Jodie was right when she spoke of women's power.

I take Fahran's hand and together we walk towards the white van.

Day 10

Ellie

In the night there was shouting, the bulldog arguing with his wife, and this morning I heard the van leave, very early.

I think I am alone in the house, but then I hear the woman crying. She's in the room below, which I know is the kitchen, and upstairs is silent so I assume that Jodie and Amina have also left in the van.

Today may be my best chance to escape, it may not come again. The woman is alone and sick with grief. If I'm going to get away the time is now.

★　★　★

I begin to call, like I did when I first arrived but soon learned not to.

'Hello? Hello? Hello?' I yell. 'I need to go to the toilet. Toilet! Toilet! Hello?' I am ready to shout for ever, but I know she won't leave me for long. Too worried that someone else will hear me.

When I hear her coming I stop shouting and get ready.

★　★　★

The door opens, but she is so different it stops me in my tracks. This woman, who has been so cruel, terrifying in her shrill power, is totally changed. Head bowed, slack-jawed, as if her very essence has been stolen away by grief and she is simply a shadow of the woman she was. 'I can't cope with you now, girl. My son is on his way to hospital,' she says.

I don't pity her. I can't.

I run at her, fast and powerful. In my hand is the small knife, its sharp point directed at her neck. It isn't enough just to threaten, I know I have to something more. She has to be too injured to follow me.

The metal tip punctures her neck and blood spurts out, unexpectedly. I did not think at all about the blood, and I can't now. The woman gasps, clutches her neck, falls back into the open doorway and keeps falling, flat on her back, her head knocking the wall behind, the blood a fountain arching over her chest. There's too much blood. She'll bleed to death, but I can't help her, I have to help myself.

The hallway isn't how I imagined, it's darker and narrow. I put my hands to the wall but all I see is the palm print of blood. Moving so quickly, after so long, leaves me dizzy. *They may still be drugging my food, I can't walk straight. But I have to, I have to leave.* Then I hear a voice, a girl calling from behind me, from the stairwell that leads to the next level of the house.

'Take me with you,' she says.

I turn and see Jodie, standing at the top of the stairs. She is shaking and her hair is damp with sweat. Her eyes are dark with purple bruises and she wears a skimpy vest with some jogging bottoms. I can see her arms are like wires and there are bruises in the shadowy crooks of her elbows.

'Please, Ellie.'

I hesitate, the floor sways beneath me. The woman on the floor moves, her eyes are closed but her mouth is open, calling too.

I must hurry. Downstairs, not knowing which way.

Jodie comes down just a few minutes behind me and is transfixed by the blood on my t-shirt.

'Ellie.' She steps towards me then stops. She's frightened of me, of something she sees in my face and I realise it's not just the blood. I think it's something in my eyes, and the knife is still tight in my fist.

'Which way?' I shout.

She points to behind me. Then says, 'Wait.'

She goes back upstairs and I think I'm an idiot to pause, that she could be getting the bulldog. Then I hear a sharp cry; the older woman, in pain, calling from the room that was my cell. I must leave.

I'm about to turn and run when I hear Jodie coming down the stairs once again. She presses a bundle of notes into my hand, there must be a hundred euros here or more. Then I see she has a cloth in her hands and she wipes my face. When she takes the cloth away I see it is not a cloth, but a dress, once yellow but now red with blood, but it's not my blood. There is only silence now, from the room upstairs.

311

We must leave.

We step outside, and as the warm air hits me I clench my fists knowing I'll fight like a cat rather than go back into that house. I won't go back to that room again, not ever. Jodie's hand is on my shoulder, as if she needs my support, and I'm moving, fast, pumped with the need to fight then fly.

'We must hurry,' Jodie says. 'I saw Jak and Amina leaving in the van, they took Fahran with them. But they may be back soon.'

We stagger, together, and I'm glad of Jodie who seems to know where we are. We are nowhere I have ever been before.

Cate

The morning wasn't welcome, Cate felt exhausted and even as she rallied Amelia, her bed seemed more inviting than the world outside. She was not sure she was ready for the day ahead.

Amelia ate her toast glumly, and Cate knew that she too was affected by the mood in the flat.

'I miss Dad,' she said, and Cate felt a stab of guilt.

'He's coming to visit in a month, with Sally and Chloe. You'll be able to take her to the pirate park, she'd like that.'

Amelia looked up, a world-weariness in her blue eyes. 'But that's ages away. And they're only staying for a weekend.'

Another stab of guilt.

Cate felt unable to remind Amelia of all the

joys and benefits of living there, of the school and the opportunities and meeting friends from all over the globe, because it may all be over soon.

She thought of the Ipswich probation office, of Paul's office. If Ellie's disappearance was just another case on her workload she could sit in his warm room and let him tell her what to do, remind her that this was her job, not her life.

But somehow, far too quickly and easily, she had become enmeshed with Bridget's mad world. She was no longer working with criminals, she was friends with one, a mother who had orchestrated the kidnapping of her own child. And Cate could see no way out of this, apart from moving forward and helping her to get Fahran the treatment he needed.

This was how people cross the line. In small, incremental steps.

★   ★   ★

As Cate pulled up at the school, Amelia didn't move from the back seat.

'I don't want to go in.'

Cate looked at her daughter in the rear-view mirror and saw she was crying. She turned, reached forward to touch Amelia's leg.

'You'll feel better once you're in class.'

Amelia pulled her schoolbag onto her lap, as if it was a cushion she was cradling for comfort. 'It's not safe here,' she said. 'I want to go home. Back to England.'

'We can't, Amelia. Not yet. But I promise you, you are safe.'

Amelia opened the car door and walked away, not turning when Cate called after her, 'I love you!'

★   ★   ★

Achim had already left, taking Gaynor to school and then going to his work, so Bridget was alone when Cate arrived at the house. This time the shutters were up and the house was flooded with light.

Bridget herself wasn't groomed, exactly, but she was smartly dressed in a dark pair of trousers and a plain blouse. And though Cate detected with sympathy the faintly sour odour that emitted from her, she had at least brushed her hair.

'I've been looking it up on the Internet,' she told Cate, almost panting with anticipation as she led her through to the kitchen. 'The whole journey should take us two hours and thirty-seven minutes.'

Bridget was almost manic with energy, opening the fridge for water, going back to it for apples, grabbing her phone, checking messages, then she went once again to the fridge, standing in front of it this time.

'What else do we need?'

Cate saw, with rising panic, that on the kitchen counter was a sports holdall. She could see snacks, a map. A British passport.

'Bridget, maybe this is a terrible idea. If we

just told the police . . . '

Bridget turned from the fridge to face Cate, her eyes sparked with something that looked close to hysteria. 'Not yet. For the boy, and for Ellie. There's no time to waste.'

Bridget had felt hopeless, she had handed over Ellie and lost control, but here she was taking that control back and the stress was making her blind to everything else.

'Bridget,' Cate said, as calmly as she could, 'what if Fahran becomes ill on the journey? What if we get to Heidelberg and they won't treat him?'

Bridget zipped up her bag. 'What if we don't take him and he dies? What will happen to Ellie if we do nothing?'

'I'm really not sure about this, Bridget. Amelia and Gaynor finish school at 3.30, who will be there for them?'

Bridget frowned. She hadn't thought about Gaynor. Then her face cleared. 'Eva. We'll tell Eva to meet them and take them home with her.'

'And what about later this evening? How will I explain my absence to Olivier? We don't even know how long we'll be away.'

'We won't be back late,' said Bridget.

'You can't know that.'

'Yes, I can. I know how long it will take to assess if the boy is suitable for treatment. I did the assessments myself, many times. And I also know that if he is suitable, it will start soon. They could even offer to keep him in overnight, start the proton therapy tomorrow. They won't delay when a life is at stake.'

It was too late. Cate knew she was already in too deep.

★ ★ ★

The car seemed to be going too fast, Cate had the strong sensation that she was about to crash and around her cars felt too close. She told herself it was just stress, to calm down. Beside her, Bridget was breathing heavily but deeply, her eyes fixed on the horizon.

The meeting point was over the border, forty minutes away. Bridget had the details on her phone, though she kept getting distracted, staring into space, so in the end, Cate pulled over and typed the German town into her sat nav.

'Merzig. Whereabouts in Merzig?'

'The forest. It's near the wolf park.'

Cate didn't comment.

A big part of her didn't really believe there would be a real boy waiting for them in Merzig, or that they would then drive him to a cancer hospital. It was all unreal, but then so was Ellie's disappearance. A bizarre string of happenings that led to a wolf park in Germany.

★ ★ ★

Cate knows she is in the right place when she sees a white wolf gazing at her from behind a fence. It is beautiful, and its fur looks so soft that she imagines touching it, pressing her face against its velvet snout. She parks the car and

316

steps out, but as she approaches, the wolf bares its teeth, long and sharp, the gums a reddish pink and edged with black. She had mistaken beauty for tameness.

She leans back against the car and looks around, but there is no other human in sight. Bridget remains in the car, and Cate is glad to be separate from her, if only by a few feet. She needs to breathe.

She feels swept along by the energy of the other woman, by her desperate need to save Ellie, and if she allows herself to stop and question what she is doing she knows it will all collapse. So Cate needs things to press on, to move forward. *Let's get the boy in the car, onwards to hospital, let's see if they can treat him.*

The white van arrives just minutes later, the swimming pool she so recently visited depicted on the side. Cate can see an older man is driving, he must be Jak. By his side is someone she recognises, the young man in his woollen hat. The girl is more of a surprise. In the back seat of the van is Amina from the nail bar, and she is cuddling a young boy on her lap.

The van door opens and the older man gets out, approaches Cate and offers her his hand. Cate hesitates. This is the man who kidnapped Ellie, yet his face is not hard or cruel, it is tense. She takes his hand and registers the sweat, the anxiety.

'I am Fahran's father. I am very grateful to you for this.'

Before anyone can say anything there is a

howling rush as Bridget opens the car door and runs at the man, slapping his face, hard. 'Where is she, you bastard?'

He opens his arms, showing her is empty palms as if this is proof enough of good intentions. 'Bridget, please understand, this was not my plan. My wife only told me last night about your meeting. I would never . . . '

'You betrayed me, Jak! You promised to return Ellie the next morning.'

'But the police were in your home, they were parked on the street. I could not bring her to you safely, we would both have been arrested.' He speaks desperately, running a hand over his face which is now red from the slap.

'You promised to help and you have gone back on your word.'

Jak hung his head, but his voice was steady. 'This is true, and it was not my intention to gain anything from my promise, *wallah*. But as our plan did not go as it should have I can now see that this is the best solution for everyone, and this I did for my boy. So, please, see that we are not so different you and I. Or do you think that your daughter is worth more than my son?'

'Of course not!' spat Bridget, and Cate saw that she was unsteadied by the man's logic.

Jak gazed at Bridget, and for a moment there seemed to be a moment of familiarity between them.

'You asked me to take your daughter, to teach her a lesson. This is something I can understand, and I also understand that when this game did not go your way you became mad. But I also want to do the best for my child. I have promised my wife this, and I am not a man to break my word. Please, let me show you my son, Fahran.'

He returned to the van, and took the boy from Amina's arms.

The boy looked younger, by months if not years, than the five years he had lived. And a large bandage covered his eye. Cate was afraid to see what was behind it.

The boy tried to cling to his father, but he was obviously heavy and his wriggling made him awkward to hold, so the man put his son down. There the boy stood, gazing up at Cate with his one good eye, his brown bear held tight to his chest. Cate knelt down and smiled at him. 'It's okay. We're going to go for a drive, to see a doctor. To try and get you some medicine . . . ' But the boy was backing away, leaning against his father, shaking his head slowly as if every movement pained him. His father's resolve was not going to be swayed by such tactics and he firmly set the boy forward, reaching for Bridget so he touched her shoulder.

'You helped me once to save a child. Please help me again, my friend.'

Bridget nodded, eventually agreeing to keep him informed at all times via text. They arranged a meeting place, a handover for Ellie, and then she watched Jak walk back to his van. At the final moment she called, 'Next time we meet, Jak, I want my daughter back. Bring her to me.'

Once again Jak and Bridget considered each other. '*Inshallah*,' he said. 'It will be as we have planned.'

The van's engine was started and Fahran looked like he might run in front of the vehicle to return to his father if only he had the strength, so Cate reached for the boy and felt how shaky he was. But he did not know her, he was scared, and he began to cry, silently as if only his mouth knew what to do but no words would come. The van was moving away when the passenger door opened and Amina jumped out, landing on the rugged pathway. The white wolf stood by the fence and watched, its eyes glinting at the spectacle of human folly.

Fahran stumbled towards Amina and the two children clung to each other.

'I'll come too,' she told him, stroking his cheek. 'I'll look after you, little brother.'

★ ★ ★

The boy is sleepy, so much so that Cate wonders if he's been given some medicine to make him that way, until she remembers that no medicine has been available for this boy. Her foot presses the accelerator until she's driving along on the Autobahn, an empty open road ahead, and Cate sees in her mirror that Amina is soothing the boy.

'It's okay,' she coos, stroking his hair. Fahran is buckled in, but somehow also curled onto the seat with his head on the girl's lap.

With any luck they could be in Heidelberg by midday.

★ ★ ★

Fahran started to slip into a deeper sleep, one that left his eye half open with only the white showing.

'Oh, please, Madame!' Amina said. 'Pull over, pull over.'

But Cate couldn't pull over, there was nowhere to stop. And they had nothing in the car but the mandatory first-aid box, fat lot of good that was.

'Call his mother,' Cate said to Amina. 'She must know what to do.'

She handed her mobile to Bridget and told her to scroll for Beauty Asiatique.

'It's ringing,' Bridget said, leaning through the gap between the front seats to stroke Fahran's hair away from his damp brow.

'But no-one's answering.'

Cate thought of Olivier. If she called him, he would tell her to drive back to Luxembourg. She could go to the nearest town, find an Accident and Emergency unit, but they wouldn't have the proton treatment the boy needed or that they had agreed to get him.

'Keep driving,' said Bridget, as if reading Cate's mind. 'It's the only way I'll get Ellie back. We have to keep going.'

The sat nav said there was still two hours to go and Fahran was drooling, deeply asleep. Cate didn't want to know just how deep he may have slipped, she just wanted to watch the miles pass.

Glad for the Autobahn, Cate drove at a speed she had never driven before, both hands clutching the wheel, barely noticing the tall pines with the second canopy of trees beneath, the height of the bridges she travelled, the pretty towns and industrial towns, the BMWs and motorhomes, the many wind farms that ran the ridge of the hills. She saw nothing but the road ahead, the miles melting, and the distance giving way to signs, finally, for Heidelberg.

★ ★ ★

In the rear-view mirror Amina sat taller, staring out of the window as if in amazement at the German landscape. Bridget too was captivated.

'God, it's only been eighteen months since I was last here but it feels like a lifetime.,' she said, as if to herself.

They had to slow down driving past Manheim, fifteen minutes from Heidelberg, the cars increasing in number as they passed the sprawl of industry. As Germany's oldest university town, Cate had been visualising a version of Oxford or Cambridge, but this was more Sheffield or Coventry. Chimneys pumped hot smoke into the hot air, banks of cars stood waiting to be bought, a red-and-white Coca Cola factory dominated the landscape.

Again checking the rear-view mirror, Cate saw that Fahran was trying to speak, but his mouth was opening and closing without sound. 'Is he okay?' she asked, pressing her foot down on the accelerator.

'He's in pain,' replied Amina.

Bridget was distracted by the surroundings and seemed completely unconcerned about the boy in her care. 'I'd forgotten how much I liked living here.'

Cate wasn't interested in Bridget's trip down memory lane.

Fahran moaned, and slipped further down in the back seat, seemingly supported only by the seat belt that was tight across his chest and Amina's small arm, now around his shoulders. Cate took the turning for Heidelberg, failing to register the change in speed limit, and there was a green flash across the front of the car. *Shit, a speeding ticket.* Then she looked in the mirror, saw the sick child being cradled by Amina and thought that a speeding fine was the least of her concerns right now.

The scenery changed, gone were the car dealerships and factories, now the surrounding area was a mix of modern flats and period houses, students pushing bikes, mothers with prams.

'Achim and I, we were happy here,' said Bridget, watching a mother cross the road speaking into the pram at the baby inside as she walked. 'We ate out, we hiked the Philosopher's Path at weekends, I was happy at work. It wasn't as exciting as being in the field, but there were days when it was still life and death.'

'You make that sound like a good thing,' said Cate, frowning at the signs and wondering which car park to go for.

'For me, it was. It's good to feel you are saving someone.'

They parked underground, Cate lifted Fahran from the car and together with Amina helped him up the stairs, arriving on a path just in front of the Neckar river. Opposite was a mountain, studded with Italianate villas, and Heidelberg Castle. There was beauty here, but no time to appreciate it. Fahran was weak, stumbling, and she wished they had a pushchair. Amina knelt down to him. 'We're going to see a doctor now, Fahran. Then you'll start to feel better.'

Bridget was still looking around, lost in memories of the past. Fahran had ceased to exist for her, and Ellie too. Cate could see the extent of her madness, the woman's grip on reality was tenuous.

'Okay, Bridget. So your colleague is expecting you?'

Bridget looked blank, as if still caught in a dream.

'And the money, you have it in your account? It's all in place?'

'Yes, yes.' She seemed irritated. As though she was annoyed to be pulled from her daydreams.

'Okay, let's go. Which way?'

★ ★ ★

Despite the fact that she had lived in Heidelberg for several years, Bridget seemed uncertain as they made their way into the old town, the streets of bistros and boutiques, the university buildings were scattered across the city.

Fahran was tired, and also nervous. Though supported by Amina and Cate, he moved slowly and Cate could feel his tension, his hesitation with each step. Amina spoke to him constantly, enthusiastic pronouncements about them being nearly there, and how a nice doctor who was going to make him feel better. She wasn't sure if Fahran could even understand Amina's broken English. But Cate thought at one point that she was actually speaking to all of them: *We're nearly there. It will all be okay soon. Everything will feel better.*

★ ★ ★

As they approached the hospital entrance, Bridget came and replaced Cate's hold on Fahran with her own, and began speaking in a low, steady voice. The boy looked up at her with his one good eye, his head cocked as though he was listening. Bridget became a different woman. Calm and patient. Cate saw her now as a nurse, how she would have soothed the sick.

'Fahran, I'm going to tell you what will happen when we go through those doors, okay? Because you might feel nervous, but everything is going to be fine. And you will see what a special place it is, because the machine that will heal you is really amazing. And big, too, like a spaceship or a rocket. You won't see that side, you'll just see the bed, which is white, it's like a mini-spaceship just for you. For your special journey.'

Amazingly, perhaps picking up on Bridget's encouragement, Fahran smiled, and Bridget bent to hug him. She kissed the boy's cheek, just where his bandage stopped.

'And because you are an astronaut, you'll have something around your head. You have to lie very still, Fahran, but you'll be given a little buzzer right here.' She took the boy's hand and pressed his palm. 'And if you feel frightened you just press it and you'll be slid out of your spaceship. But I don't think you'll be scared, even when the noises start. Because it's just the noise of you landing on the moon. And the knocking is just the friendly aliens, who want to invite you to see their home. And they will knock for a long time, but that's okay. You can just think about them, and say hello to them in your head. And then you can imagine waving goodbye, because it will all be over.'

★   ★   ★

Heidelberg Ion Therapy Centre looked more like an airport than hospital, a glass modern structure, gleaming in the sun.

Cate stepped aside. 'You'll be okay, Fahran.' She nodded to Amina. 'You're in good hands.'

Bridget's face snapped round. 'You're not coming in?'

'I've got you here, Bridget. I'm already risking a great deal. Don't ask me to do any more, please.'

Bridget dropped Fahran's arm so swiftly that he stumbled, clinging desperately to Amina who was also looking at Cate with a terrified expression.

'You make sure that Fahran is registered, that he is admitted for assessment. Then you call me and say it's done, and I'll call Jak, as we agreed. I'll come and get you once I have Ellie.'

Bridget clutched Cate, hugged her tightly and whispered in her ear, 'Make sure my daughter is safe. Nothing else matters. Just make sure you get Ellie.'

Amina

When Fahran coughs there is blood on his brown bear, and some pus is coming from under the bandage of his eye.

Amina is glad to be at the hospital. The journey was unpleasant, the British woman drove fast, and Amina was scared by the world outside the car window.

As they travelled towards the hospital she could see that Germany was not like Algeria. The sky here was bigger, the land was very green. The rain was the main difference. In Algeria the rain comes rarely, but when it does it is to be feared, it makes fierce rivers flow through the town.

Fahran leans his head on her shoulder, sitting in the waiting room. He is such a good boy, but she knows he wants to be with his mother. Amina begins to hum, a song that Omi liked when she was cooking or busy about the home. It makes Amina feel content, and she hopes to pass some of this to the sick boy.

He leans against her, his face nestled against her arm, and they wait for the doctor to arrive.

Ellie

We stagger along the road, Jodie and I, as though drunk. I feel it too, unsteady and confused. If

327

anything, she's shaking harder, and she rubs her arms constantly even though it's a warm day. As we pass a bin she drops the bloodied yellow dress into it, it hardly makes a sound.

'Now the knife, Ellie.'

I don't want to give it up, but I know I must, and it goes in the bin with the dress. I lift my face to the sun, feeling its warmth for the first time in what feels like a lifetime. I can't believe I'm actually out. I'm free.

'Let's knock on the nearest house,' I say, but Jodie pinches my wrist hard with her fingers.

'Idiot! You think any place here will help us? You, with your dirty yellow t-shirt covered in blood. Me.' She does not say why they would not help her, though I cast a glance at her track marks. Her face is red with heat and her hair is matted with sweat. Around her eyes, old mascara is thick and clogged. She is right, any normal person would turn us away.

* * *

We walk farther and the street becomes busier, there are people leaning on walls exchanging money, and alcohol bottles line the edges of the path. I know where we are now, this is the rue de Strasbourg and soon we will be at the Gare. And then I see a police officer, monitoring the activity around the front of the station.

As I approach he looks up and his face takes in my appearance dully, maybe judging me to be a prostitute or a junkie. Jodie is close to my side, pulling me away, and I think of the bloodied yellow dress hidden in a bin just a few hundred yards away.

'Jodie,' I say, urgently. 'None of this is our fault.' But still she will not walk with me. She stands, watching, as I approach the police officer. He is in full uniform, which must be hot, and his bored expression tells me he has been standing there a long time. It is only when I speak that his eyes spark to life, as if he finally has a task.

'My name is Ellie Scheen. And I have been the victim of a kidnapping.'

★   ★   ★

Twenty minutes later I am being driven, but this time it is different.

I am not puking my guts up, trying to stay conscious. This time I know where we are going: to my mother.

The police officer at the train station radios in the news and another man arrives swiftly; he tells me his name is Detective Massard. He drives carefully, so we are constantly overtaken by flashy cars, even by Dutch caravans. My eyes are greedy, hungry for the sun on the river, the blue sky over the wooded slopes as we leave Luxembourg for the meeting point with my mum.

It is all happening so quickly. He hasn't told me where this meeting will be, but he did say it would take a few hours. Just a few hours and this will all be over.

Safe. Back with Mum. The two ideas jar, contradict each other.

'I was told the kidnapping was organised by her,' I say, wanting him to correct me. He keeps his eyes on the road, he doesn't say anything, he doesn't need to. Jodie's story makes perfect sense. And that says a great deal about her, and about me.

'Will Jodie be okay?'

'She'll be fine.' He softens then, his voice drops to a more human tone. 'She's going to help us with the police case against your kidnappers. She'll be given a place to stay and an allowance. She'll be looked after, Ellie, I promise.'

I shiver, though I'm not cold, it's actually too warm in the police car. There's no air conditioning and I'm starting to feel sick.

So this is what it means, to be rescued. To be safe.

Why then do I still feel so afraid?

Cate

Cate was clutching the phone with both hands, waiting for it to ring. It vibrated first, and she answered the call, desperate to know if the crazy plan had worked.

'Bridget? What's happened?'

'Fahran is in admissions. They've taken his blood, to test for type, and he's in a gown. They'll do an MRI next. Everything is underway, Cate. I've done my part, now it's Jak's turn.'

Cate called Jak's number and told him the news, then waited for confirmation about the handover of Ellie, but the response that came was not in words. She heard a choking cough, then a sob.

'I think Fahran is in excellent care,' Cate told Jak. 'Heidelberg hospital was the first to use proton therapy in Europe, and it's world-class. And Bridget told me she's paid in full. Fahran will have all the treatments he needs.'

Breathing came, heavy and jagged. The man was trying to control himself and failing.

A younger voice, also male, took over.

'Cate? It's Malik.'

Malik. The baby that had been saved in Algeria, his life had bound Bridget and Jak forever, and somehow led to this moment.

'Malik, I'm going to drive to the meeting place and wait for you to bring Ellie,' she said. 'How long do you think you'll be?'

There was silence on the other end of the phone.

'Malik? Is everything okay?'

Then the line went dead.

★   ★   ★

Twenty minutes later, Cate sat on the topmost level of the Thingstatte. After Malik had hung up on her, she proceeded to the meeting place. It was deserted, a good choice for Ellie's handover.

The sun warmed her, but looking down to the open platform at the base of the amphitheatre, Cate shivered, imagining the ghosts of Germany's past. Youths in brown uniforms, tired from the walk up the mountain but excited to be hearing words from their leader, who would walk through the entrance and throw his voice so it resounded around the stadium, calling on them to serve their country.

Cate closed her eyes. She felt exhausted, she could fall asleep right now if it was not for her heart pumping blood in her ears.

Let it be over now. Let it be okay.

Her palms sweated on her phone, though all the calls had been done. Bridget was still at the hospital with Fahran, who was now receiving his first treatment. Ellie would be brought here, soon, and then it would be over. They could all go home.

★ ★ ★

Cate scrolled through her contacts and didn't allow herself to consider what she was doing before she pressed MUM.

The answer came on the second ring. 'Cate?'

'I'm sorry I haven't called.'

A silence. 'Your sister is here. I'll put her on.'

Cate panicked. 'Just tell me what happened, Mum? Is Dad in prison?'

Another pause. 'He got what he deserved. Speak to your sister, you need to.'

Cate could hear them talking, could imagine Liz saying she wouldn't speak to Cate, her mother insisting. Finally, she heard her sister's voice. 'How are things, Cate?'

'Fine.' Then she decided she was too tired to lie. 'Fucked up. I might be home soon.'

'We'll be here for you. Mum and me. I've

moved in with her.'

'Is she drinking?'

'Not yesterday. Not today. One day at a time.'

Cate paused, struggling to take in this glimmer of good news. 'Is Dad in prison?'

'He did a plea bargain, so his sentence of five years was suspended. He changed his plea to guilty, Cate. It was all I wanted.'

Cate sighed. So there had been no interrogation in the witness box. He had spared Liz that.

'I'm going to be okay, Cate. So is Mum. It's over now. But what about you? You don't sound well.'

Cate ran a hand through her hair and held the phone away from her ear, not able to stand her sister's sympathy when she had failed to be there for her. Cate cried, wept hot tears, for the life she was about to lose and the mess she was in. From the phone she could hear Liz calling her name, and she lifted it back to her ear.

'It's okay. Whatever it is, it will be okay. I promise you. And I've been to hell and back, so I should know. When you have family, things can be fixed. I love you, Cate. Mum does too.'

Hardly able to speak, crying hard now, the two sisters said goodbye.

She was wiping her face when a car drove into the car park and second later, two figures began to walk through the entrance in the distance and out into the performance space of the stadium. A man, whom she recognised from his walk even before she saw his face, as Olivier. And next to him was a teenage girl. Ellie.

Cate pushed up from the stone step and began

to clamber down, taking the wide steps too fast, stumbling but quickening downwards, towards the girl, who was now in the shadow of the dramatic proscenium entrance. Then she was there, on the platform, with the girl, grabbing her, holding her to check she was real.

'Oh Ellie, oh thank God.'

Ellie collapsed, letting Cate take her slight weight, both clinging to the other, two strangers locked together by a nightmare, now woken to find the world, for ever changed.

As she held Ellie, Cate looked over at her lover, searching for blame or anger but found only fatigue etched on Olivier's face.

He touched her arm and she couldn't hold back, she leaned into him, still holding Ellie, wanting for one last time to be held by him. For Olivier to love her, before he discovered what she had done. She needed this moment, his warmth, the spiced smell of his skin, his arms around her.

Then she pulled away, and as the three of them separated Ellie stepped aside, as if needing some space. She wandered a few feet, gazing out at the stone steps of the amphitheatre. Then she sat down, her head bowed.

Cate took the opportunity to draw closer to Olivier, not wanting Ellie to hear her. 'I can tell you where to find Bridget. You were right, she organised the whole thing. You were right, Olivier.'

He looked at her. As if he too knew that this was the end for them.

'I know, Cate. We've known for days now. We've been watching.'

'Watching the house?'

'Listening to calls too. Achim has helped us. We just needed to make sure Ellie was safe before we could arrest Bridget.'

Cate saw it then, that he had known all along, every move she and Bridget had made. 'You knew about the trip to Metz?'

'Of course. I was in the cathedral with you.'

Anger shot through Cate, unjustified though it was. He had hidden things, too.

'Will I be charged?' she asked, thinking it was deserved.

'Not if you help us to prosecute Bridget. We'll need you to give a statement, and to appear in court, but that won't be for many months yet.'

'She's sick, Olivier. I don't think she belongs in prison.'

'That's not for you or I to decide, Cate. We're both done with it now. This is in the prosecutor's hands.'

They stared at each other, only two feet but many miles apart. Cate approached Ellie, and sat close beside her. She had never met the girl before, but she felt she had known her since birth. Olivier followed and looked at his watch.

'How did you know to come here?' Cate asked Olivier.

'Jak. Once Jodie told us the address it was very quick. He's in police custody, but he told us about the meeting point. He's very distressed. He just wants to know that his son will still get the treatment.'

Ellie looked up at Olivier. 'And will he?'

'I don't know, Ellie. There's not really a

precedent for things like this. But I hope so. Cate felt how Ellie's body was shaking. She looked exhausted, dirty too, and there was dried blood on her t-shirt. But she was here. That was what mattered.

'What happens now?' Cate asked, placing her arm around the teenager.

Olivier gazed at Cate, for a long time there was only the two of them in the world. In that moment there was love enough, without the anger and blame that could follow. Despite the trust that had been destroyed. Then he looked at Ellie, to the girl who was patiently waiting to see her mum for the first time in ten days.

'We go home,' he said. 'All of us.'

Epilogue

Dear Ellie,

In that instant, when I saw the police officer walking into the hospital waiting room, in his navy Luxembourg uniform, I knew. I knew it was finally all over. And I felt something like relief, that I could stop pretending.

I was clutching the boy's teddy, he had left it behind when they led him to the treatment room. Amina was with him, and I knew he was safe. I had done my part, just as I'd promised Jak. Fahran will be treated.

They drove me back to the same police station I visited just three days ago, they put me in a different cell though. This one, I think, is for special prisoners. It has cardboard furniture so I can't harm myself. As if it was even possible for me to do any more damage.

I was allowed one phone call. It was enough, to hear Achim say that you are home. Showered and fed and tucked into your bed. Safe.

It is enough, to know that you came home, eventually. And so I have just one question for you, one thing I need to know: have you learned your lesson?

Are you going to be a good girl now?

They sent a psychiatrist to see me and he has said I am sick. I could have told him that! Sick with worry for my little girl, whom I have not seen for ten days! Tomorrow he will tell the judge about my illness, and then they will see about getting me some treatment. And soon, very soon my solicitor says, I will be home.

Because none of this was my fault, I was sick and soon I will be well.

And you were bad but now you will be good.

Everything is okay, Ellie.

Mummy will be home soon. I promise.

Acknowledgements

I am indebted to the following people who gave their time so willingly, and answered so many of my questions:

Firstly, thanks to Laurence Hever, Assistante Sociale at the Association de Soutien aux Travailleurs Immigres (ASTI), whom I found through a Google search, and thank goodness I did. When I was exploring the subject of illegal immigration, and the difficulty of finding medical assistance for a sick child, I called her up, asking, 'Could this scenario happen in Luxembourg?'

Laurence replied, 'Ruth, I had a family in my office just today, with exactly this issue.' Whilst I was reassured that my plot is therefore authentic, it saddens me that such a wealthy country as Luxembourg is not providing for the most needy. Laurence, and the work she does at ASTI, is both essential and admirable.

Thanks also to Joseph Sadler, Commissaire en Chef with the Police Judiciaire, who gave me an alternative perspective on human trafficking and also an insight into how Luxembourg faces the challenge of organised crime, as well as answering several random questions on police procedure.

I am grateful to the Association Luxembourgeoise des Visiteurs de Prison (ALVP) who, despite my terrible French and non-existent Luxembourgish, welcomed me into their ranks. I am in awe of the voluntary commitment they offer prisoners in Luxembourg, visiting regularly for months or years. Their stories and insights gave me an additional viewpoint on crime in the city.

For my research into Algeria, I am indebted to Kheira Si Larbi. Thank you for a pleasant afternoon looking at photos of the Djudura mountains, and chatting over what it means to live in Tizi Ouzou. The prayer mat, the gallet stone, all derive from this conversation.

And to Kamilla, who made our weekly waits in the driving range car park so much more interesting, and who answered my questions with such vigour.

As always, thanks go to the wonderful team at Legend Press, especially my editor, Lauren Parsons.

And to my writing group, Lizzie Ferretti, Morag Liffen (got it right this time!), Jane Bailey and Sophie Green. Thanks to my probation colleague and friend, Janet Wood, for her eagle eyes and advice on current practice.

Finally, thanks to my husband, Andrew, and children, Amber and Eden, who were frequently press-ganged into strange outings to places such as Heidelberg hospital, Mertzig wolf park, and the dodgier parts of Luxembourg. I love you all.

The character name 'Achim Scheen' was supplied by its original owner, who won the right to have it featured in *Nowhere Girl* during a charity auction to raise funds for Make-A-Wish Foundation, Luxembourg.

Achim, thank you for having such an interesting name, and I hope you like the book!